LONESOME, PARTY OF SIX

LONESOME, PARTY OF SIX

A. AINSWORTH

FAMILY STORY LEGACY PUBLISHING

Lonesome, Party of Six Series

1: Lonesome, Party of Six
2: Lonesome Reunion

AUSTEN

1

Austen would admit that hers was a first-world problem. Still, she reflected that nothing seemed worse than sitting around the Thanksgiving table waiting for *the question*. The family would line up in the kitchen for turkey and dressing before making their way to the table for the rest of the feast. The volume of food could feed the entire family four or five times. Grandma Vick would join them after her fifth query of "Does anybody need anything?" She would stir her gravy into her mashed potatoes, take a tiny bite, and set her fork down. Then, as if it was an idea original to this year's meal, Grandma would ask, "Well, what is everyone thankful for this Thanksgiving?"

Austen could thank her middle brother for an extra day to ponder the question this year. When he was preparing to go to Starkville for the annual Egg Bowl, she considered going with him. The maroon top she bought two weeks earlier was cute, and she had the requisite cowbell covered with stickers from games from previous seasons. Those were games she attended with Mick, her ex-boyfriend. He would be there, though, and Austen couldn't bear to witness him with the girl who took her place while she third-wheeled with her brother and his girlfriend. She had moved past Mick in many ways, but she didn't want to risk her progress by seeing him. *With her.*

Thanksgiving, the holiday she defended so passionately, was closing in on her. No Christmas tree until *after* Thanksgiving, she admonished her mother when the decorations began appearing in the corner of the den. Having already decorated her classroom at school on Friday before the break, Hannah Lynn Thomason couldn't wait to start on her home. Austen protested one shouldn't decorate for *the holidays.* You give Thanksgiving its day first. Christmas should be off limits until at least Thanksgiving night. Every year, they engaged in the same debate. Dad took her side. Her brothers antagonized both sides. Mick sided with her mom. It was a petty annoyance, much bigger on this side of their breakup.

Mick. Looking back on their time together, *Mick* sounded like such a silly name now. *I dated a mouse.* Austen laughed out loud.

"What's so funny?" Hannah Lynn asked from the front seat.

Lost in her own pondering, Austen forgot she was in the car with her family, sans Hunter, on the way to an afternoon matinee. "Nothing, Mom."

"Well, you didn't laugh at nothing." She wasn't about to ignore it. "Come on, share with the class."

Austen caught a glimpse of her dad's hand moving over to touch his wife's knee. She followed Justin Thomason's arm to his face, where she caught him mouthing to his wife, "Just let it go." Austen ducked her head so her mother wouldn't catch her smile.

"I just wanted..." Hannah Lynn trailed off. "Never mind. Have we decided which movie we would like to see?"

"Mom, you know you always end up deciding." Jack's keen sense for saying the most inappropriate things at the most inappropriate times had offended every member of the family more than once. Almost halfway through his freshman year of high school, Jack's embarrassment at being seen in public with his parents was approaching its apex. However, Mom had insisted they do this as a family. Austen felt sorry for Jack, even as she bristled at his approach that she recognized as her own at his age more than she would care to admit.

Mom flushed but let the judgment pass. "Why don't you decide today? How about that new animated movie? You loved the first two."

"And I was four and six when they came out."

"Austen, wouldn't you like to see it? Isn't that kind of what you do with your storytelling thing?"

"Mom, I've told you visual storytelling is nothing more than graphic design and marketing. It's not coloring and story time. Think outside your third-grade classroom." She stopped there, not wanting to insult her mother's career choice that she admired.

"She makes more money than we do, hon," Dad offered. He was a career teacher who never aspired to school administration and its accompanying higher compensation. As he closed in on a retirement he hoped he could afford, Dad found net worth a handy score-board. Though Hannah Lynn had pushed Austen toward becoming an elementary school teacher like herself—and Austen had the requisite skills for it, he thought—he was glad she chose something just as fitting to her personality.

"Doubtful, Dad."

"More disposable income, for sure."

"Hey, I'll be glad to move out and get my own place any time you say," Austen said, referring to her living arrangements in the apartment above the Thomasons' detached garage.

"You know I'm just kidding. We don't know if you're home most of the time. Plus," he added, chuck-ling, "without you at home, your mom would slip away during the Fourth of July barbecue to decorate the house for Christmas." Glancing at the pouting face to his right, Dad grinned and said, "You have to admit I'm right."

"Go ahead, gang up against me again. Make a choice, Jack."

"I don't care."

"That's not a choice. Pick."

"You pick."

"You're the one who said I always choose the movie. Now you choose it."

"I don't care."

"Fine. Why don't we watch the one about a little boy who gets made fun of and feels left out? Let's go see that one. Perhaps his story will make us more *thankful* for our *supportive* family."

"Splendid idea," Dad said, giving his wife a thumbs up. "Our kids at school read the book in seventh or eighth grade, and they all seem to like it."

"Seventh grade," Jack mumbled.

"But did you like it?" Mom asked.

"Sort of."

Austen poked her little brother in the ribs. "And there it is: that's freshman-speak for, 'I actually read and enjoyed it.' He just doesn't want to admit it."

"Sure, if you say so. Did you have to read it when you were in seventh grade?"

"No, it hadn't come out then."

Unable to resist, Jack poked back. "Sometimes I forget how *old* you are."

"Cut it out." Austen forced herself to reciprocate her younger brother's gamesmanship. She was sure he did not understand how deep his cut hurt on this Thanksgiving afternoon.

ONE YEAR EARLIER, she thought this would be her first Thanksgiving to argue for her favorite holiday in her own home. It would be a small apartment for the first year as she and Mick decided where they wanted to start their careers. Her thoughts took her to Tupelo or

Madison or even closer to her Harriston home. When he considered where they might live, he talked of Dallas or Nashville or Atlanta. The closer he moved toward his golf management degree, the more the lure of making a name for himself in the industry drew him. Austen's suggestions that there were plenty of golf courses closer to home seemed to her a normal part of career conversations. But her hints exploded into accusations from both of them about deeper motivations. Mick was all about money and fame. Austen was incapable of breaking away from her mom. Mick didn't appreciate his parents. Austen wouldn't think bigger than her hometown. Mick might become a workaholic. Austen was just like her mother.

As the calendar turned from September to October to November, the barbs became sharper and more frequent. Austen's Starkville apartment, where she lived alone, transitioned from school decor to her beautiful Thanksgiving display. Mick and his three roommates decorated with dirty dishes and clothes strewn throughout the house. Austen hadn't stepped foot in it in since the last time she cleaned it for them right after Halloween. As far as his visits to her place—once daily —he had become a more infrequent guest after midterms. She should have seen the breakup coming. For her, though, making him the perfect Christmas gift to mend the part of their relationship she considered her fault dominated her thoughts.

When Mick texted that he was meeting with a study group from his human resource management class again, Austen removed a hand-sewn quilt from her closet to put the finishing touches on his Christmas present. They hadn't talked about where they would spend Christmas this year, their third as a couple. They had met in a sophomore marketing class and started dating in October that year. Recalling their first Christmas, she chuckled at the gifts they had exchanged before spending the break with their families apart from each other. She gave him a superhero T-shirt and received an "I Love Chick Flicks" T-shirt from him.

For their second Christmas, the gifts became more personal and more expensive. Austen bought Mick golf shirts from the last three PGA Championships. He gave her a customized laptop skin adorned with the logos of the brands she admired. She might have insisted if took their relationship to the Christmas-with-the-families level, they visit hers first. Instead, Austen played the long game because she fully intended on Christmas being her family's holiday after they married. She spent Christmas Eve with his family in the Delta and reported to her family all the ways they might make "her" Christmas more inviting the following year.

During the fall semester of their senior year at Mississippi State, two thoughts superseded the rest of Austen's next-to-last term: Christmas at home with Mick and the expectation of his popping the question. Though they had barely mentioned marriage in their two years as a couple, it seemed the next natural step. When they talked about their individual futures, each of them included the other. Homecoming came and went. His fraternity's fall formal came and went. So did the home football schedule, and finals were approaching.

Each event that passed without a proposal led to Austen's belief that he would ask her on her home turf at Christmas. *That's it, he wants to ask my dad in person.*

Austen put the finishing touches on his quilt she had sewn to match her own, almost. The centerpiece of hers was the chick flicks T-shirt he had given her for their first Christmas. His contained the superhero shirt she had deftly swiped from the back of a chair in his kitchen. Thinking ahead to chilly nights next winter with nothing in particular to do at their apartment, she imagined continuing their practice of a best-of-three game of rock, paper, scissors. The winner picked the movie. They would snuggle under the quilts on wintry nights while binge-watching shows and munching on popcorn. Her vision of their future so vivid she could smell the popcorn.

Austen had wrapped the quilt, topped it with a bow, and stored it in her closet by the time Mick called and asked if it was too late to come by. Sure, no problem, she told him. She was having trouble studying for her consumer behavior test for thinking about Christmas with Mick and her family, anyway. When he said he wanted to talk about their plans for Christmas, she encouraged him to come right over. In the twenty-minute interlude between his call and his expected knock on her door, Austen took his quilt out and put it back in her closet three times. Since she had started on it, her antagonism toward Mick had dissolved. Who cared whether they lived near her family. Nobody ever said they had to continue living where they started. Perhaps they would move back to Mississippi at some point. Maybe what he said about her picking up on some of her mother's traits was true, too. Some distance between mother and daughter might do them both some good. *Since Mom wouldn't be able to wait to give a personal gift like Mick's quilt, I will make myself wait to prove I'm not like her.* Austen was walking into the den when she heard Mick's tentative knock on the door.

"Get on in here, you," Austen said, grabbing his red Christmas scarf with both hands and pulling him in for a kiss he hardly returned. "Tough night at study group?"

"Austen..."

"Oh, you know what, it doesn't matter." When Mick sat on the couch, she snuggled next to him. "Before we talk about plans for Christmas, you need to realize I'm showing great restraint tonight. I want to give you your present right now, but I am forcing myself to wait until you're at my house when I can give it to you in front of everybody. But I can't stand waiting!"

"Stop, Austen. I want to break up."

ALMOST A YEAR HAD PASSED since those six words had devastated her existence. She sleepwalked through her test the next day and through class the following week. When a friend insisted she accompany her to her family's lake house the next weekend, Austen stayed curled up on her bed for two days, pretending to study. The drive home was a blur. Everything was a blur. Except her. *Molly Blankenship.* Austen didn't hate her as much as she detested seeing Mick's laughing with her around campus everywhere she turned. It wasn't fair that he rebounded first. He had dumped her and found her replacement within two weeks and with a girl Austen couldn't bring herself to envy, no less. She didn't want him back—heck no. She just wanted the knot in her stomach to go away. Feeling enough emotion to cry herself to sleep one good time would help. It would also be nice for somebody to ask her out, even if she didn't want to go.

———————

As HER FAMILY exited their sedan and walked toward the mostly vacant theater, Austen contented herself with an extended version of what her tribe had deemed *her holiday*. She gave thanks in her mind for Hunter's girlfriend that the rest of the clan didn't know about. She appreciated her mom's willingness to swallow her pride yet again to engage her little brother with the rest of the family. As for her banter with Jack, it brought a laugh when she needed one, even if his jokes were at her expense. She smiled as her dad slipped an understanding arm around her shoulders.

2

The volume of people at The Log Cabin on a Thanksgiving evening surprised Austen. She made small talk about the movie with the hostess, one of her high school classmates she still saw around Harriston now and then. "Is it always this crowded?" she asked.

Laticia laughed out loud. "Girl, you ain't got no *idea*. I've been working here three years—still trying to finish school—and Thanksgiving is the fullest day of the year."

"You've worked the last three Thanksgivings? That stinks."

"Girl, they treat us *good* around here. My manager throws us workers a big feast before folks start coming in for lunch. He always tells us it's a privilege to serve people their Thanksgiving meals. Some of them ain't got no people around here—to be honest, he's describing several of us. I thought his hype was silly that first year, but then I started paying attention to why folks come to a restaurant for Thanksgiving instead of eating at home with their families. And he's right. It's a privilege to attend to them."

"We're here because Hunter went to Starkville for the Egg Bowl. We're doing this *and* eating at Grandma's tomorrow." She lamented how both meals might affect her girlish figure, but a glance at Laticia's rounder frame caused her to pivot. "Spill the tea—why are people here alone on Thanksgiving?"

"Aw, girl, could be a lotta things. Kids don't prefer the traditional Thanksgiving meal, but the parents do— that's a big one. Let me see, can't afford to travel to see family way out of town—that's another one. Those are the regulars; work here long enough, you learn why they're here."

"I guess I've never considered what Thanksgiving was like for anybody else. I assumed everybody ate Thanksgiving lunch the same as my family does. Think I've been a wee bit sheltered?"

Laticia threw her hand on her hip as she rolled her eyes. "Mm hm, you reckon? Come here, girl, let me show you something." She motioned for a cashier to take her spot.

Taking Austen by the arm, Laticia led her—pulled her—around the corner where Austen's dad stood near the dining room while her mom browsed the Christmas merchandise near the register. "Look around, Austen."

It took a minute.

"Oh, my goodness. My goodness, Laticia, I... I don't..."

"They got unique stories, girl. Sometimes I hear them, most times I don't. I won't ever see most of them again."

"But they're so... they're so a*lone.*"

"Mm hm. They're the reason I prefer working every Thanksgiving. They come in and you can tell they notice the families sitting around them, but they try to act as if it's any other day. I know better, though, so I give them my best *how you doing?* I tell the servers they better give them the best service they ever had with the biggest smiles they'll see all day. They don't take care of my lonesome people, they got me to answer to, you understand what I'm saying?"

Austen nodded.

"I'll have my turn with them, too, coming *and* going. The adorable old man in the corner—he's my buddy. He comes in here with his son about every Tuesday. He likes him some flirting from the girls, so we put a little extra butter on his bread, you understand what I'm saying?"

Again, Austen nodded.

"His son's sick today, so there he sits. He's as sharp as a tack—good tipper, too—but I can tell he's in the dumps today. His wife died a long time ago, but his son never married, so they spend lots of time together." She looked around the dining room, and continued, "The rest of them—I don't know why they're here. Could be any number of reasons they're eating by themselves, but I want you to look at them. *See 'em*, girl."

Austen counted six solitary figures in a room full of family get-togethers. She liked the elderly man in the corner right away. His waitress looked to be in no hurry to leave their conversation, smiling and laughing as she chatted with him. Two women sat alone on the left side of the room, each one deep into her cell phone. A good looking, well-dressed man in his twenties filled his empty table with the busyness of three devices in front of him. A pleasant-looking elderly gentleman looked around the room with gentle eyes from the corner opposite Austen. Another girl about her age sat alone at the smaller tables to her right.

Laticia stirred Austen from her thoughts. "See what I'm talking about? Before the lonely folks leave here today, they'll be loved on, know what I'm saying? That's something I *can* do." Austen nodded as Laticia's substitute announced another party's invitation to the dining room.

"Hey, girl, that's your family Gina just called. Y'all have a wonderful meal, now. I've gotta get back to work."

Austen reached over for a quick hug. "Thanks for showing me this, Laticia. You're a special person to notice the lonely people today. If I were in your position, I'd feel sorry for myself for having to work on Thanksgiving."

"Girl, you remember having Ms. Millie Shelligan for science class?"

"Yeah."

"You remember how she used to pray for us sometimes before a test?"

Austen smiled. "How could any of us ever forget? She closed her prayers with, 'And, Lord, please bless

—'" She paused, and Laticia joined her, "'—the sick, sad, and lonely.'"

"Girl, I'm an answer to that woman's prayers. Understand, most of these folks'll be fine if they can just survive today. I'm gonna do my part to help them get through." With that, Laticia took her glowing countenance back to the hostess station, and Austen joined her family at a table near the fireplace in the front of the dining room.

THE THOMASONS HAD no sooner reached their table when Mom started in with the questions.

"That was Laticia Brooks you were talking to, wasn't it?"

Austen took a deep breath, still processing what Laticia had shown her and not ready to put her emotions into words. Mom was always too quick with questions.

"I remember teaching her. She was the sweetest little thing. She's not a little thing anymore..."

"Mom!"

"What?"

"That was rude."

"What was rude?"

"Mom, just because you're still the same size you were..."

"No, no, honey, I wasn't referencing her weight. I wouldn't do that. All the kids I taught are way bigger than they were in third grade, that's all."

Austen cooled. "Okay, sorry, I just…"

"Laticia was always so respectful, especially when you considered what she was going through." Austen cocked her head to the side. "Oh, that's right, you were in Ms. Peabody's class because you didn't want to have your mom for a teacher."

"Hannah Lynn, let it go," Dad interrupted. "We both agreed it was best for you not to teach this little dynamo." He rubbed Austen's head and winked at her on the sly.

"Like I was saying," Mom continued, flushing red, "that was the year Laticia's mother was diagnosed with breast cancer. Her father had left them the summer before, so Laticia was struggling with that when her mother got the news. I remember meeting with Ms. Brooks during open house and thinking I had my room mother for the year. I gave it a week and called to ask her. It was the day after she received her diagnosis. I'm sure I came across as selfish, but she was gracious and told me she still wanted to help when she was able. It felt empty, but I told her if she needed anything, to please tell me. She said—"

The server arrived to take their drink orders—a quick "five sweet teas, please." Mom continued, choking out the words, "Laticia's mom said, 'Just take care of my baby girl. She's the only thing I've got. I couldn't have any more kids after her, and her daddy left us. If she loses me…' Well, I cut her off right there and told her she was going to pull through just fine. I told her how they had made so much progress fighting cancer, and I told her my Aunt Sue survived breast cancer twice. It got quiet on Laticia's mom's end of the phone, so I stopped talking for a minute."

"Miracle," Jack said, not exactly under his breath.

Mom huffed and continued. "Her mama said she *would* fight that cancer with everything she had, but they were on public assistance and couldn't afford top-notch health care. We took up collections for her several times that year at school. Her church did, too, but it didn't amount to much compared to the cost of fighting cancer. Her mama died a week after school was out, and Laticia went to live with her grandparents. They didn't have much either, but they were good folks. I saw in the paper where they both died recently, too. She must be a lonely young lady without..." The server arrived with five sweet teas and a plate of biscuits and took their dinner orders.

After a quick sip of her tea and a nod of approval, Mom straightened up in her chair and cleared her throat to shift gears in the family conversation. "I thought we might go around the table saying what we're thankful for this Thanksgiving."

Jack threw up his hand in objection. "That's Grandma Vick's question!"

"Okay, fine, mister smartypants, do you have a better one?" Mom countered, flustered.

"How about our favorite Thanksgiving tradition?"

Mom's jaw dropped. "What an excellent alternative, Jack. You can go first since it was your idea. What is your favorite Thanksgiving tradition?"

"That Austen wins the battle every year for you not to take us straight from Halloween to Christmas."

Mom threw up her hands. "And there it is."

"I'll tell you mine," Dad intervened. "Seriously," he added, combating his wife's eye roll. "Mine is that even though we might have other stuff going on—such as Hunter's going to the Egg Bowl this year—we make our enormous meal together at Grandma Vick's a priority. And I like that we do it with no electronic devices at the table."

Jack slipped his phone into his pocket. "I have a serious one. I love the food Grandma fixes every year and that us men go to the den after lunch to watch football... and take a nap."

"There," Mom said, "was that so hard?"

"Wait, there's more. I'm a fan of the tradition that Grandpa only unzips his pants halfway when he kicks back in his recliner after lunch."

Dad chuckled, "I'm with you on that one, bud. That man scared me to death the first Thanksgiving I spent at their house when your mom and I were dating."

"Ooh, old Mom and Dad dating stories," Austen encouraged. "Keep going, Dad—tell us about your first impression of Mom's family."

"Well, I figured if I married into her family, I could count on a solid meal every Sunday after church with enough leftovers to carry us through the first part of the week. With your mom's being a teacher, too, we would be able to ride to school together and save on gas. Your Uncle Dennis had a solid reputation as a mechanic, so we could save on car maintenance since most teachers drive their cars till the wheels fall off. Your Uncle Scott had started his landscaping gig, which set me up for summer work. All things considered, I'd say marrying your mom was a solid business venture." Before she could jab his ribs, he winked at his wife. "Plus, she's eternally cute when she gets riled."

"I don't understand why y'all have to pick at me all the time."

"We don't *have* to," Jack said. "We *want* to."

Dad added, "You *are* an easy mark, hon. Your turn. Tell us your favorite Thanksgiving tradition in your rush to sneak in a Christmas movie."

"Contrary to popular belief, I *am not* opposed to Thanksgiving. I just love Christmas so much. Thanksgiving is more enjoyable since everybody gets a week off from school now. When our only vacation was Thursday and Friday, that meant finishing up school on Wednesday and going straight to the kitchen. I had to have the sweet potato and green bean casseroles ready to take to Mama's the next day. I am very fond of everybody's being home. Of course, Austen, you're always home."

"Mom…"

Dad stopped Austen. "Hannah Lynn, you know good and well that Austen does outstanding work; she just does it from home. With the internet she can…"

Mom waved off the rest of his spiel about Austen's working remotely and making a good living and staying in the garage apartment because she wanted to and not because she had to. If they wanted her to stay, he argued, she better stop nagging her about her flexible work schedule. "I just wish she would answer my texts when I need something during the day."

"Dear, do you want her to work or be your errand girl?" Dad sneaked another wink in Austen's direction.

Mom huffed and admitted, "Both, I guess. An-y-way, I cherish our recent tradition of having dinner together each night during Thanksgiving break before the boys head back to Hunter's room to play video games. Austen, you will, too, when you have kids and they're nearly grown. It's not much, but it means a lot to me."

"See, Mom, that wasn't so hard, was it?" Jack shot across the table.

"Watch it, you. You would be mighty sad and lonely if you didn't have any family with which to spend Thanksgiving. Take Laticia there—I bet the holidays are a tough time for her."

"It might surprise you," Austen said, wishing right away she had kept her mouth closed. Her mom was not one to leave a conversation loop open.

"What do you mean?"

"Nothing."

"Come on, you mentioned it. Wait, does she have a serious boyfriend?"

"It's nothing, Mom. I don't want to talk about it."

"Because of Mick?"

"What? No, Mom, what are you talking about?"

Mom was in full stealth mode now and not to be denied. The mention of Mick brought Austen a tinge of sadness, but with it a reminder she had dated a mouse. She worked hard to suppress a giggle while her mother continued to press for more information regarding Laticia's dating life. Austen leaned forward to hide her face and the grin creeping up on it. It drove Mom crazy for someone to have other thoughts during her part of a conversation.

Dad noticed. "Austen, you okay?"

"Fine," she mumbled. "Biscuit caught in my throat."

Mom didn't notice Austen had long since finished her biscuit, and then their food arrived to further distract her. Austen lost herself at once in her hamburger steak and gravy until Mom snapped, "Blessing. Justin—"

"Got it," Dad said. "Heavenly Father, we thank You for your blessings. We thank You for our family and the time that we have had together and will have together this week. We ask You to bless this food and bless Hunter as he drives back home in the middle of the night. Bless the sick, sad, and lonely this Thanksgiving season." He hesitated and added, "And, Lord, please bless Laticia's boyfriend that we don't even know she has. Amen."

Austen's mouth fell open even as Mom was scolding Dad for joking during prayer. She hated it when he did that, which didn't discourage him from the practice. Dad turned to Austen and whispered, "Your mom was looking at Christmas decorations. I was five feet from you and Laticia with nothing to do. Sorry."

Austen nodded. "It's okay. Thanks." Turning back to her food, she thought she was home safe from the earlier discussion.

Mom sampled the mashed potatoes and green beans and then turned back to Austen. "You didn't answer Jack's most excellent question. What is your favorite of our Thanksgiving traditions?"

Austen had been developing her answer during a few quiet moments after the food had arrived.

"Well, if I might offer a unique perspective..."

"Of course *your* perspective..."

"Hannah Lynn, let the girl answer the question, for crying out loud." Dad uncurled his palm, offering the floor for Austen to continue. "Sorry, young lady. Please continue."

"As I was saying, I kind of like what we have done today as maybe a fresh Thanksgiving tradition, at least as long as Hunter is at State. Maybe when Jack goes away to college, too, if he goes to State or Ole Miss and wants to go to the game."

"Hotty Toddy," Jack said without looking up from his plate.

"I'll be honest—I have dreaded the 'what are you thankful for' question at Grandma's this year. She won't remember that Mick and I broke up, or she'll figure it's a temporary thing and bless my heart a couple dozen times. It'll be fine, but I think I've mostly put that behind me. Now, when he comes to mind..." She stopped, realizing she hadn't shared her new inner joke with them.

A sharp glance from Dad stopped the question Mom wanted to blurt. After two bites of mac and cheese, Austen continued, "Today has been a real eye-opener for me. Mom, I'm glad you pushed for us to do this, and I'm glad you picked the movie you did."

Validated, Mom placed her hands in her lap and sat up straight. "Honey, I love the Christmas season because of the time we get to spend as a family, and, well, there's no reason Thanksgiving shouldn't be like that. I hate you and Mick broke up, but it's all for the best. We get the benefit of having you with us more."

"Mom, it's not actually about that...." Suddenly, Austen pushed back from the table and fairly ran around the corner to the restroom.

"What's the deal with her?" Hannah Lynn asked, her eyes following Austen.

"Talking about Mick made her want to puke," said Jack with his mouth full of chicken.

"Don't talk with your mouth full. That's uncouth." Turning to Dad, she said, "Let me go check on Austen."

"Let her be," Justin said. "Give her space. She'll be okay."

"But what if..."

"Give her a few minutes, dear. If she doesn't come out in three minutes, you can go check on her. You've got to let her grow up."

"But she's my..."

"Three minutes. The clock starts when you stop resisting."

"Fine." Hannah Lynn checked her watch every ten seconds. At the 2:40 mark, she looked up to see Austen talking to Laticia at the hostess station.

"There she is. I'm going to check on her now."

"Does she seem okay to you?"

"Yes, but..."

"Then let her talk. She'll come back to the table when she's ready."

"God knew what He was doing, not making you a mother."

"Truer words were never spoken. They say passing a kidney stone is as close as a man comes to understanding childbirth. I'm fine with never experiencing either."

"Dad, I'm trying to eat over here," Jack said. After a stern look from his mother, he finished chewing before he added, "Quit talking about sick stuff at the table. Good thing I have a cast-iron stomach."

Austen returned to the table with a spring in her step and a twinkle in her eye. "Sorry, everybody. Something I ate didn't agree with me, but I'm fine now."

"What were you talking to Laticia about?" Mom asked.

"Just how grateful I was to everybody here for serving us this meal today."

"But I thought you felt..."

"Doesn't matter. Not their fault. No other restaurant is even open for us to enjoy a wonderful meal together."

"What's gotten into you?"

"Nothing, Mom. Just thankful. It *is* Thanksgiving Day. Doesn't a girl—a young lady—have a right to be thankful today of all days?"

"Yes, you do. Does anybody need a to go box? I'd hate for this food to go to waste."

"Hon, when would we eat it?" Dad asked. "We'll eat for a week on the leftovers from your mom's tomorrow. That's one reason I married you, remember?" He kissed his wife on the cheek and stood up.

"Did you forget the check?"

"I have an inkling it has been covered." He winked at Austen, who nodded.

"What…"

"Outside, dear."

"But…"

"Hon, outside."

"I don't understand…"

Jack blurted, "Austen paid for our meal, Mom. Even I can figure that out. Now, can we go? The game is coming on in fifteen minutes."

3

I nside the family sedan, Mom turned around to Austen, sitting opposite her in the backseat. "Thank you, Austen. You didn't have to do that."

"I know."

"I just hate you weren't able to enjoy your own dinner. They should have let you order something else."

"Mom, it's fine. I've never appreciated a meal better than that one."

"If you say so. I'm glad you had such a satisfying time with your family."

Dad caught the eye roll and gleam that had not passed from his daughter's eye. He waited until they arrived home, and Hannah Lynn and Jack had rushed into the house to don their Ole Miss gear. Austen was three steps up toward her apartment when Dad reached up to touch her arm. "Just a second, Austen." After the door to the house was safely closed, he leaned in close.

"That episode in the restaurant meant more than paying for our meal—am I correct?"

"You caught my conversation with Laticia, right?"

"Yes."

"Dad, I paid for those people eating by themselves, and I've never felt more light and free." She reached over the rail to give her father a hug.

"And there it is. I've never been more honored to be your dad, especially after the year you've had."

"I know, right? Even though I've always considered myself a charitable person, I'll be honest—I wouldn't have noticed those lonely people if Laticia hadn't pointed them out to me. The more Mom rambled on about our precious family time, the more I noticed they didn't have it... at least, not today. It made me want to do something. I figured when Mom brought up Mick, that was the perfect time to fake sick and pay for their meals before any of them escaped."

"You were never sick?"

"Not in the least. I pulled it off like a pro, don't you think?"

"Especially with two teachers who usually recognize 'fake sick,' as you call it."

Austen reached over for another hug. "Dad, can I share a secret with you?"

"That's a loaded question."

"Not a deep, dark one. Every time somebody mentions Mick's name, my inner voice tells me *what a dumb name. You dated a mouse.*"

"That's funny. I'll enjoy catching your eye and attempting to make you laugh out loud every time someone mentions his name. For instance, when you are supposedly choking on a biscuit you finished five minutes earlier."

"You detected that, huh?"

"I did. Can I share a secret with you?"

"A deep, dark one?"

"Nope. When your mom opened her investigation of your sudden disappearance from the table, Jack told her mentioning Mick's name made you want to puke."

Austen laughed. "Not even a mention of his name would ruin today."

"Enough of this benevolent kindness. Let's go put on our State jerseys and agitate the heck out of your mother and brother with our cowbells for the next three hours."

"One more hug," Austen said. She held him longer than usual. "You'll tell Mom later?"

"Always. She'll be just as proud of you as I am."

———

"AUSTEN, girl, where have you been? I've been trying to call you for hours," Laticia blurted as soon as Austen returned her call.

"Watching the State-Ole Miss game with the fam. I left my phone upstairs in my apartment and didn't want to go back to get it. What's so urgent?"

"Girl, you ain't got no idea. Here, I'm gonna send you a picture."

Austen fumbled her phone when she saw her six lonely people seated together at The Log Cabin drinking coffee. "What... how..."

"Soon as you left, they started leaving. Pops stood up first, not two minutes after your family walked out. I called him over and said, 'Pops, somebody wanted to bless you tonight. Your meal's been paid for.' Course, he started looking around and wanted to know who did it, but I didn't give you up, girl."

"Thanks, Laticia. So what did he say?"

"He teared up and started telling me about his son being sick and all. He told me about feeling lonely lately and thinking nobody ever noticed him or called his name anymore. It was enough to make me wanna cry right there in front of everybody, girl. I'm telling you, Austen, I didn't do nothing but tell that little old fella somebody had paid for his supper, and he opened up to me like I was his therapist."

"That's incredible, Laticia. Did you talk to any of the rest of them?"

"Girl, I'm just getting started. I talked to every one of them. I suspect the good Lord stopped new customers from coming in every time one of them got up to leave. And He kept them from coming in till we finished talking. Austen, you ain't got no idea what you did tonight. Those folks were so lonely that I worried about some of them leaving. But when they found out a stranger had paid for their meal, it seemed like they snapped outta whatever funk they were in."

"Such as?"

"How long you got, girl, because this ain't no short story. It's more like a novel."

"Long as it takes."

"Well, I'm gonna be honest with you, I enjoy

working on Thanksgiving Day because the holidays get kinda lonely for me. I ain't got no family to spend them with."

"Hold on, Laticia, what are you doing tonight?"

"I thought I was talking to you...."

"No, I mean are you at home right now?"

"I'm at my apartment, yeah."

"You remember where I lived in high school?"

"Mm hm."

"Well, I'm living in the apartment above the garage now. Why don't I start a pot of coffee, and you come tell me in person?"

"That ain't putting you out?"

"Not a bit. I've been lonely, too, even with my family around me. Your story will be the highlight of my day, I can practically guarantee. I would rather you share it in person."

"You got it, girl. Give me a few minutes to change into my sweats, and I'll be right there."

THIRTY MINUTES LATER, Austen was curled under a fleece throw, savoring her favorite blueberry cobbler blend from Strange Brew from her panda mug.

Laticia said, "Girl, this here's some fine coffee."

"It's imported," Austen giggled, "all the way from Starkville. I'll send you home with a bag—I received three for my birthday this year. Guess I'm easy to shop for."

"I'll take you up on that."

"Okay, back to your report. Give me the goods."

"I was telling you how folks stopped showing up every time one of our lonesome people got up to leave, so I could stop them all on the way out and tell them somebody had bought their meal."

"Yep."

"It was funny how it worked out. They left several minutes apart but spaced out enough for me to talk to each of them. I didn't do it on purpose, but after a while, they stacked up right near my hostess station."

"Stacked up?"

"Yeah. Like I told you, Pops was the first one finished. He wasn't in a rush to go home, so we stood there talking for a few minutes before One Month Sober got up to go." Laticia answered Austen's upturned eyebrow. "I named them in my mind because of why they were there so I could learn them better. Along with Pops and One Month Sober, I named them Army Mom, Pastor Widower, Mr. Important, and Inconvenient Heart Attack."

"*Inconvenient* Heart Attack? As opposed to a convenient heart attack?"

"She didn't have the heart attack; her husband did, and he's over at the hospital across the highway. Anyway, I'll tell you their stories, but let me get through how I came to know them in the first place."

Austen let her missed attempt at humor pass. "Take your time. I'll try not to interrupt you anymore."

"All right, here goes. Pops and me were talking when One Month Sober finished. I called her over to where we were. When I mentioned her meal was free, she did the same thing Pops did and started dropping her story on me. She hadn't started good when Mr. Important got up to leave, though."

"The guy with the computer and tablet on the table?"

"That's the one. When he got up, I figured I needed to catch him quick before he slipped out. So I handed off One Month Sober to Pops, and they started talking. I never would have figured it, but you touched Mr. Important by paying for his meal. He couldn't figure out why because I guess he knows one look at him and anybody would know he can afford to pay for his meals. So he asks me why anybody would do that, and I told him somebody spotted him eating alone and requested to pay for his meal.

"He says, 'So somebody felt sorry for me?' I said to him, 'Consider it somebody who understands, instead.' That shut him up long enough for Pops to step over and tell him his wasn't the only meal that the guy paid for. He kinda looked at me when he said *the guy*—like he was looking for a clue to who did it—but I acted like I hadn't heard him. From then on, though, the entire group assumed it was a man who paid for all the meals, so I guess you're safe in staying unidentified."

"Cool." Austen sat her mug on the coffee table and settled back for more.

"I'll tell you their individual stories in a minute," Laticia continued. "Pops and One Month Sober were standing there talking to each other and telling their stories. Soon, Pastor Widower, Army Mom, and Inconvenient Heart Attack joined Mr. Important, and they

A. AINSWORTH

were still near my hostess station. They'd figured out by now that *the guy* had paid for everybody sitting alone, so they figured they'd just stay till everybody flying solo had finished.

I didn't have much to do, so I stood there listening to our lonesome people, still standing there swapping stories and enjoying one another. They didn't seem too restless to leave—not even Mr. Important after a while—so I asked if they wanted a table where they could have some coffee and pie. Pastor Widower said that would be nice.

"Nobody had come in since they had, and it was about the time we slow down, anyway. My manager had heard what was going on with our lonesome people, so he said, 'You can take care of your group there' and tips his head over toward them.'"

"So you got to stay with them?"

"Yep. By the time we cleared two tables next to each other to accommodate them, they were the only group left in the waiting area. They weren't bit more paying attention to me than the man in the moon, so I picked up the microphone and called out, 'Lonesome, party of six, your table is ready. Lonesome, party of six.'"

Austen laughed. "You said that?"

"Yep. None of them noticed at first, but Army Mom caught me looking at them and said, 'Y'all, I'm pretty sure she called for us.' I grinned at her and they came on in to the same tables where you and your family ate. I got them started on some coffee and even slipped in some pie that would have gone to waste if somebody didn't eat it. One Month Sober noticed theirs was the only table I was working and invited me to join them. My manager said it was okay—special circumstances and all. I put two pots of coffee on the table with plenty of cream and sugar and hung out with them for a solid two hours after that."

"No way."

"Yes way. I was getting paid time-and-a-half to listen to these amazing stories."

"Cool," Austen said. "You need more coffee?"

"Bet. We're gonna be here a while, girl, but between coffee and adrenaline, I'm good."

Austen filled both of their mugs, tossed Laticia a quilt Mom had made her last Christmas, and coiled back under her own fleece. "All right, tell me about Lonesome, Party of Six. Start with Pops. He's an adorable little old man."

Laticia laughed. "Don't let him hear you say it. He's harmless as can be, but he can flat lay the flirt on a pretty girl like you, and don't imagine his ninety-two-year-old self can't do it, either."

POPS

4

Jimmy Lee Yates was ninety-two years old. He would pay for that newspaper until his obituary appeared in it. Every morning, James Junior stopped by to drink coffee and read it with him. It was a shame Mrs. Right hadn't come along for his son, but Pops enjoyed the company. For his part, James Junior recognized when to leave before he'd outstayed his welcome, too, which was nice because they both had plenty else to do.

On Thanksgiving morning, Pops read the paper alone. James Junior thought he might have the flu and didn't want to give it to him, so he stayed home. Pops still made mention aloud of items of interest, as he always did. He shook his head and said, "Guess Old Man Crowley was ready to go. He fought a good long fight. You realize he'll be three doors down from Catherine, right?" Pops kept a close watch on the new tombstones "in the neighborhood." Crowley had been his high school math teacher, a scant three months out of college and four years older than most of the seniors. It made Pops a little uncomfortable knowing his remains would one day be that close to a former teacher. But his interaction with Mr. Crowley at the corner market through the years made him seem more than a teacher. "I thought they all lived in the school basement," he once remarked to James Junior.

When Pops saw the ad declaring the The Log Cabin would be open on Thanksgiving, he declared to the empty house, "I believe I'll eat some of their hamburger steak and gravy. I'll wait till tonight, though, when it's not so crowded."

Catherine's birthday fell on Thanksgiving some years. She would have been ninety this year. Although cancer took her some twenty years ago, Pops sensed an extra twinge of sadness every Thanksgiving. It was her last pleasant holiday because she put off the doctor's appointment on purpose until after her favorite day of every year. Finding out a few days earlier wouldn't have mattered, though, the cancer was so far gone. At least she was able to enjoy the day in ignorance, Pops always said to console himself. She died before Christmas, and James Junior began showing up at his house to read the paper every morning within a week.

If James Junior wasn't going to get married and give him grandkids, Pops figured his son's regular companionship was the next best thing. They drank coffee and read the paper Monday through Thursday and met some of James Junior's old high school buddies on Friday mornings down at Hazel's. The food wasn't great, but they sat and talked as long as they wanted with no pressure to give up their table. Now that most of James Junior's friends had retired, they worked to perfect their ability to break down every ball game, political race, and Sunday sermon like nobody's business. Sometimes they would stay at Hazel's for two or three hours on a Friday morning. Pops always lagged to help Dorothy clean up the mess their breakfast bunch created, and she returned the favor with a "Thanks, sweetie" and a kiss on the cheek.

Pops reserved Friday afternoons for fishing and working on the land he owned out from town. He gardened behind his house in town, but he still liked to get out on the tractor and clean the trails and the edge of the pond, his practice since he had inherited the place. He and Catherine once planned to build their dream house there after they finished paying for James Junior's journalism school.

The younger Yates wrote for the local paper for years —never made much money, but the locals thought he did a fine job covering the high school and college teams all those years. Sometimes James Junior rode with them to the out-of-town games in their RV when the college team was playing well. The dream house took a back seat while they delighted in traveling the country. Their favorite experience had come during Sparky Powell's last season as the football coach when their team played in the Tangerine Bowl down in Orlando. He and Catherine decided then that when they retired, they wanted to have a winter home in Florida. That was the second dream home they never built.

These days, Friday nights meant high school football in the fall. High school basketball was already underway by the time football was over, and high school baseball followed in the spring. Pops was such a fixture with James Junior in the various Harriston High press boxes through the years that nobody shooed him away when James Junior didn't accompany him. The booster club fed him well and kept him warm. Mark Carmichael, who called the action on the internet broadcast for Harriston High School's teams, enjoyed interviewing the school's most experienced sports fan from time to time.

Pops knew most of the Tiger fans by name... or at least as Billy Frank's boy, who hit that game-winning shot against Murphyville. Or Alice's grandson, who intercepted that ball in the end zone to save the conference championship back in '94. Or one of the Carson twins—boy, they could knock the cover off a baseball. Everybody knew him, too, but only a handful of the current crop of fans could call his name. They identified him as Pops—the adorable old man who never missed a game, that newspaper reporter's dad, or the occasional guest on the school's athletic broadcasts. During the last few months, Pops realized he came across as more of a cuddly old mascot than a seasoned chronicler of Harriston High. It hadn't helped when he ran into Jerry Glen's wife at the first basketball game a few weeks ago. Martha Gail was from somewhere up near Jackson, and he didn't care for her anyway because she was so much younger than Jerry Glen, who was James Junior's age. That night, she had the audacity to tickle his ribs and greet him as *Mister Pops*. Without a word, he walked away. His ninety-two years gave him the right to walk away when provoked.

On Saturday mornings Pops strolled to the end of his driveway by five o'clock, an hour earlier than usual, so he could read the paper before James Junior showed up to take him fishing. Most of the time, they drove out to their land and their pond stocked with bass, bream, and catfish. James Junior fished for catfish, but Pops didn't appreciate sitting still and waiting on the fish. Plus, he liked the fight of a good bass on the line. Most days, a seven-inch watermelon-flecked worm with a glass rattle inserted by the hook did the job just fine. When they passed the Barlow place driving to the pond, they looked to see if their cows were laying down. If they were, Pops would say, "Son, you can fish today if you want to, but you won't catch fish when the cows are laying down." James Junior believed it to be true. What he hadn't determined was whether the fish didn't bite because the cows were laying down or because Pops made so much noise on those days bush hogging around the pond.

Pops had the run of pretty much every other fishing hole around Harriston. He'd stick his nose in just about any fishing conversation he overheard around town, wait for the right moment, and offer a piece of his experience with a certain lure. Any fisherman worth his salt would listen to the advice of a man his age, and he'd walk away with an invitation to fish a new honey hole. He'd take them up on it, too, at least once or twice.... unless the cows were laying down. Occasionally, folks he didn't recognize would see him out in public and walk up to him and introduce themselves. "Are you Pops, by chance?" they'd inquire before asking him for a fishing tip or two. His go to response was, "I can show you better than I can tell you," which always led to an invitation to fish a new spot. Even as his fame as a guide spread, Pops realized most folks didn't bother to ask his name.

During football season, his rule was to make his last cast by ten o'clock. The college games started at eleven, and the SEC game of the week came on at 2:30. Pops never missed those, even when he was out of town with James Junior to cover the local college. He enjoyed the road trips, though not as much after Catherine passed. One benefit of being his age was the food he enjoyed at everybody else's tailgates. He loved the Cajun food at Southwestern Louisiana—they changed their name some years ago, but Pops was having none of it. Ditto Memphis State, where the ribs were killer. This year, he kept score of the people who called him by name and those who called him Pops (or nothing at all). Not a single person called him *Jimmy Lee Yates*. He wondered, *when did people stop remembering my name?*

Like most ninety-two-year-olds, Pops' social calendar was dominated by doctor visits. Two of his doctors had retired, and one of them moved about ten stones down from Catherine a month ago. After his check-up this summer, his fifty-year-old general practitioner told him, "Mr. Jimmy Lee, there's almost forty years between us, but our biological ages are about the same." The doctor had smiled when he said it, so that was fine, but all Pops carried away from the consultation were the words *Mr. Jimmy Lee*. It started him down the lonely rabbit hole of pondering his own meaning at this stage of his life.

He always looked forward to his high school reunion —almost all of his class of forty-six from '46 had either stayed nearby or moved back when they retired. His classmates appreciated the real Jimmy Lee Yates. They developed regular meeting spots around town through the years, but they especially enjoyed the reunions. Their sixtieth reunion had been their last, though. He and Roni Lu Crenshaw were the only ones left, and she lived in a nursing home near her son in Atlanta. On the night his class would have celebrated their seventieth reunion, Pops told James Junior to go to the game without him. While poring through the aged yearbooks, he had cried a little.

The longing in the pit of his stomach reminded him of the homesickness he endured in Korea during the war. The ache eased a little after that night, but he couldn't get past the pangs of loneliness that hit every time someone called him *Pops*. He liked the attention of the college girls down at the cheap taco place where he tried to have lunch often while school was in session. Adept at walking the fine line between cute little flirt and dirty old man, his motivation to melt the college girls by flashing his dentures had weakened.

Around town, the restaurant owners he had known for years called him *Pops*, too, and so did the folks at the grocery store and the pharmacy. "James Junior's friends started this," Pops said to his empty house when he laid down his paper. It was heartwarming back when they first started congregating at his and Catherine's two-bedroom house on 12th Avenue. They called her *Mama*, and him *Pops*, just like their only son did. James Junior didn't know it then, but his parents once wanted more children. After he was born, the doctors warned them of the dangers of another pregnancy, so after much prayer and a second opinion, they decided Catherine would have a total hysterectomy. They had talked about adoption, and Pops often wished now that thoughts would have moved to plans and action, but they never got around to it. *Maybe if we would've, I'd have some grandkids running around here on the holidays*, he imagined in his lonelier moments. Every month since Catherine died, he had sent a check to a children's home in Harriston.

POPS EXPERIENCED another lonesome moment the Sunday after the day the doctor called his name. John Smith, one of the regular greeters at 12th Avenue Baptist Church where Pops had faithfully attended since childhood, greeted him with, "Hey, Pops, how's life treatin' ya?" He asked the same question every week and raised his voice a little when he asked it, Pops had noticed. *Does he believe just because I'm ninety-two years old, I'm hard of hearing? I can hear that he has the most generic name on the planet—what, is he in witness protection or something?* Martha's spot was still empty on the pew in front of him. The only church member older than Pops for the longest time, Martha had moved a few doors down from Catherine earlier in the year, having shouldered the weight of being the congregation's oldest member long enough. Pops sat alone, but James Junior would be on directly. He usually showed up about halfway through the first song, often with a hint of fish smell leaking through his fruity-smelling hand soap.

Church had transformed over time, but Pops didn't mind change as much as the younger old folks tried to avoid it. He remembered July 14, 1935, as if it were yesterday. He was seven and wanted to invite his friend Jeremiah to come to church with him that morning. His daddy said no—black folks had their own churches. That was also the day his daddy said he thought it better if his son stopped hanging around with Jeremiah. Before young Jimmy Lee argued, his daddy bolted for a deacons' meeting. He said they would talk about it later, but Robert E. Lee Yates never rescheduled.

It took sixty years, but Jeremiah Johnson became the first black person to walk through the doors of 12th Avenue Baptist Church with his friend Jimmy Lee. A third of the church's members didn't return, but Jesus was pleased, even if the church folks weren't. His church boasted the most diverse membership in Harriston now, more than the two large suburban churches. None of the current members realized why except him and James Junior and perhaps a few other old folks. *I wonder what ol' John Smith—or whatever his name was before witness protection,* he imagined—*would think of ol' Pops back in '95 when he was a "real" person.*

"JEREMIAH, this is Jimmy Lee. Are you ready?"

"I was born ready, my friend. But are all them white folks ready for Jeremiah Johnson to walk through them white doors?"

Many wouldn't be. Another small-town Mississippi church had made national news in recent months by refusing to marry a long-time church member and his mixed-race fiancée. The pastor of the church was aware of the girl's ethnicity but told no one. His secretary tipped off the chairman of the deacons, who called an emergency meeting to "maintain the purity" of the church. The pastor caught wind of the meeting and stepped in to defend his decision. The chairman of the deacons reportedly told him they could send him packing quicker than he had arrived in town. After the pastor married the couple at an alternate site on a Saturday, he had moved out before nightfall.

In many ways, the culture of 12th Avenue Baptist Church mirrored that of their sister church across the state. Jimmy Lee was encouraged by the church's move away from the deacon model of leadership that seemed to him to be hypocritical to the biblical position. The new pastor, Brother David Caraway, seemed open to the change Jimmy Lee had felt was his duty to bring to 12th Avenue. They had met about the possibility of Jeremiah's visit and the fallout sure to follow. It was the same conversation he had sparked with a half dozen other pastors since his daddy had first rejected Jeremiah's visit so long ago. Bro. David encouraged him to bring his friend, but urged Jimmy Lee not to advertise it. "Let's see what happens if we just thrust it upon them like its not even a choice." He didn't seem to fear any more for his own future with the church than he did for Jeremiah's safety. Jimmy Lee wasn't as confident about either.

"Ready?" Jimmy Lee asked again after parking within sight of the front door.

"I was born ready," Jeremiah repeated. "If I'm shaking, it's out of excitement, not fear."

Jimmy Lee knew that to be a stretch of the truth, but he gathered his worn black leather Bible and reading glasses from the backseat. "All right, let's do this."

The two friends walked through the double white doors like they had done it every week since they were boys. Three men in their early to mid-forties stepped forward one by one from their various conversations around the foyer.

"Coach Johnson!" the first called from halfway across the spacious room.

"Welcome!" shouted a second from a little further away.

The third, standing near Jimmy Lee and Jeremiah, wrapped the church's first black visitor in a bear hug. Just as quickly, he introduced him to a friend as his son's football coach, a mighty fine one at that. All three men parked their families near the third row where Jimmy Lee guided his friend.

At lunch on Wednesday, Jimmy Lee confessed he had manipulated Jeremiah's first entrance to the church. He wanted to give 12th Avenue its best opportunity to greet Jeremiah properly. By his standards, they had done okay, but he wanted assurance Jeremiah felt the same.

"Okay? I'd say it was better than okay. I felt downright welcomed."

"Don't give them too much credit yet. Next Sunday will be a more proper test."

"What do you mean?"

"The folks who know you and the pastor and me played our cards this week. Now that they know where we stand, some of them will get together and figure out how they're going to respond. Likely, they'll try to force the pastor's hand, or they might just never show back up."

Over the next few months, 12th Avenue purged a full third of its six hundred members, though many of those who left mainly came for Christmas and Easter and business meetings. Jeremiah never came back, but several black parents from his youth football team did. Jimmy Lee and his three sentinels invited and invited and invited until the church was a picture of the community's diversity. As one of them once summed up that season of life at 12th Avenue, "we lost a lot of friends but gained a lot of brothers and sisters."

5

On this beautiful Sunday a quarter of a century later, Pops seemed to himself an outsider in his own church. James Junior slipped in beside him during a contemporary version of "Come Thou Fount." The gleam in his eye indicated a fruitful morning of catching fish, and his presence snapped Pops back to the moment.

"Have we raised our Ebenezer yet?" James Junior whispered.

Pops giggled like a far younger version of himself. "Nah, they skip that verse in all the remakes." Just like that, one of many inside conversations between him and James Junior erased the encroaching loneliness. "Too much work explaining it nowadays. How was the fishing?"

"Not quite the 153 the disciples brought in, but I would've caught the limit if it hadn't been time for church."

"A little past time, as usual, you mean."

"Perhaps, but we'll eat good this week. We can invite the preacher to come eat with us if that'll make it better."

Pops shook his head as Pastor Dean promoted the revival services coming up in three weeks. "Doctor says I shouldn't eat so much fried food."

"I can grill them if you'd prefer. But you're ninety-two years old. Why don't you tell that doctor you will eat whatever you want to eat? Your diet works pretty well, wouldn't you say?"

Pops smiled at that and turned his thoughts toward lunch.

After lunch Pops slipped over to the other side of town, where the Shady Grove Missionary Baptist Church was just letting out from their Sunday service. Pops parked his truck a quarter of a mile down the street at the elementary school to give the folks a few minutes to clear the parking lot. When they moved, he pulled under a shade tree near Jeremiah's place.

"Hey, buddy, sorry I'm late. They went a little long today. Have I ever told you I wished you had hung around long enough to get you a place in mine and Catherine's neighborhood?"

He imagined Jeremiah's reply: *Just every Sunday, that's all.*

"The message at 12th Avenue was out of John 10 today. Here, I'll read it to you first, and then I'll tell you all the points the preacher made." Pops read the text from the same Bible he had pulled from the backseat for Jeremiah's visit so long ago. He only used it to read to his friend now. When he finished the passage, he taught Jeremiah about Jesus' role as the Good Shepherd as much as he remembered from the notes he had taken.

When his recap of the message was over, Pops sighed. "James Junior caught a mess of crappie this morning, so lunch was good. He was late to church again. The boy doesn't watch out, he'll get set in his ways like us. Jeremiah, you can probably tell I'm beating around the bush about something, so I'm just going to come right out and say it. I'm lonely, Jeremiah, a loneliness I haven't felt since you and Catherine left me. This summer, one of my doctor's called me by my name—nothing unusual. But it emphasized how people I see all the time never call me anything but *Pops*. Don't get me wrong, I don't mind the nickname. Still, I've been thinking I'm nothing but an old man to folks nowadays. Does my life before I became an old man matter? When did that happen, anyway?

"During football season, not one person at the school called me by my name. I went to several college games with James Junior, and everybody who recognized me in the various press boxes called me *Pops*. Even at church, they don't call me by my name, not since Martha moved over to Catherine's neighborhood. I've probably told you this before, but that John Smith fella gets under my skin. Something about the way he calls me *Pops* chaps my hide more than when anybody calls me that. Did I tell you I suspect he's in witness protection? Who else goes by *John Smith*? It's too common a name for anybody in actual life, don't you think? He gives me the same greeting every week, too, word for word.

"But you don't want to hear about John Smith, do you? I don't have any other news this week. Like I said, I've been down going on several months now. Maybe the good Lord is getting me ready to join you and Catherine and Mama. It's like homesickness, Jeremiah, best I can explain it, a sadness that won't go away. Sometimes I'm happy on the surface, and I'll think I'm getting past whatever this is, and then I'll get downright lonely. Sometimes I feel like crying. Sometimes I actually do.

"Jeremiah, I've outlived all of my friends. Most of my friends now were James Junior's friends first. Besides Catherine, I miss you most of all, buddy. I wish you could have seen the change in our church after you left us. Every time I see a new dark-skinned brother walk through those doors, I remember the old days and how you changed all that. Not long ago, this fella walked in, and from a distance, he could have been your doppelgänger. When I got closer, he didn't look much like you at all except for his size, but it made me miss you all the same. I probably told you about that. I reckon I'll go watch the late game on TV and stop all this rambling. See you next week, my friend."

POPS READ the entire Thanksgiving edition—beginning with the sports page and then reading the sections he deemed less important—by a quarter after six. Before he forgot, he wrote his prediction of Mississippi State's winning this year's Egg Bowl 24-16 on a napkin so he might prove it to James Junior later. He would throw it away if he was wrong. "Seems like the favorite never wins, anyway, not even Dak's senior year," he told his empty house.

Pops was one of only a handful from his sports community who rooted for both State and Ole Miss as long as they weren't playing each other. "Southern used to whip them both before they stopped playing," he remarked to the hall closet as he reached for his Christmas tree. A former civil engineer who had worked on the portion of Highway 49 from Jackson during parts of the 1950s and '60s, he established camaraderie among his many colleagues who were State graduates. The Ole Miss fans, bless 'em, required more grace. Their brief dalliance with national relevance back in the '60s spoiled them, he thought.

"This may be our last Christmas together, Bruce Spruce," Pops announced. "I won't decorate you without James Junior, but I'll get you ready for tomorrow." Pops' seven-foot tree was the hall closet's only occupant for much of the year until its owner centered him in the front window. A decade ago, he began preparing his tree for life without him. In his mind, he imagined Bruce replying *promises, promises, old fella; you ain't going anywhere.*

Without fail, Pops pulled Bruce out of the closet on Thanksgiving. A day later, he decorated him. During halftimes of New Year's Day bowl games, he removed a lifetime's worth of ornaments and sent Bruce back to hibernation in the hall closet.

"Don't judge me, Bruce," he growled as he adjusted the aging branches. "I'm still a Thanksgiving first, then decorate for Christmas kind of guy. This year's just a little different with James Junior sick and all.... No, won't decorate you without him. I'm just getting everything out.... No, this is not a new tradition. Geez, you are so stuck in your ways, Bruce. Remind me which one of us is ninety-two again?"

At eight o'clock Pops flipped on the TV to watch the Macy's Thanksgiving Day Parade. It was one of his concessions to Catherine—along with no TV during Thanksgiving lunch—so he could watch ball games all afternoon with James Junior. What Catherine saw in watching the parade year after year, he didn't understand. Every year resembled the last, but sitting with her and feigning interest while she flitted back and forth between the couch and the kitchen was a small price to pay for hours of football. She had moved down the street to the cemetery over two decades ago, and he hadn't missed a Thanksgiving parade since.

"Oh, look at that big Scooby Doo," he said, pointing to the flat screen James Junior had mounted on the wall for him a few years ago. "Catherine would have loved that one." With that, he rocked back and forth enough to generate the momentum he required to stand to his feet. He fetched his keys from the kitchen counter and started for the door. "Bruce, I'll be back directly. I'm going down the street to tell Catherine about Scooby Doo."

"SWEETHEART, you should have seen this big Scooby Doo float in the parade today. I couldn't wait to tell you about it. Remember, James Junior was in college when that show started, and he used to mimic Scooby all the time. It drove me up the wall sometimes, but you told me I would miss it when he stopped doing it. You were right, as usual. Every once in a while, when he's rambling on about something I'm not particularly interested in, I'll imagine him using that voice. Don't tell him I said that. He'll believe I'm losing my mind and put me in a home. I'm just kidding. Next place I'm moving is right here next to you.

"James Junior thinks he might have the flu, so he's staying home today so I don't get sick. I hope it's just a little bug so he can help me decorate the tree tomorrow. I got Bruce Spruce out today—that's right, you've never met Bruce—but I didn't start putting ornaments on him yet. You would have my hide for decorating for Christmas before Thanksgiving lunch. I'm going to go over to The Log Cabin early this evening before the Egg Bowl to eat my Thanksgiving meal. I'm going back over to my house now to get the ornaments sorted out before the game comes on TV. I'll come back tomorrow to let you know who wins… like you care, anyway. I love you, sweetheart. See you soon." Pops blew a kiss toward Catherine's tombstone and started the two-block hike back home, a little happier in his spirit and a shade sadder in the deepest part of his soul. He imagined her raspy voice. *Soon, Jimmy Lee, soon. Take care of our little boy.*

THE PARADE WAS ALMOST over when Pops walked back in his house. He reached for the wall phone to call and check on James Junior. Pops was an early adopter of the smart phone—at least for his age bracket—mostly so didn't have to bug his son for ball game scores. He used it to text now, and he was even part of a few group chats about fishing and football, mostly. For talking on the phone, though, he still liked the way his wall phone laid on his shoulder. James Junior ranted sometimes about his spending fifty bucks a month for the comfort of a phone against his ear for the few times a month he used it. Pops countered by questioning why in the world James Junior would pay thousands of dollars in depreciation to buy a new car every other year because he liked the smell. They called it a draw.

"HEY, DAD."

"How did you know it was me?"

"Caller ID, Dad, same as last time. If you weren't so tied to that wall phone, you'd recognize who was calling you. I don't understand why you won't just cancel your phone service. You're better using a smart phone than some folks half your age."

"I don't care who's calling me. I'm just glad for the

conversation." It was true. Pops could outlast telemarketers and political pollsters every time. "Anyway, I figured I should call and check on you."

"Been visiting Mama this morning, I reckon."

"Maybe. She says to take care of you. So how are you doing?"

"Better. I don't have a fever, so it must be a touch of food poisoning. As much press box food as I've eaten through the years, I should have built up quite a tolerance. I may need to let you go soon, though, if you know what I mean."

Pops laughed. "Don't let me stop you. Bruce and I will be waiting for you in the morning."

"My mind is not exactly focused on food, but have you made plans for Thanksgiving?"

"Probably going down to the Log Cabin later. They'll be slammed at lunch, so I'll wait until 4:30 or so to avoid the crowd."

"You be careful. Plenty of stores can't wait until tomorrow to make that Christmas money, so the crazies will be out on the road."

"I know. I'll be careful. I'll remind you I haven't had a traffic accident since that crazy lady sideswiped me back in '87 on the way to the state championship game in Jackson."

"You had that ticket last year."

"First one in nigh on thirty years, it was. Officer felt lowdown for giving it to me, too."

"He shouldn't have. You were going nearly your age."

"I was only driving seventy-four in a sixty-five, thank you very much."

"But how fast were you actually going?"

"Seventy-four in a sixty-five. I can show you the ticket."

"So says the ticket," James Junior echoed. "I'm a reporter, remember? I have mad investigative skills, and my sources say you were doing eighty-one."

"The ticket said seventy-four miles per hour," Pops insisted. "It never showed up on my insurance, either. It also made me the oldest graduate of defensive driving school, so I've got that going for me."

"You should frame your certificate. I'm still considering having an intervention to take your license."

"Better bring an army."

"Love you, Dad."

"Love you, son. Get better soon."

THE DETROIT-GREEN BAY game bumped Pops back into his usual Thanksgiving Day routine. He had liked the Packers since local boy Brett Favre played for them, so he was glad to have a team to root for this year in the early game. He had never forgiven the Cowboys for booting Tom Landry to the curb, so he would pull for the Redskins against them later. His favorite team, the Saints, played tonight against the Panthers. He would go back and forth between that one and the Egg Bowl. He couldn't complain about the day's slate of football.

When the Packers took a 21-3 lead into halftime,

Pops turned his attention to a box of Christmas decorations in Catherine's old closet. He brought the smaller boxes of ornaments into the den to sort—he never was much on order when he took down the decorations during the New Year's Day games. "This is like unpacking the story of my life," he commented to Bruce when he brought the last box from the bedroom.

Pops had thrown his ornaments into a plastic box eleven months earlier with no rhyme or reason. As he pulled each piece from the box now, their order seemed well planned. Pops liked the proximity of Thanksgiving and Christmas on the calendar. Thanksgiving reminded him to give thanks for his memories with Catherine and to celebrate her birthday. During the Christmas season, he shared the the story behind each ornament with James Junior, who had now heard them dozens of times. James Junior didn't complain, and Pops enjoyed repeating the same old stories.

"Guess I'll tell you the stories this year, Bruce. This one is one of your favorites and mine: It's the little school building that Ms. Georgia, my third grade teacher, gave us to paint that year. The boys at my school all fell head over heels in love with her, so we would have done anything she asked us to do. She figured the ornaments were an efficient way to keep everybody quiet and busy on the day before our homeroom party. I'm sure I've told you about Mark Carmichael—he does the broadcasts for all the games at the high school. Ms. Georgia was his grandmother. She's a few rows down from Catherine, died a few days before her. I would have gone to her funeral, but I couldn't leave Catherine's side during those days. When I look at this old ornament, it always makes me think of my first love and my forever love living in the same neighborhood now.

"You'll hide this one again for me, won't you, old buddy?" Pops clutched the rebel flag carved from a piece of cedar. Its colors had faded, and Pops' grip on it threatened to break it into pieces. "My daddy made this himself. I'm not proud of it, Bruce, but I'm a man of my word. He made me promise to always put it on my tree, but I didn't promise I would put it where anybody could see it. Bruce, this reminds me of how much difference one man can make in breaking generational garbage like racism. My daddy cost me years with my best friend, but if Jeremiah can forgive him, I reckon I can, too. This ornament reminds me of who Daddy was and what a wonderful friend Jeremiah was—God rest his soul. I wish we could live in the same neighborhood after I'm gone from this earth. That rebel flag also reminds me to keep things right between me and James Junior so he doesn't have to deal with my junk after I'm gone. Let's hide it behind your branch here in the back, Bruce, so James Junior doesn't find it this year.

"This is the first one Mama gave me, the year I left home to work over in Alabama. I couldn't make it home for Christmas, so she sent me this little metal wreath in the mail; she got one just like it for herself and told me it would connect our hearts on Christmas. She repeated it the two years when I was overseas in the service—here's the Christmas tree from the first year and the little bird from the next year. We were together on Christmas except for those three for the rest of her life. She made sure we were together in our hearts and minds on those years. I had no clue back then how hard it must have been to live with my daddy. She made Thanksgiving and Christmas special for all us kids, even when he was drunk and acting a fool. I need to go talk with her a spell next time I go visit Catherine. She's in the older part of the neighborhood, you know."

"This is the last one Mama gave me. I've told you this story before, but she understood she was eaten up with cancer. It would be her last Christmas. She had her wreath, tree, and bird from the years we were apart on Christmas melded together into one ornament. She only awakened for a little while on Christmas Day, but she called me over to her side before she had to push her morphine pump again and pulled out this ornament. When I recognized what it was, I cried, but she said, 'Son, I don't have long now, so I need you to listen to me. You've got Catherine and James Junior to lean on, but I want you to always keep a piece of me, too. We may have been sad, but we got along all right on those years you weren't home for Christmas. This'll be our last one together for a while, but you will be okay. Just promise me you'll never stop thinking about me at Christmas time.' She held on a few days, but she was never coherent enough for us to talk again. That's why this one gets to be front and center, Bruce, but I reckon you already knew that."

Pops continued sorting through the ornaments, telling Bruce about each one, until he reached his special box marked *Catherine ornaments*. After a deep breath, he gently opened the box. He found the pair of turtledoves from the year he married her. He was twenty-four and one of the oldest of his high school classmates to marry. She was nineteen, but an old soul. Her mother had given them an ornament every year of their marriage. She died a year after Catherine, so both Christmases became especially lonely. Pops paused over the fiftieth anniversary ornament, a golden treasure chest. He sobbed, softly at first and then in heaves. He had bought it at a Hallmark store on the year of their golden anniversary, even though Catherine couldn't celebrate the occasion with him.

"Bruce, I'm sorry, I've got to go down the street to see my sweetheart. I'll drop by to look in on Mama and Catherine's mama while I'm at it. Hold down the fort for me while I'm away and take a message if James Junior calls. I'll be back directly."

THE PACKERS-LIONS GAME was over by the time Pops walked back into his house. His emotions were spent except for the loneliness that gripped his soul. The lingering idea that nagged at him was how almost everybody who cared about him was dead and gone. He wondered why there didn't seem any end in sight. *God, nobody even knows my name anymore.* He had made the rounds, visiting Catherine and her mama and then his own mama before making the loop back around to Catherine's grave. He stared at his headstone, especially the blank after the dash. *Dear Jesus, I'm ready when you are. I'll hang in here as long as you want me to, but if you haven't taken me because I haven't told You I'm ready, then I'm declaring it. I miss them, Lord, I miss them real bad today.*

Halfway home, he felt a peace and heard a quiet voice in his spirit. *Jimmy Lee Yates, I know your name. I'll call it when I'm ready.*

Pops turned the station to the Cowboys' game. They were up two touchdowns on the Redskins, so he clicked it off. "Bruce, I'm going to get ready to head over to The Log Cabin to eat my Thanksgiving meal. I plumb forgot to eat lunch, so I believe I'll eat turkey and dressing and the whole nine yards over there. We'll finish getting you decorated tomorrow after Thanksgiving." Pops turned back around when he reached his bedroom door. "Bruce, I'm a little lonelier than usual this Thanksgiving without James Junior. Say a prayer for me, please, sir."

6

Pops didn't like to drive after dark anymore. His eyesight was remarkably strong, but he didn't trust his reaction time at night like he used to back in his eighties. He at least wanted to arrive at the restaurant before the sun set, hoping traffic would thin out by the time he was ready to drive home. Dressed in Levis he had worn for the better part of two decades and the flannel shirt James Junior had given him for his birthday last year—or was it the year before that—Pops said goodbye to Bruce and locked his door. The engine in his old Chevy fired right up as it always had, and Pops backed out of the carport and turned around in his driveway. Before he pulled out into the street, though, old Mrs. Leviston came running across her yard next door, waving her arms like a crazy woman.

Ethel Leviston was only in her upper sixties, but Pops privately called her Old Mrs. Leviston because she had an old name, and she dressed... well, old. More often than not, she traipsed to the mailbox in the mid-afternoon in a fluffy old bathrobe and slippers. Curlers in her hair was not at all unusual for her, either. *And I've been guilty of calling Catherine an old soul. At least she was a sharp dresser, especially in public.* Old Mrs. Leviston's husband was twenty years her senior, and he lived a few blocks over from Catherine now. *He must have left her plenty for her to sit inside all day. I wonder what today's disaster of the day is.*

"Pops, I have a question for you before you leave, real quick like."

Right.

"I noticed Mr. Otis down the street pruning his crepe myrtles earlier this week, and I was a-wondering if I should trim mine back, too."

You mean, get me to trim them back for you. "Really, fall or winter will work, Mrs. Leviston."

"I've told you, sweetie, call me *Ethel.*"

I'd really rather not. And I'd rather you not call me Pops, either. "Ethel, then. Like I said, cut them back before spring."

"Sweetie, you think you might help me cut 'em back again this year?"

Help you? You mean cut 'em for you, load the branches in my pickup, and haul them away for you. "Yes ma'am, I'll be glad to. May take me a few days to get to it."

"You are a such a sweetheart. Now, you make sure and holler at me when you can help me with my crepe myrtles, you understand, so I can be ready."

Ready to schedule a doctor's appointment or a visit with your aunt at the nursing home or a trip to your daughter's or... could be a new excuse this year. "Yes, ma'am, Mrs.... Ethel, I sure will. Now, I need to go."

"Where are you going, Pops?"

"To The Log Cabin to eat my Thanksgiving meal. I missed lunch, so..."

"Oh, I love The Log Cabin. I always told Ed—God rest his soul—if I had one place to eat out, it would be The Log Cabin. Their country ham is to die for, don't you think?"

"Yes, ma'am. I..."

"It reminds me of the way my grandma used to cook it. Sometimes I get the chicken 'n dumplings when I have a hankering. Don't just anybody make chicken 'n dumplings nowadays, you know."

"Yes, ma'am. Well, I better be..."

"Takes too long to make 'em if you ask me. Our generation is the last with that kind of patience. Everybody's too busy. Take me, for example. I'm way too busy to fool with making dumplings."

"Yes, ma'am." *I wonder if she'd notice if I just pulled out. Doesn't seem like one of us is necessary for this downright scintillating conversation.*

"Sweetheart, I'm going to need you to let me go. I see Mr. Otis coming, and he's going to help me hang my Christmas lights tonight. You enjoy your evening, you hear?"

Pops smiled. "Yes, ma'am, sorry for keeping you."

DROPPING the gearshift into drive and pulling out of his driveway, he noticed the sun losing its fight to light his way across town. "That woman would talk the horns off a billy goat," Pops said to his dashboard. "Catherine would be proud of me, how I minded my manners when I wanted to give her a piece of my mind instead. She always said kindness didn't cost anybody anything. Better she never met old Mrs. Leviston. Ethel. *Ethel.*"

A car honk yanked Pops back from his thoughts at the four-way stop east of the college. Unaware of whether he or the college kid in the silver sports car to his left had arrived at the stop sign first, Pops froze. *I don't reckon he would honk his horn if it was his turn.* Pops eased his car into the intersection at the same time the kid did. They both stopped. Pops started again as the kid did. They both stopped. The kid was losing it, Pops observed. He could read the boy's lips: "Move, old man!" A third time, Pops tried crossing the street, this time with no interference. *Young fella, my driver's license photo is older than you are. You need to slow your butt down and not be in such a hurry to get wherever it is you're going.*

By the time Pops pulled into The Log Cabin parking lot, he had little appetite. The emotion of the day, the conversation—if you could call it that—with old Mrs. Leviston, and the encounter with Mr. Impatient at the intersection made him consider turning around and going home. *Dadgummit, nobody's going to stop me from eating my Thanksgiving dinner. Lord, remind me what I have to be thankful for today.* He pulled up on the door handle and added, *please let Laticia be working today. She's always so friendly, and I could use a little friendly right now.*

"Good evening, Laticia," Pops said, stepping up to the hostess station.

"Well, hey, there, Pops! Just you tonight? Where's your son?"

"He's a little under the weather today. Thought I would come down here and eat my Thanksgiving meal today."

"I'm sorry to hear about your son, but, honey, you've come to the right place for a wonderful Thanksgiving supper. You want your usual table or you want to sit somewhere different tonight?"

"I'm feeling a little lonely today, Laticia. I had to walk down and talk to Catherine two different times today, and I thought about my mama a lot. You see that table in the corner?"

"I sure do. We'll bus it in just a minute, and I'll save it for you. I sure am sorry you're feeling down today, Pops. We're gonna treat you special and get those spirits up. We can't have one of our regulars leaving here low, now, can we?"

Pops from Laticia sounded more suitable than from most people lately. He smiled. "No, I reckon we can't. Still, that corner table would be great."

She stepped around her hostess station to give Pops a quick hug. "You bet, honey. We gotcha taken care of. I'll call you up as soon as it's ready."

POPS FOUND a seat in the waiting area and lost himself again in his thoughts. *Was I as impatient as that kid in the sports car at his age? I wonder if other people see me as bothersome as old Mrs. Leviston—would they say anything? Should I tell her? Heck, no, I'd never get away from that conversation. Still, I'm sure there's a reason she goes on and on so. Catherine probably wouldn't have paid it any attention; if she had, she wouldn't have told a soul. I sure miss her. Catherine, that is.*

Laticia tapped him on the shoulder. "Pops, your table is ready."

"Oh," Pops said, embarrassed, "did I miss your calling out my name?"

"Aw, no, honey, I came and got you myself. I told you we're gonna take great care of you tonight. Now, this is Vanessa," she said, pulling a brown-aproned server alongside. She doesn't usually work Tuesdays when y'all come, but she's real good, and she's gonna take you back to your corner table now and take excellent care of you."

"Thank you, dear. Have a good night."

"Oh, you bet I will, honey. Vanessa, you take care of Pops now. I'm gonna let you take him on in. Pops, you make sure you stop by to say goodbye on your way out now, you hear?" She winked at him.

"Yes, ma'am, I will," Pops smiled.

"HERE WE ARE, sir. May I get you started with something to drink?"

"Tea, please."

"Sweet or unsweet?"

"Honey, this is Harriston, Mississippi. There ain't but one kind of tea."

"One sweet tea coming up." Vanessa chuckled, spinning away from Pops' table. *The old fella's got spunk, just like they said.* She had never served Pops and James Junior, but all the servers who had done so talked about them all the time. She knew better than to raise her voice like she did with most seniors because his hearing was fine. Another server warned not to call him *Pops* until he invited her to do so and to flirt with him a little. She already knew he out-tipped everyone else in his age group.

Pops scanned the room, feeling conspicuous, even from his seat in the back corner of the dining room. He wondered why several other people were there eating alone. The others were connecting with the outside world through their phones, so pulled he his readers from his shirt pocket and joined them:

You DOING ANY BETTER?

...

Some. What did you do today?

...

Watched part of the Lions-Packers game. Rescued Bruce Spruce from the closet and sorted the ornaments.

...

You didn't decorate without me, did you?

...

I never start until Thanksgiving night. Catherine would kill me.

...

How was your visit with her?

...

Went twice today. Talked with Mama and Catherine's mama, too.

...

That's a lot of visiting in one day, Pops. You okay?

...

Better now. I'm down at The Log Cabin, about to eat my Thanksgiving meal.

...

They surprised to see you?

...

A little. Surprised my sidekick is missing. Laticia is her customary friendly self. (I think she might have a crush on me.) New server—haven't decided about her yet. She didn't yell at me like I was hard of hearing, so she's got that going for her. Asked me if I wanted sweet or unsweet tea—what kind of question is that?

...

Don't reckon she'll ever ask you that again, huh?

...

Reckon not. Here she comes.

"Sir, here's your *sweet* tea. We have to ask—somebody might be dealing with health issues or be from somewhere north of here."

"I reckon so," Pops answered. *Let's see your smile, Ms. Vanessa.* "I've been drinking sweet tea most of my ninety-two years and don't see any reason to get all health conscious now. Doctors tell me to eat less red meat and cut back on the sweets, but I can tell their hearts are just not in it. They aspire to live as long as I have."

She grinned and didn't rush him to place his order. She left him and returned with a basket of biscuits. "Figured you for a biscuit man instead of cornbread."

"You figured right."

"What else can I get you tonight?"

"Thanksgiving special. Not what I figured on ordering earlier today, but I changed my mind."

"Yes sir, superb choice. They fed all us workers before we opened today, and it was *some kinda* good."

Pops held up a biscuit and announced, "Ms. Vanessa, you can call me *Pops.*"

She blushed. He saw it. "Pops, it would be an honor. I'll get right on your order."

SHE'LL DO.

...

Got her wrapped around your finger already, old man?

...

Maybe, son, maybe.

...

Give her permission to call you Pops already?

...

73

Perhaps. She made up for the unsweet tea thing by tabbing me as a biscuit man.

…

You realize one of the other servers probably told her, right?

…

I know, but she doesn't have to realize I do.

…

You are such a dang flirt.

…

Watch your mouth. And don't tell your mama.

…

She knows you didn't flirt with anybody but her when she was alive.

…

I'll confess to her later. Besides, flirting keeps the brain warm. I'm harmless, you understand.

…

So says every girl in Harriston.

…

You understand your mama was the only girl for me forever and always.

…

I realize that, Dad. I'm just giving you a hard time.

…

There's a lot of people eating here by themselves tonight. They're all on their phones, trying to look like they're not lonely on Thanksgiving.

…

What do you call what you're doing?

…

...

...

Dad?

"Here ya go, Pops. Turkey, dressing, cranberry sauce, green beans, corn. Careful with that corn. It's hot. Do you need anything else right now?"

"No, Vanessa, this looks delicious. Thank you."

"I'll check back with you in a few minutes and top off your *sweet* tea." That evoked an exchange of smiles between the new friends.

Pops stopped her. "Vanessa, do this many people eat by themselves every Thanksgiving?"

She looked around the room and shrugged her shoulders. "This is my first Thanksgiving working here and to be honest, I've been so busy I hadn't really paid it any attention. I'll ask Laticia—she's the old pro for Thanksgiving at The Log Cabin."

"No worries, sweetie. I just wondered. My son usually buys a couple of Thanksgiving plates from—I don't rightly know where he gets 'em—and brings them over to my house."

"That so? Well, I hope everything's up to your standards. I'll be back to check on you."

Pops' appetite returned like gangbusters when he leaned in to smell the dressing. He consumed it like he always did, stabbing a piece of turkey, a dab of cranberry sauce, and as much dressing as he could fit on the rest of the fork. Memories of Catherine's dressing came flooding back. It had taken her the first ten years of their marriage to get it like she wanted it. Pops judged it edible by year three, tasty by year five, and perfect two years later. He argued against further tweaks to Catherine's recipe, but he told her the dressing became "perfect-er" each year until she was finally content. This dressing wasn't bad at all—he would compare it to about year six of Catherine's journey. Before his review of his wife's culinary process was complete, that part of his plate was clean, and he went to work on the sides. Though they were less satisfying to his palate, they carried memories of their own.

By the time Vanessa returned to pour some more tea in his still half-filled glass, he was stabbing at the stray green beans that had escaped earlier attempts. "Wow, you had quite an appetite tonight, didn't you?"

"Forgot to eat lunch today." Pops dabbed the corners of his mouth and dropped his napkin on his plate, patting his belly as a definitive act of satisfaction. "That was good eating, Ms. Vanessa. My compliments to the chef."

"I'll be sure to pass that along. Did you save room for dessert?"

"I better not. If you're not in a hurry for the table, I'd like to sit a spell longer and enjoy my sweet tea."

"Sweetheart, you stay as long as you want. I'll leave you to your thoughts, but you wave at me if you need anything at all."

"Yes, ma'am, thank you."

I wonder what the young lady in the other corner's story

is. She looks like she's been rode hard and put up wet, like Daddy used to say. Jittery. She's worried about something.

"YOU NEED SOME MORE SWEET TEA?" Vanessa asked. After enjoying his drink and finishing his thoughts, he had beckoned her.

"No, ma'am, I reckon I'll call it a night."

"All right, then. Pops, let me tell you what a pleasure it has been to meet you at last and serve your Thanksgiving meal tonight. Laticia told me to tell you to make sure you stop by to see her on your way out, okay?"

"I will." He stared at her for an awkward moment. "Aren't you forgetting something, Ms. Vanessa?"

"No sir, I don't believe so."

"My check."

"Oh, that. See Laticia about your bill." Her mischievous grin was not lost on Pops.

"Okay, thanks for taking such fine care of me tonight. You should work Tuesday nights so you can visit with me and my son."

"Well, I just might look into that. Make sure you check with Laticia, now."

Pops picked up his phone and put it in his pocket. He still had not responded to James Junior's latest text. He would get to that later. His curiosity focused on Vanessa's grin. Laticia was waiting for him.

"So, Pops, did Vanessa give you outstanding service tonight?"

"She sure did. I invited her to work Tuesday nights. She said to see you about my check?"

"That's right. Pops, someone has paid for your Thanksgiving dinner, tip and all."

"But I can pay for my own…"

"Not about charity, honey, not at all. One of our customers just wanted to bless you tonight, that's all."

"Who was it?" he asked, scanning the dining room intently.

"No need looking around. They're gone. Didn't want credit for it. Just wanted you to leave smiling."

Indeed, Pops was smiling. "Well, at least give me my total so I can leave Ms. Vanessa a good tip."

"Uh uh," Laticia answered, shaking her finger at Pops. "They told me to tell y'all… to tell you they left a real generous tip and that you shouldn't pay a thing."

"Y'all… you said y'all. Who else…"

"Slip of the tongue," Laticia lied. "I'm used to you and your son being in here together. Sorry about that. Tell him I hope he's better by Tuesday night."

Pops bought it. He wasn't ready to leave, and Laticia wasn't particularly busy, so he kept talking. "Haven't you earned enough seniority by now to spend your Thanksgiving at home?"

"Honey, I ain't really got much family to speak of. My daddy left and my mama and grandparents died, so I come up here and try to make everybody else's Thanksgiving good for them. Besides, I'm a little late getting through college—paying for it as I go, so every bit helps."

"If you ever need a place to come on the holidays,

you can join me and James Junior, least while I'm still around."

Laticia threw her arms around Pops. "You ain't got no idea what that means to me, Pops. Hey, can I ask you something personal?"

"I expect so. What is it?"

"I figure you probably have an actual name, not just *Pops*."

Pops teared up, and she feared she had crossed a line of some sort. "I'm sorry, Pops. I thought..."

"No, sweetheart, it's fine. It's just that..." Pops cleared his throat and walked her through his internal struggle of the past few months. "For someone to care enough to ask my name—well, you couldn't have known how much that would mean to me tonight."

"You still haven't told me."

"Haven't told you what?"

"Your name. You told me all about how you want people to call you by it, but you haven't told me what it was."

Stretching to his full five feet seven inches, Pops announced, "Laticia, my name is Jimmy Lee Yates."

ONE MONTH SOBER

7

"Excuse me," the jittery girl from the corner interrupted. "Sorry to break up your... my server said I should see you for my check."

Laticia broke away from Pops. "Mr. Jimmy Lee, don't run off now." Turning to the embarrassed young lady, she said, "Ma'am, another one of our guests has paid for your meal, generous tip and all. You don't owe a thing."

"Wait, what..." she started, but a family stepped up to the hostess station, and Laticia excused herself.

"Excuse me, young lady," Pops said, "but I heard that somebody bought your supper, too."

"*Too?*"

"Someone paid for mine, as well. No need to search for them; they've already gone. That's all I could pick up from Laticia. She told me to just count it as a blessing, so that's what I'll do. And let me tell you, I needed a blessing tonight."

"Me, too." She dabbed the corner or her eye with her sleeve, struggling to escape Pops' notice.

"I was throwing myself a little pity party when I arrived an hour ago, but I'm feeling better now." He hesitated and continued, "This old codger is an excellent listener… if you need one."

"If you're serious, I *could* use one right now."

"Jimmy Lee Yates." When Pops extended his hand, she accepted it. "And you are—"

"Tara. Tara Cates. I want to be forthright with you, Mr. Jimmy Lee. If I don't make it through the next couple of hours, I'm afraid it'll be real rough for me."

"Young lady, are you in some kind of trouble?" Pops asked as she wiped several strands of hair that had escaped her tight ponytail from her forehead. Keeping his voice down and leaning in toward her, he continued, "If you need me to, I can call the police."

"No, nothing like that." She shook her head, her eyes moistening. "Mr.—I'm sorry, I've already forgotten your name." Despite her strongest efforts to control them, the tears flowed.

"Jimmy Lee Yates. Call me *Pops*. Most people do, and it'll be simpler to remember."

"I'm sorry, I'm so sorry. Here I am falling apart in front of a complete stranger."

"Not a complete stranger, Ms. Tara. We've met twice now. And I am not going anywhere. You take your time."

That produced a smile. "All right, here goes my life story in three words: I'm a drunk."

"You? You can't be over twenty-five years old."

"I'm twenty-three, but I drank away half my life."

Now that she had delivered the difficult first line, the details overflowed.

Tara stood erect and threw her shoulders back. "I'm one month sober today." Her stray blond hairs flopped against her forehead. She wiped them away and with them, her tiny moment of confidence. "When DHS took my little boy from me about two months ago, I reached rock bottom. After two or three weeks of trying to drown my pain and only making things worse, I decided I wanted to quit drinking, and I mean quit forever. One day, I was out for a walk near my house. I passed by a church whose sign out front said something about a recovery ministry."

"Celebrate Recovery," Pops said.

"Yeah, that's it," she said, surprised. "Wait, are you..."

"No, just familiar with it. Our church is one of several in Harriston that have Celebrate Recovery ministries. My son is a newspaper writer, and he helped them write some advertising copy when they first started."

"Oh. Anyway, I live in my grandmother's house—actually, it was my great-grandmother's. She always tried to get me to come to church, but I'm jumping ahead. I have been doing pretty well so far. My sponsor is relentless. It's like she understands my triggers and stays a step or two ahead of my next drink. She advised me that the holidays were especially tough and to brace myself. She and her husband open up their house to the CR folks on every holiday, but they had to go out of town to be with his dad, who had a stroke. They'll be home by nine, but I'm not sure I can last that long without a drink. I want one real bad, Pops, and I doubt I can be strong enough to hold out." She crossed her arms and clutched them to her sides to control her shaking.

"Do you have any family you can call?"

"I wish. I come from a big family, Pops, but I have burned most of those bridges. They let me stay in Granny's house, but I'm on my last chance to stay there. When DHS took my son, most of them wrote me off."

"Most of them? Isn't there one person you could ask to sit with you for a few hours?"

The shock of hair on Tara's forehead was back, and her best efforts to shoo it elsewhere were in vain. She wiped her face and both hands and blurted, "I'm so weak right now, I wouldn't make it a block from here without stopping at a liquor store." Her shoulders slumped, she forced her eyes to meet Pops'. "I hoped you might talk to me since we both had..."

She turned her head from side to side, wanting suddenly to be anywhere besides here embarrassing herself in front of a kind old man who had done nothing to deserve this kind of outburst from a complete stranger. Those words again. *He's not a complete stranger —I've met him twice.* "... since we've both had our meals covered tonight. I'm sorry, that sounds silly to even say."

"Ms. Tara, don't worry about a thing. My night driving leaves a lot to be desired, and I should wait until the traffic thins out."

"Gosh, where should I start?"

"My wife—God rest her soul—always said to start at the beginning, a very good place to start. I expect she stole that from a movie or something."

"I'm sorry."

"About Catherine? Nah, she's been gone twenty years. She lives down the street from me now, and I'll be joining her soon enough."

"Wait..."

"My wife passed away years ago, honey. Her grave is walking distance from my house, so we visit all the time. We spent forty-eight years together, so I really don't need to listen to her side of the conversation out loud; I already know what she would say, so we have some pleasant talks. I walked down there to see her twice today, in fact. But enough about me. Let's return to your very good place to start."

"When I was twelve, I picked up my first drink. It was at a stupid middle school party, and two boys pulled out a bottle of whiskey one of them had stolen from his parents' cabinet. I wasn't scared of anything, so I accepted the bottle when they passed it around and took a swig. It was like liquid fire going down, but I had to one-up the little twerps who brought it to the party, so I took another drink before I passed it on. Don't you know they thought I was all that. When the bottle worked its way around the circle, the rest of them— there were about ten—went back to doing what middle schoolers do at parties, talking about kids who weren't there. They left the bottle sitting on the counter, and I took another drink when they weren't looking and felt a little buzz. I slipped the bottle in my purse, told them I needed to go, and strutted home like the big shot I thought I was.

"After the party, I seemed destined to be a drunk—hair of the dog, you might say. There was never any alcohol in our house except for a little whiskey my dad used every once in a blue moon to mix with peppermint and honey as a homemade cough syrup. I didn't dare touch that, but alcohol found me, even at that age, you know? My friend group changed. It's easy to find the rebellious kids, and they'll accept you. CR is similar, but on the flip side of addiction.

"My parents were fine folks—*are* fine folks—but they were clueless until I was too far gone. But I understand—who expects their freaking *twelve-year-old* to be hitting the bottle? It was on my sixteenth birthday when it all came down. I'll tell you the story if have time and want to hear a recovering alcoholic ramble on."

Pops reached over and touched Tara lightly on the arm. "Honey, you talk all you wish. If you don't make it until your sponsor is ready to help you through tonight, it won't be on account of this old man." She brushed the pesky shock of hair away, took a deep breath, and told an almost complete stranger about her darkest day.

8

"Tara!" Jeri Cates yelled upstairs. "Can you come give me a hand with these streamers? It's not every day you celebrate Sweet Sixteen!"

Tara didn't come down, just like she hadn't come down the two previous times her mom called her to help, though she heard Mom's impassioned cries well enough. The fact is, she wasn't coming down to help, nor for her party. She was considering not leaving the upstairs bathroom alive. The pregnancy test lay beside every bottle of pills from the medicine cabinet. Even though she didn't understand the prescribed purpose for many of those pills, she figured if she took the lot of them, they would do the job.

"HEY, YOUR HOTNESS, I'M J," he had introduced himself at a sophomore class party. "One letter, one wonderful time."

She cocked her head to the side and tossed her hair behind her ear. "Prove it, tough guy." Sober, Tara would have laughed the unknown kid's weak pickup line right out of the room. The party was just a few blocks from her house, though, and she had told her parents she would walk over with some friends. They left early "to help with setup" but stopped in a back corner of the neighborhood park to down a bottle of rum instead. Before they walked through the door of the party, they were drunk.

She went to bed with J an hour after she met him and was pregnant before the Sweet Sixteen party her mother had planned for years. She ignored her first missed period, but she found ignoring the morning sickness impossible. When Mom insisted she take Tara to the doctor, she blamed the pressure from her chemistry class for her biological struggles. Sitting on the floor of her bathroom listening to her mother's shouts for help, chemistry and biology were now foremost in her mind. *I've got to tell her. I've got to tell her. I've got to tell her. Now.*

Tara struggled to bring herself to her feet to make the longest walk of her life. She was three steps from the bottom when her mother looked up and knew something was wrong. "Honey, what's the matter?!?"

"Mom, I'm... I'm..." Her mouth wouldn't form the words, and her eyes continued to study the runner on the stairs. She still wanted to die, but her mind willed her arm forward.

"What's this? A pregnancy test?!? Tara, you're..." Jeri Cates couldn't say it, either. She staggered to the couch, staring at two lines that changed the trajectory of this day and promised to change the rest of her life.

Tara didn't imagine it possible to feel lower than the moment she watched her mother enter her new reality. She was wrong. The front door opened at just that point, her dad and brother returning from a morning in the woods with her nine-year-old brother's face covered in blood.

Before the door was completely open, Stu Cates announced to anyone within shouting range: "John David Cates killed his first deer today!" John David's moment in the family spotlight vanished when Stu spotted his wife on the couch with her arms around her knees, her sobs deep and her breath hard to catch. "Honey, what happened? What's wrong? Talk to me!"

Tara remained frozen on the stairs as her mother handed the pregnancy test to her father, who stood perplexed. "You're pregnant? But I had…"

His wife caught her breath and turned her tear-streaked face in his direction. Her three-second stare told him everything she couldn't bring herself to say. As Stu's face turned mechanically toward the stairs, John David said, "Tara's pregnant?" Tara fled up the stairs before her father locked eyes with her. John David didn't particularly like his sister anyway—he knew far more than his parents about her extra-curricular activity —but he might never forgive her for stealing his moment in the family spotlight. Forget that he wanted to go hunting on the day of her special party; they both already recognized her Sweet Sixteen as a farce.

The pill bottles were back in place before Tara's

father tapped on her bedroom door. She didn't answer, but he opened it anyway to find her facedown on her bed. "Tara, sit up." He extended his arms, and she melted into them.

"Dad, I'm so sorry, I'm so sorry, I'm so sorry."

"We will get through this." Tara forced her face up to look him in the eyes but couldn't help but notice John David in her doorway wearing a disgusted expression. He flung his head back into the hallway and stormed down the hall to his room, slamming the door for emphasis.

"Oh, Dad, what have I done to our family?" It seemed the first coherent thought since she initially tasted alcohol almost four years earlier. *John David will hate me more than ever. Mom will be so ashamed, she may never leave the house again. Dad will act like everything's okay, but he's going to consider himself a failure. Oh, Tara, what have you done?*

"Look at me, Tara. Let's get the cards on the table so we can make the best decisions for everyone." *Everything with Dad was always about moving forward.* As bad as she despised the last ten minutes of her life, spilling the details would be beyond humiliating. Dad's sturdy arm around her shoulders gave her the strength to give him the slightest of nods.

"First, were you… was it…"

Tara didn't make her father say the words. "It was consensual, Dad. He didn't rape me." His relief showed through his pain. "Tara, who's the father?"

"I don't want to say."

"Honey, I will not sugarcoat this part. It doesn't

matter that you're just sixteen years old now. This was a grown-up decision, and you're looking at big-girl consequences, but you didn't create this baby all by yourself."

Baby. *Dear Jesus, make this stop! I'm too young for this.*

"Tara, I'm not going to seek the guy out and kill him, but if this was consensual like you say, he's got an obligation in it, too."

"Please, Dad, no. It was a mistake. I don't want to…"

"He doesn't get a pass just because it was a mistake."

"I don't want to…"

"Look, Tara, he should take responsibility for this child, too." He was doing his best to keep his composure, but Tara sensed her father's temper growing shorter by the moment.

She blurted, "Dad, I want nothing to do with him! I was nothing but a conquest to him, and he has hated me ever since."

"Does he know?"

"No, I never want him to!"

"Had you been dating this guy long? I don't remember your bringing a boy around here."

The shame threatened to take her, but she had to say it. "Please don't hate me, Dad."

He nodded and braced himself.

"I met him the night of the sophomore party. He was new, and I liked him, and we ended up…" He would have to figure out the rest on his own.

"Tara, I will ask you again, and you *must* be honest with me. Did he rape you?"

She might as well tell him the complete truth, that

she was drunk when she arrived at the party and that her drinking already spanned several years.

He waited.

She drew her breath. "Dad, I..."

"Stu, stop!"

Mom hugged the door frame, barely holding herself upright. Dad arose from the bed, caught his wife before she slumped to the floor, and helped her to their bedroom downstairs. Tara followed at a distance and overheard everything they said for the next hour from her perch on the stairs. If Mom had given her two minutes, her secret would have been out in the open. She would have said *I have a drinking problem and I'm pregnant because of it*. But the moment passed, and Tara began to harden.

THE NEXT OPPORTUNITY TO say out loud what had happened came at Tara's first pre-natal visit when she realized the doctor would ask about alcohol consumption. Even though her mother might have a come apart later, Tara had decided she would tell the truth. When they pulled up to the doctor's office after the silent drive, though, her mother touched her arm and told her to wait a minute.

"Your father and I have been talking, and since you made the grown up decision to engage in sex before marriage, we think you should handle the results of your decision like a grownup. Since you're going to be a mother, you've got a lot of growing up to do. You can start with seeing your doctor alone."

We? You mean, you. From Tara's place on the stairs a week earlier, she had heard her mother's true thoughts.

———

"STU, do you realize what she had done to us... what she has done to me? I'll have to call off the party and tell everyone why. Do you understand how embarrassing that will be for me?"

"Jeri, slow down. The reason's not important. Just tell them Tara is sick, and we need to cancel the party."

"Do you really assume we'll be able to hide the truth? Don't be so naïve, Stu."

"I didn't say we should hide the truth. We just don't have to tell them today. Let's give ourselves some time to process this. Let's start with what's best for our daughter."

"What's best for *her*? Did she think about what's best for her family when she was off getting pregnant?"

"It was a mistake, dear. We all make them."

"Stu, listen to yourself! It's not like she was working a multiplication problem and forgot to carry the *one*. This will change everybody's life. We'll have to change churches... we'll have to put her in a different school..."

"Jeri, this is not the 1950s. We can't just send her to a home for unwed mothers or send her away to live with another family member."

"I'd like to know why not? My Aunt Suzanne lives in Texas. She has a gigantic house and nobody living there with her. She raised five kids, so she knows how to take care of a baby."

"How are you going to explain away her absence? How will you explain that to Tara? Are you just going to forbid her to text her friends or—God forbid—post anything on social media? Come on, Jeri, be realistic, for crying out loud. Say it out loud. Tara's going to have a baby. You're going to be a—"

"Don't say it! I am nobody's grandmother! I'm only thirty-eight years old—I'm not old enough to be a *grand*parent."

"You'd better get used to it."

"I will not!"

Tara could not listen anymore. She slipped silently up the stairs and cried herself to sleep. That would be her practice for the next three weeks until she moved in with her Aunt Suzanne an hour north of Dallas.

"Your mother made you move away?" Pops asked.

"Yeah, but it was okay and probably for the best. She got what she wanted—at least, what she believed she wanted. John David was happy because he figured he would get all of my parents' attention. And Dad didn't have to argue with Mom anymore."

"What about you?"

"Mom and I agreed about one thing: I didn't want anybody to know I was pregnant, especially J. As much of a disaster as my son's life has been so far, the one thing that would have made it worse is for his father to be a part of his life. Every time I would see him after the night we… you know… he had this smug expression on his face, and if he bothered speaking to me, he was so condescending. Pops, I looked up synonyms to describe how bad a mistake my hooking up with J was, and I landed on *colossal*. It was a colossal mistake."

"I hope you don't see your son as…"

"Oh, no, no, no." Tara shook her head, and the shock of blond fell once again on her forehead. She flipped it away and continued. "Zan is the joy of my life."

"Zan? That's an unusual name."

"I named him after my Aunt Suzanne. I told you the move to Texas wasn't so bad, at least in the beginning. Aunt Suzanne was amazing. She took care of me and loved me and listened to me whenever I needed to talk. She set me up with an understanding doctor, and she was there in the room with me when I gave birth. When a nurse asked me if I had a name for my baby, I'll never forget the look on Aunt Suzanne's face when I said his name. I hadn't told her about naming Zan after her."

"So what happened?"

"Well, after Zan was born, I couldn't keep my eyes off him. I wanted to hold him constantly. I wasn't drinking all this time, mind you, and I was making good grades in my online classes. Then, one night, Aunt Suzanne told me I needed to get out and do something. She would take care of the baby, but I needed some time away from him, she said. She handed me twenty bucks and the keys to her car and told me to go. I didn't want to leave, but I went to a baby store and bought an outfit for Zan. I stayed gone an hour, tops, and Zan did just fine without me. After that, she would make me leave the house without Zan at least once a week. She encouraged me to stop for ice cream and not be in such a hurry to get home.

"That worked fine for a few weeks, but my demons returned with a vengeance. Aunt Suzanne attended a big church probably twenty minutes from her house, and I was on my way there to a concert one night, the first time I was to spend over two hours away from Zan. Anyway, I had almost made it to the church, feeling good about where I was in life. I don't know what made me turn into the parking lot of a bar along the way, but I did. I figured if I could give birth, I had earned a single drink to take the edge off before being around a crowd of people. Because I was so far under the drinking age, I didn't imagine they would let me in, but they did. One drink led to two, and before I realized it, I was drunk and in a fix. I texted Aunt Suzanne, told her I was having an enjoyable time, and asked her if she would put Zan to bed so I might go out for coffee with friends I had met. She did, and I headed down that road again. I felt lower than low for lying to Aunt Suzanne and everybody."

"Everybody?"

"Yeah, Dad texted me every day and came to see me. He has to go out of town for business every few weeks, so he would fly through DFW and add a day to his trip. He would rent a car and come visit me and Zan. I don't think he ever told Mom."

"Did she ever come see you?"

"For less than two full days when Zan was born. I

don't think she could stand seeing me happy, though. I was supposed to be at Aunt Suzanne's to 'think about what I had done.' I replayed my mistakes, for sure, but I wasn't about to share that with her. Anyway, as soon as I came home—well, my new home at Aunt Suzanne's—Mom told Dad she wanted to go back to Mississippi. Dad didn't put up much of a fight, so they left the next morning.

"Oh, and I heard from my granny—that's my great-grandmother—pretty much every day. I thought it was cute how she texted me because she was almost ninety then."

"Hey," Pops interjected, pulling his smart phone from his pocket.

Tara threw her hands up and laughed. "Obviously, I'm not as familiar with your generation as I thought." She needed the comedic break.

"You speak about your granny in the past tense," Pops noticed.

Tara tried her best to hold back her sobs. Unable to force out any words for a solid minute, she nodded.

Pops reached over with a comforting hand on her arm. "Take your time, sweetie."

While Tara caught her breath, Pops noticed Laticia was talking to other lonely eaters. From their surprised responses, he recognized their meals, too, had been covered. He didn't want to break away from Tara's story, but he wanted to talk to them, too. When they moved to the side and started talking to one another, he turned his attention back to Tara, who seemed to have regained her composure.

9

"Pops, I hope you won't hate me for what I'm about to tell you, but the worst is yet to come." When he reassured her, she took a deep breath to begin. Just then, her phone rang, and she answered. "It's my sponsor," she whispered. "I need to take this."

Pops held up his right index finger to show he would be back in a moment. He interrupted the conversation of the two lonely diners to introduce himself and see if they minded sticking around for a while. "This young lady is telling me her story, and she needs it to be private, but I sure would like to meet you folks." After they assured him they would stick around, he excused himself for a quick bathroom break and returned to Tara, who stood nearby, still talking on the phone.

"I'm talking to this friendly man at the restaurant right now. He said he would stay with me until you were home... No, Karen, nothing like that. He might be in his eighties... Here, do you want to talk to him? Okay... okay... I will... okay... bye."

"Ninety-two," Pops said.

"What?"

"I'm ninety-two and proud of it."

"You don't look a day over—I'd say—eighty-two."

Any other time, Pops would have accused Tara of flirting with him, but he stood silent, waiting for her to continue her story.

"Okay, where was I?"

"Old people texting."

Tara blushed. "Granny texted me every single day I was in Texas. Even though I didn't always answer her, I understood she cared. I felt real bad about the double life I led, but I began going once or twice a week to the same bar. I started staying out late on Friday and Saturday nights. I would mention the tremendous friends I had made from the young adult ministry at the church to Aunt Suzanne. She would ask to meet them on Sunday mornings, but I told her most of them attended other churches. I can't tell you if she suspected me at first. By the end of my time there, I'm pretty sure she did."

"*Pretty sure?*"

"Okay, Pops, brace yourself. This is where it gets bad. After I tell you what I'm about to reveal, I wouldn't blame you if you hated me."

"Sweetheart, I'm ninety-two years old. If you don't quit beating around the bush, you might not have the chance to tell me."

"Guess I am beating around the bush. All right, here

goes." Tara took a deep breath and exhaled. "I had been living a double life for a year, weekends mostly, but some weeknights, too. One day, Aunt Suzanne informed me I needed to go to work. I had finished school online and earned my GED, and I was about to turn eighteen. If I say so myself, I stayed levelheaded about it, and I started looking around for a job. I saw it as the perfect opportunity to start walking straight again. Zan had turned a year old, and I didn't want him to think of his mama as a drunk.

"I decided to blow it out one last time that weekend and turn the page on that part of my life. I shouldn't have. Aunt Suzanne was watching Zan, as usual, but she didn't feel well. I was selfish, though, and left anyway. Earlier in the week, I had told my bar friends that Saturday would be my last chance to hang out there, so they planned a good time for me. I shot pool and sang karaoke and danced and drank free drinks. Messing up scared me enough that I would quit drinking before eleven so I wouldn't be as drunk when I drove home at midnight or a little after. Around 10:30, I stopped, but one of my friends acted like I hurt her feelings when I turned down her offer of a drink.

"I drank another rum and coke and figured I would leave a little later than usual. At 11:17—I'll never forget the time—I got a text from Aunt Suzanne: *Heart pains. Please come home.* She had never texted me while I was out, not one time, which gave me a false sense of security. Well, I didn't consider other options besides driving there to help her and check on Zan. Fear sobered me up as I started home, but not as much as when I drove up the driveway and saw emergency lights everywhere. She had called 9-1-1 either right before or just after she messaged me.

"The cops refused to allow me in the house at first. When I told them I lived there, they asked if the little boy was mine. I said yes, so they let me inside. I hurried upstairs to look in on Zan first. He was sleeping, so I ran back downstairs to check on Aunt Suzanne." Tara's chest and shoulders heaved again. "Pops, she was gone. I never imagined she would be dead."

"I didn't sleep that night, trying to figure out how to wiggle out of the jam I created for myself. That policeman who tried to keep me out of the house must have smelled my breath. He understood I must've driven drunk to get home. It's a thousand wonders he didn't arrest me, but I guess he figured Zan needed me, even in my condition. If I stuck around, I figured they would come and take my baby from me. Being honest with myself, I was not a very fit mother, but I couldn't let them take Zan from me.

"Wisdom said stay and face the consequences, but I needed to make myself scarce. I had stashed some cash from the money Aunt Suzanne had given me, plus she had told me if anything ever happened to her, she wanted me to have her car. With Zan and all my belongings, I moved into a motel until after her funeral in the middle of the week. None of my family from Mississippi came. As soon as the service ended, I started driving home. Like *home* was even an option. I couldn't risk giving up Zan, though.

"I stopped for the night somewhere in east Texas and

developed a plan. I texted Granny, who said she was worried about me. I told her I was driving to Harriston, but I hadn't talked to Mom and Dad. I didn't know if they would let me move back in their house. Granny informed me I was welcome in her home and that we would figure it out together. So I drove straight to Granny's house, and that's where I have been ever since.

"I stayed straight until earlier this year. I got a decent job as a receptionist at a law office thanks to an acquaintance of Granny's. Zan went to daycare at an older lady's house and enjoyed it. Pops, I hoped my troubles were behind me. At first I resisted attending church with Granny, but when she suggested I try one of the mega-churches east of town where they have more people my age, I did and liked it. They didn't judge me, and I found a few other single moms to hang out with and to have play dates for our kids.

"Everything skipped right on along for almost two years, and I believed I had put my demons behind me. Then, one mom in my church group offered her house for New Year's Eve. Everybody planned to spend the night. The kids played until a little past their usual bedtimes, and we made pallets for them to sleep on in her son's room. It took a while to finish the *I want a drink of water's* and *I need to go to the potty's*, but after a while, we single moms sat together in a quiet house. While we soaked up the silence, our hostess walked into the kitchen and came back with a bottle of wine.

"She had been saving 'the good stuff' for a special occasion. My instincts said get Zan and leave. Still, everybody was so relaxed, and the kids were all asleep, so I took a glass when she gave it to me. As you might imagine, I heard a little voice on one shoulder telling me I was not the person I used to be and I deserved a few sips of wine. A voice from the other shoulder was like, RUN!!! I told myself I would drink the one glass and stop. The girl kept walking around refilling everybody's glasses, though, and I didn't want to—no, that's a lie. But I convinced myself I was sticking to my plan since my glass never ran dry.

"Anyway, we talked and watched the New Year's Eve shows on TV and had a delightful time. A few minutes before midnight, here comes our host with a bottle of champagne. The angel voice kept saying NO!!! RUN!!! The demon voice said it was a one-time occasion, I didn't need to offend anybody, and besides, I wouldn't be driving. So I drank one glass and then another. We were all drunk by then and acting like middle school girls.

"We stayed up late and awoke the next morning to take care of our kids like responsible adults. I took Zan home, and we ended up spending New Year's Day with my parents. My head throbbed from a hangover, but I still believed my life had reached a point where I could handle alcohol as an adult.

"A week later, the same girl who hosted the first night sent out a group text asking when we wanted to have another 'Girls' Night In.' I wanted to ignore it, but the other girls started replying and offering some times like *yesterday* and *not soon enough*. So I joined in, and we planned a get-together for a Friday night in late January. And then again for Valentine's. We all gave one another unspoken permission to keep doing these girls' nights. If anybody had suggested that drinking with our children right down the hall was a bad idea, we would have stopped. Of the entire group, it should have been me who said *no* first, but I kept letting the evil voice convince me it was okay since nobody was getting hurt. It didn't affect my job or even church. We would get drunk on a Friday night and show up to church on Sunday. Some of us even worked in the nursery or kids' ministry. We might as well have worn bright T-shirts that read *Hypocrite.*"

"How long did this go on?" Pops interrupted. He didn't wish to rush her, but some more of the lonesome eaters were talking to Laticia now, and he didn't want to miss them. Pops enjoyed watching the reactions of the others as Laticia gave them the news of their free meals. When they joined the two who were already talking, Pops turned his attention back to Tara, who didn't notice his focus wandering.

"For the better part of a year. I never liked myself after these sleepovers. It's an awful look for half a dozen moms to get soused in the den while their kids are sleeping down the hall. Every once in a while, one of them—thank goodness, never Zan—woke up and needed his mommy. Even though I didn't like the guilt these gatherings produced, I kept going. Like I mentioned, if any of us had spoken up, we'd all have stopped.

"Well, one night we were celebrating some holiday or another at about twelve-thirty in the morning. The girls had moved on to harder stuff by then, and I had drunk too many rum and cokes. I pulled out my phone and noticed a missed a call from Granny a little after midnight. She left a message lasting seven seconds that I figured was a hangup, but I clicked on it, anyway."

Tara took a deep breath and repeated the well-rehearsed line: "The last word I ever heard from my grandmother was *help*, and I was too drunk to help her."

"Oh my," was all Pops could muster.

"Like a fool, I drove home, and it seemed like I was driving back to Aunt Suzanne's all over again. Only this time, my parents were there, and they realized I was drunk when I staggered toward the door. My dad hung his head in shame, and my mom walked straight to one of the policemen on the scene. I couldn't hear what she said, but I saw her pointing to me and then to Zan, who was still in the car. The policeman nodded and walked toward me in what seemed slow motion.

"He asked, 'Ma'am, have you been drinking?' I started explaining our girls' nights in and how careful we were, but he cut me off cold. 'Ma'am, have you been operating this motor vehicle while impaired tonight?'"

10

Tara sighed and continued. "I went to jail that night for drunk driving. My parents took Zan home with them, and DHS took him from me the next week. I take complete ownership of my awful choices, but it was also one of the best things that ever happened to me."

"How do you mean?"

"I can finally admit I am an alcoholic and that I need help. See, Mom wouldn't let Dad bail me out, so I stayed overnight in a holding cell. Spending the night behind bars was beyond humiliating, but I survived. I don't hold Mom's decision against her. Still, the embarrassment of jail wasn't as horrendous as knowing I would lose Zan.

"I had so many chances and blew them. Aunt Suzanne couldn't have been any better *to* me and *for* me, but I hung out at a bar, anyway. Granny gave Zan and me a place to stay and pushed me to the right places, especially church. But I still found myself drunk with a bunch of freaking church moms. Sorry for the language, but I get so mad at myself sometimes. What kind of loser am I?

"The women who extended me my second and third chances both died while I was out drunk. I've come to grips with the fact that nothing I might have done would have saved either of them, but they died alone. At both of their funerals, I kept thinking how they died by themselves and helpless. Neither of them deserved that."

With nothing fitting to say, Pops clarified, "So they took your son?"

"Yes, but Mom and Dad agreed to take him. I didn't know if that was a workable solution, but I was hopeful. John David hates me more than ever. He feels I'm still one-upping him through Zan, which I accept. Dad jumped at the chance to keep his grandson in the family, though. Even though Mom puts up a tough front, Zan has won her over, too.

"They've been strict regarding visitation for me, though, and I'm glad. They let me visit Zan for two hours on Saturdays and an hour on Sundays, but only with my parents in the room. I don't know what they've told him, but he never asks to come home with me. He seems sad when I come for visits, but I can tell they're taking wonderful care of him. Still, it's not the same as Zan's being with his mother. Look, I'll wrap it up so you can chat with the others, too."

"I'd rather both of us talk to them. While I sat in the corner during supper, I wondered why everybody was here eating alone tonight of all nights. Plus, it might pass the time until—Karen, I think was her name—is ready for you."

Tara nodded. "To wind up my story, they didn't schedule Granny's funeral until the Friday after she passed so her out-of-town relatives would have time to get here. After many of my relatives arrived, word spread about what I'd done. They treated me better than I deserved, and two of them even came clean about their own battles with addiction. One of my older cousins told me Celebrate Recovery had impacted his life after he became hooked on pain medication. He offered to help me locate one. Turned out Granny's church has CR, and their meetings are on Friday nights. Danny took me that night, and I shared my story right off, before I chickened out. Pops, I'm determined to heal and make sure Zan never experiences another tragedy of my making."

"You've got to choose it for yourself, too, you understand," Pops said.

"Yes, sir, I do. After living with Granny for a while back when things were going well, I explained the circumstances of Aunt Suzanne's death. I didn't sugarcoat any of what I did, and Granny didn't judge me, just like you're not now. She shared with me that the Bible says we will comfort others with the same comfort God has shown us. Well, that's..."

Pops cocked his head to the side, and Tara paused. "Tara, who was your great-grandmother?"

"Her name was Martha Reynolds."

"Oh, my goodness. It hasn't occurred to me this whole time that your granny was Martha Reynolds."

"You knew her?"

"She sat on the row in front of me at church for over fifty years, that's all. And the Bible passage you mentioned—it's in 2 Corinthians. If I heard Martha quote it once, I heard her quote it a hundred times. I knew she had her great-granddaughter living with her, but I had no idea it was you. I hope you realize she has quite a story herself."

"Granny?"

"Ms. Tara, do you believe in miracles?"

"I'm beginning to."

"We will have to get together again real soon and discuss Martha Reynolds. She lived a remarkable life, but God did a tremendous work in her once upon a time. You will appreciate her story."

"Oh my gosh, yes, the sooner the better."

"So you go to CR at 12th Avenue Baptist—do you attend services on Sunday, too?"

"Yes, sir, I sure do. I slip in late on Sundays and sit in the balcony, but if it's okay with you, I'll come sit with you this Sunday morning."

"Let's do better than that. My son, James Junior, and I will move up, and we'll all sit together on your granny's row.

Tara threw her arms around Pops and hugged him tight. When she released him, they both blushed when they realized the rest of the lonesome diners were staring at them. Pop broke the awkward silence with a shrug. "What can I say? Ninety-two and still got it."

After introducing himself to the group as Jimmy Lee Yates, he invited them to call him *Pops*.

"And this beautiful young lady is my friend, Tara. She is going through a rocky season and needs a little support to make it to 9:00. Can we help a pretty girl who obviously can't keep her hands off of me?"

They laughed and introduced themselves to one another. The group was lost in conversation when Laticia announced, "Lonesome, party of six. Lonesome, party of six, your table is ready."

MR. IMPORTANT

11

E aston Sterling found it hard to believe only one restaurant was open on Thanksgiving in a town this size. The master of manipulating a schedule, he closed sales over power lunches in one city fast enough to make dinner in another. The company sales records he broke this year would be his own. Nobody dared argue with his success, but even his most aggressive rival cowered at his schedule, which took no note of holidays.

Neither he nor Sherrill could persuade the CEO of the Harriston County Hospital to meet with him on Thanksgiving. He insisted instead on a seven o'clock breakfast meeting on Friday morning, so Sterling made the drive a day early. He despised the wastefulness of a ninety-minute drive from the airport in Jackson and a hotel stay in Harriston. Give him an eighteen-hour day with multiple flights and a solid five hours' sleep in his own bed, any day. When he told Sherrill he had rented a car for his trip, she gave him the cockeyed glance she used to warn him about burning the candle at both ends. He responded with his usual obligatory excuses.

During his drive to The Log Cabin, Sterling thought about his mother. Her stroke last year confined her to an assisted living facility, even though she was only sixty-four. Easton's dad had died of a heart attack two years earlier. He went to his grave still trying to "beat the man" and boastful about his son, who had become "the man." He looked forward to Easton's sporadic visits, knowing they would end with a hundred-dollar bill from his son and an admonition to "do something for yourself, old man." Begging him not to be a stranger, Margie Sterling refused her son's similar efforts.

He knew he should have visited his mom. He wondered if she cared to ask what her family was thankful for after the last few years. There was plenty, for sure, for Easton. He remembered the first two hundred dollar Eton white shirt he bought at Oak Hall the day after his first bonus check. It cost more than the suit he wore on his first sales call. That didn't matter, though. His sales from his first six months outpaced all but a handful of the company's sales force throughout the South. The casual khakis, button-down oxford, and brogans that he wore on this rare quasi day off eclipsed the thousand-dollar mark. While growing up on the ball fields of suburban Memphis, Tennessee, Easton expected success; it just hadn't looked like this.

It was rare for Sterling to experience the pangs of loneliness, but he did tonight. Sherrill had told him she would not answer if he called on Thanksgiving. She scheduled his trip, but that's where it ended. When she dropped him off at the airport early Thursday morning, she said he could fire her if he wanted, but she was spending Thanksgiving with her family, uninterrupted by Easton Sterling. He huffed in response, but they both knew no assistant he might replace her with would keep pace with him like Sherrill did. He would leave her alone.

Easton wondered why today seemed different, strange. Since he had become intoxicated by the deal, he didn't long for family gatherings. The cafeteria at the nursing home would take care of his mom, and his brother and sister wouldn't miss him. Their kids might, but he had excused himself from such family events for so long now that they no longer expected him. Today, he missed them... just a little.

ALTHOUGH HIS DAD named him after a bat brand, Easton made his mark as a left-handed pitcher. His six-foot-three frame carried his two hundred ten pounds well. He could have had his pick of girls on campus, but even then, his schedule would not allow for leisure time in his quest to be the best pitcher in the game. The fire in his belly for the sale arrived after a torn ulnar collateral ligament in his elbow curtailed his baseball career. After several prominent publications tabbed him a pre-season All-American before his junior year, he expected a hefty bonus after that June's Major League Baseball amateur draft. That was before the injury.

When his elbow gave out near the end of his junior season, Sterling maniacally pursued his return to the game, doubling up on his rehab exercises. The Rockies selected him in the twenty-ninth round of the draft in June, hoping for a bargain and a full recovery. An assistant to the general manager called and offered him $195,000 to sign, an insane offer for a late draftee. It represented a far cry from the million-dollar bonus Sterling envisioned, though, so he hung up the phone as soon as he heard the amount. Determined to make it back to the top of the game, Easton used the lowball offer as fuel to propel him toward one last college season.

While he rehabbed that summer, he took a job at Mid-South Med Services, a hospital equipment company. He accompanied Barry Needham, one of the senior sales reps, to his local calls and helped deliver samples. On the drive to their first call in Jackson, Tennessee, Needham turned to his young protégé and growled, "Just smile and keep your mouth shut, kid. Your role is eye candy for female execs and autographs for any of the guys who waste their time following sports." Sterling did as he was told and learned the art of the upsell from Needham.

When Needham called in sick on the day of an important presentation in Jonesboro in late July, he gave Sterling the "big boy job" of working out another time with the decision-makers there. Instead, Sterling drove to Jonesboro alone, closed the sale, and signed his own name to the paperwork. When he returned to the office, he tossed the papers on the desk of Tom Silverman,

Needham's boss who had hired Easton as his ride-along. "Needham called in sick. He'll be ticked off, but whatever. Your 'eye candy' closed the deal." He wheeled around to leave Silverman's office, content with the last hurrah of his summer job.

"Hey, kid, wait." Silverman followed Easton to the hallway. "No need to rush out."

"Headed back to be an All-American," Sterling said, waving over his shoulder and continuing to walk away.

"You'll get the bonus on the sale," Silverman said in desperation.

Sterling stopped without looking back. "How much?"

"Ten grand."

Sterling turned. "Are you serious?"

"As a heart attack. Come on back to my office and let's talk."

Tom Silverman was a career salesman. Rarely had he seen this gumption in even his best salesmen, and he didn't want this one to get away. "Kid, you might end of making millions as a ballplayer, or you could tear up that left shoulder of yours and never earn a dime. I'll give you a full-time sales job in a nice region tomorrow, and you'll make big money the rest of your life, perhaps more than you would as a ballplayer and definitely easier on your arm."

The wheels were turning in Sterling's mind as he envisioned a new scoreboard. He might never enjoy this kind of leverage again. He sucked in a deliberate breath —a technique he learned to control the flow of adrenaline during pivotal moments of a game—and took his time pushing the air through his pursed lips.

"You've got one offer. Make it your best."

"I can start you at a hundred thousand dollars. You'll double that with commissions in a decent year. Company car, 401(k), whatever training you want." Silverman had never offered a job without vetting an applicant, nor had he offered near this compensation for a rookie. But Easton Sterling had "it." He couldn't let him off the hook.

"Let's talk bonuses."

"Bonuses?"

"Twenty-five grand if I meet my sales goals, fifty if I'm number one in sales from now till the end of the year. I pick my assistant."

"You're an arrogant little cuss."

"I have options."

Silverman rocked back in his chair, tapping his fingertips against one another. After a lengthy pause, he relaxed. "That attitude will make all of us rich, I believe. I'll have my secretary draw up the paperwork. You start Monday. Go buy yourself some suits this weekend. Your days as a delivery boy are finished."

The conversations that followed weren't easy, but Easton's decision was firm. Dad's dreams of being a big leaguer's father flew out the window. He accused Easton of wasting the money he had spent making sure he was the best lefthanded pitcher in the country. "Fine, put a price tag on it and I'll have you paid back, with interest, in a year," Easton had responded.

Father and son scarcely spoke for a year. But when

Easton arrived the following Christmas with a brand new Corvette and ten thousand in cash for his dad, the elder Sterling's missing sense of pride in him magically returned. He drove the Corvette to the plant once for the boys to give it a once-over and informed them their cracks about his washed-up baseball player son should stop. Easton bought the car to spite him, though, and their relationship never recovered. That his father's heart attack and death had barely stirred Easton's emotions still bothered his mother and siblings.

12

Telling his coach he was leaving the game was the last time Easton had felt anything genuine deep in his soul. Coach Johnny Thorpe was the pitching coach who had recruited him since he pitched a no-hitter in the fourteen-year-old state championship for a team from north Mississippi. Instead of telling Easton how great he was like he was used to hearing, Coach Thorpe had encouraged him to envision his future and pursue his potential. With a track record of coaching four pitchers who had made it to the big leagues, his credibility held Easton's attention for the next four years.

While other recruiters were fawning over Easton, Thorpe reprimanded him for poor body language as a freshman. He encouraged him as a sophomore to work on a changeup when his fastball and slider were already causing older players to swing and miss. After Easton led his team to a state title his junior year, Thorpe pushed him past complacency before his senior season. Along the way, he explained the benefits of pitching for him in college instead of taking the money the pros offered to a top high school draft pick. Easton never regretted his decision to play college ball, though turning down the $100,000 the Red Sox offered him didn't sit well with his father.

***

"COACH THORPE, can you spare ten minutes?" he remembered asking. The hesitation in his voice caught Jon Thorpe's attention.

"Come in, Sterling. Close the door. What's going on?"

"Coach, I appreciate everything you've done for me."

"I don't like the sound of this, Easton," his pitching coach said, immediately concerned. "What's going on? Is your arm giving you problems?"

"No, nothing like that. I'm just looking in a different direction."

"Hold on, son." Coach Thorpe almost turned his desk over getting out of his office. He disappeared down the hall and reappeared seconds later with head coach Seth Garry, whose face was as distraught as his pitching coach's.

"Hey, Easton," Garry began, "Coach Thorpe tells me you're talking about going a different direction. What does that mean?"

"Coach, I want to tell you how much this program has meant to me."

"Hold on, Easton, stop with the farewell speeches. What is it that's got you so ticked off that you're ready to up and transfer and throw away everything we've set up for your future?"

"Nothing."

"Nothing? Then what...?" Garry was on the verge of exploding, flailing his arms in frustration and anger with his star pitcher, who remained calm.

"Just going to give you a minute to calm down so we can talk."

"Give me a min—" If Easton had been an umpire, Garry would have been in his face earning himself an ejection. Instead, he turned and flung open the door. His footsteps pounded down the hall of the otherwise empty building and returned with a little less force. He forced himself into the chair that sat at a forty-five degree angle to Easton's and asked through half-clenched teeth, "All right, Easton, I'm calm. What is it that has stirred up this talk about transferring?"

"I'm not transferring, Coach. I would never do that."

Garry looked at Thorpe with raised palms, as if questioning a call on the field. Thorpe's eyes returned the sentiment.

"I've been working at Mid-South Med Services back home during the summer while I've been rehabbing."

"I didn't know about any job, but yeah, I understood you were back home rehabbing. Easton, did you take something banned by the drug policy?"

"No, Coach, I'm clean."

"Then what?"

"If you would give me a few minutes, I can explain everything. The program is not in any danger of violations on my account, drugs or otherwise."

Garry leaned back in his chair and waved the back of his hand toward Easton, bidding him to continue.

"This job—it's a medical supply company. Anyway, they had me tagging along with one of their salesmen during the summer. He was one of their best, and they had me helping him deliver equipment and sitting in with him on his sales calls. This guy said they hired me as 'eye candy,' and I suppose he was right. Anyway, like I said, he was one of their top salesmen, but he seemed way too satisfied to me. Maybe that's why they had me ride along with him—I'm not sure. I signed autographs and posed for photos with his clients, but I paid attention to his pitches, too. He was good at upselling. Once he sold one product, he convinced the client to add to his order, which sometimes added thousands to his bottom line."

Both coaches were about to come out of their skin waiting for their own bottom line. Thorpe alternated between drumming his fingers together and scratching the back of his head. Garry tapped his palms on the arms of his chair.

"I was doing all my rehab ahead of schedule, but this sales thing was pretty intriguing, too. Friday should have been my last day."

"Should have been?"

"I did something out of line."

Garry wanted to ask about the legal ramifications of

Easton's *something out of line,* but by significant effort, he remained silent.

"The salesman I was working with called in sick, although he wasn't sick. He told me all I needed to do was call the client and reschedule the appointment, count all eight hours on my time card, and call it a summer. That's what I should have done."

Garry fidgeted, waiting for the other shoe to fall. "What did you do?"

"Instead of calling the client, I went on the call. From the company's standpoint, I thought I should show up like we committed to do. It wasn't my role or my job to close the sale, but it also wasn't right for my boss to take a sick day when he wasn't sick."

"Easton, are you in trouble? Because we can help you with that."

"No, I closed the deal."

"You what?"

"I showed up in Jonesboro in my boss's place. After watching him all summer, I understood what to do. I added some auxiliary products to the sale, signed the deal, and drove back to Memphis by mid-afternoon. I waited until around four o'clock, when everybody but my boss's boss would be gone for the day. When I tossed the contract on his desk and told him what I had done, I half expected him to fire me, even though it was my last day. I didn't care because I felt like I had represented the company better than my boss had. He had been a jerk to me all summer, so I didn't care if he got in trouble. I walked out of the big boss's office, but he yelled after me that I would get the commission on the sale."

Thorpe stopped drumming his fingers together. "How much?"

"Ten grand."

Garry responded with a long, low whistle. "Yeah, that might be a problem. Have you received the check yet?"

"No, they'll cut it at the end of the month."

He exhaled slowly. "Good. Tell 'em to keep it. Tell 'em to give it to your boss. Either way, don't take that money."

"Why?"

"The NCAA will see that as an improper benefit. If you never get the check, we'll be fine."

Easton smiled when his mind caught up to his coach's logic. "Coach, this is not about getting paid too much for a summer job and breaking a rule. Mr. Silverman didn't just give me the commission on that sale. He offered me a job."

Both coaches sat dumbfounded now that they had reached the gist of the most bizarre player conversation either of them had ever had. Thorpe spoke first, straining to keep his temper at bay. "You mean to tell us you are leaving baseball to take a sales job?"

"That's right." The ease with which Easton responded struck panic into the hearts of his coaches.

"Son, do you realize how much your left arm is worth?"

"Between two and three million dollars if everything goes right with the potential of nothing if it doesn't."

Garry's chair could contain him no longer. Thorpe's office allowed him three paces in each direction between walls and furniture. He took full advantage, revealing his angst with gyrations usually saved for the game. "What about everything we worked so hard for this coming season—conference championship, regional, super-regional? With you throwing the first game of every round and the depth we have coming back, we should make a legitimate run at Omaha. It's not every year a school our size gets a shot at the College World Series. What am I supposed to tell your teammates, for crying out loud?"

"Nothing. I wrote a letter to each one of them explaining the whole situation. I will drop them in the mail as soon as I leave here."

"And this doesn't bother you a bit, what you're doing to them, to us, to your school?"

"I don't expect you to understand this, Coach. To be honest with you, I don't, but I am convinced it's what I need to do. You've been around baseball your entire life, right?"

"Since I was six years old, cutting box scores out of the paper. Never wanted to do anything else."

Easton turned to Thorpe. "Coach?"

"Sold insurance for six years after my last high school job."

"Did you like it?"

"It was okay. I made enough that Kim could stay home until the kids started school."

"Why did you return to coaching?"

Thorpe recognized Easton was leading him toward

something, but he couldn't determine what. With an ulterior motive of his own, he answered, "I took over an office for a guy who was retiring. I started with enough of his old clients to scrape by. The higher ups wanted me to survive on what I inherited, but be hungry enough to build the business from there. During those first couple of years when I was struggling, my wife needed another car, and we couldn't afford it. I built a bullpen in my backyard and started giving pitching lessons, just a handful of former players at first, but I made enough to buy my wife a decent car.

"I didn't just do it for the money, though. Over the next couple of years, those first guys I worked with kept coming back, even after they started pitching in college. To a one, they told me I was better than the pitching coach they had in college. My mind drifted that way, even after the insurance business picked up. My wife saw the passion I had for coaching and the lack of desire to grow my business, and she suggested we make a plan. I would grow the business for three years, put enough money in the bank to supplement our income until she was ready to return to work, and see where we stood. We followed through with the plan and saved enough to survive my three years coaching at a junior college before coming here. I can tell you this: I never would have loved selling insurance like I love developing pitchers." After a few seconds, he added, "Like you."

Easton pressed, "But what if you had loved selling insurance like you loved coaching. Coach, I love sales. I can show you my plan to be the best within the first two years."

"I don't doubt it," Garry said. "But I can't help but feel they've manipulated you. What if they're just using you? What if you work hard for whatever piddling amount they've promised you, and it turns out to be a pipe dream?"

"Like making it to the big leagues, you mean?"

"But Easton, making the show is not a pipe dream for you, don't you get that? Even an average season by your standards, and you'll be a millionaire in less than a year."

"Followed by several years making a *piddling amount*, as you call it, in the minor leagues."

"But you're special, Easton. I can imagine your being in the big leagues in three years. You realize what the minimum salary for a big league ballplayer is?"

"Half a million."

"More than that soon after. Pitch well for the first few years, your next contract will set you up for the rest of your life."

"And one arm injury, I'm done for life. No minimum salary, no next contract. What then?"

Garry snorted, "Then you sell medical equipment."

The room stayed silent until Thorpe said, "It's not like you to take the negative side like this, Easton. I'll be so bold as to say it sounds like you're playing scared."

"Sure, it might sound that way, but I'm just refuting Coach Garry's logic. I took this job because sales lit me up like nothing since I picked up a baseball and started throwing it. I'm good at it, just like you're good at fixing a pitcher's mechanics or getting inside his head to change his mindset."

Thorpe nodded as Garry continued to pace. "What did they offer you, Easton?"

"Hundred grand to start. Commissions could double it first year." Garry stopped pacing and sat. The number held their attention. Easton outlined his conversation with Tom Silverman and laid out his two-year plan. "Coaches, you've seen how hard I work. You know how focused and relentless I am. Coach Garry, consider your plan for my life over the next ten years, and consider mine. If you remove passion from the equation, which plan is better?"

"I still say baseball has more upside, but I can't argue with the risk side of it," he conceded. "Research shows the biggest indicator of major arm injuries is prior arm injuries. And here you sit a year after the big one. But here's the thing, Easton. When you're thirty-five, I don't want you to wonder what might have been. This is your only shot to be a professional baseball player, something you've dreamed of since you started playing ball. You can start sales later, with this company or another one."

"I've considered that. But, Coach, when I closed that deal this summer and saw the potential in sales, a switch flipped inside of me, and all my passion for baseball started flowing a different direction. Plus, have you ever known me to be the guy who looks back with regret? I only move one direction, straight ahead."

Thorpe nodded and smiled for the first time during the conversation. Tilting his head in Garry's direction, he said, "He started sending me out to talk to you on the mound because he couldn't get you to come out of a game."

"I had to save face with the crowd," Garry said, his face softening. "Coach goes out to do his job and make a pitching change, and his dang lefty won't give him the ball—not a good look in this profession."

"How many times did I escape the jam, though, Coach?"

"Most of 'em. This should have been a special year. I hate this for all of us. Is there any part of you..."

Easton maintained eye contact with his head coach as he shook his head.

Garry stood, followed by Thorpe. "Well, Easton Sterling, this is a first for me, but thank you for everything you've done for this program and, to be honest, for our careers as coaches. It will be hard to pivot from our plans for the season, but we did it last year when you injured yourself, and that kind of comes with the territory. We'll start damage control when it gets out that you've quit baseball."

"I have a lunch appointment with Rob Jarnigan at the end of the week," Easton interrupted, speaking of the *Harriston Daily News* sports reporter who covered the team. "I'll lay it all out for him and say a dozen times how much this program and my coaches and teammates mean to me. Rest assured, I'll tell him how my decision is not reflective of anything with the program, perhaps play up how hard rehab has been and how it has taken the joy of the game away from me. When I come back with a sizable check for whatever project you guys are working on, that should silence the doubters and help you guys build the facilities to recruit the next Easton Sterling."

"Dadgum, you've thought of everything, haven't you?" Garry said, extending his hand. Easton took it. He hugged Coach Thorpe and walked through the door. Garry stopped him. "One thing, Easton. You might reconsider informing your teammates through a form letter."

"They're not form letters, Coach. I've been writing them for the last two days."

"Twenty-three personal letters?"

"Thirty-five. I wrote them to the incoming freshmen, too."

Easton waved as he walked out the door. Behind him, he heard Garry curse and say, "Thirty-five personal letters to give them the news he's quitting the game?" And then he cursed again.

Before Easton walked through the outer door into the parking lot, he heard Thorpe reply, "He never played like anybody else we ever had. Why should he go out like them?"

13

Easton Sterling's exit from baseball sent shock waves through the college and professional ranks. He paid no attention to the part of his life from which he had walked away. For him, the intoxication of the sale was immediate and thorough. Within five years of that first illegitimate sale, he broke every company sales mark on record. His hunger for more opportunities was insatiable, and Silverman was happy to feed the beast. No sales manager should have allowed such a potent salesman to keep a pace that promised early burnout, but Silverman planned to ride his golden goose all the way into retirement. No one who profited from Easton's success dared slow him down.

Easton hired Sherrill Riggs less than a year into his stint with Mid-South Med amid rumors he would sign with a company with deeper pockets and equally rampant whispers he would take Silverman's spot when he retired. He had no such intentions. While others in the office still valued a woman's attractiveness in their admins, he wanted someone to aggressively plan his schedule and take anything out that didn't make money. It's not that Sherrill was unattractive—she just cared more about adding zeroes to the end of her bank account than she did making the most of her looks. Sterling figured out a way to incentivize her position; heck, he didn't mind sharing a few thousand of what would soon become hundreds of thousands he attributed to Sherrill. They were a perfect match.

By Sherrill's third year with Sterling, she was practically scheduling his bathroom breaks. Freed to spend more time with medical execs, he found new clients to schmooze. By year five he had helped develop a propriety software for heart surgeons that made him money on each end of the sale. When his sales rose, so did Sherrill's commission checks. She found it impossible to over-schedule the man.

And then Sherrill found Jesus and started giving her money away.

EASTON MET Sherrill at one of those weekend path-to-riches seminars at a hotel in East Memphis in early January, halfway through his first year with the company. He had nothing to do on a snowy Saturday and figured he might as well hone his sales game. Her T-shirt read *I Don't Care What You Think*, and he liked her right away. He saw a hunger in her he could only describe as a mirror image of his own drive. He introduced himself during the first break by asking about her shirt.

She had not paused for formalities. "I *will* thrive in the business world one day. My friends and family can give you a hundred things standing in my way, but I do not care what they think. I wear this shirt to any training like this to remind myself to push back against the resistance."

"Seems you should lead your own personal development seminar," Easton offered.

"Don't sleep on me," she had snapped back. "I see through the rags-to-riches stories most of these charlatans are pitching. Mine is legit, no need to exaggerate."

As the last of the stragglers returned to the meeting room, Easton tested her by nodding toward the full-sized cutout of the day's speaker. "What about this guy?"

"Full of it. What makes you care about my opinion?"

"I'm looking for an assistant. You might be just the person I've been trying to find." He kicked himself for not playing his cards closer to the vest. He had just met her and wasn't sure her edginess would work for him or against him.

"What makes you think I would want to be your secretary?" she bellowed loud enough to cause guests in the foyer to stare.

"You didn't hear anybody say *secretary*."

"Call it what you will. I will be no man's personal valet. How old are you, anyway?"

"Twenty-three. You?"

"Close to that. What kind of assistant are you looking for, somebody to help with your frat parties?"

"Tell you what—what did you say your name was?"

"Sherrill."

"Mine is—"

"Easton Sterling."

"You remembered."

"I pay attention."

"So you do. Well, I'll tell you what, Sherrill, I'm top three in sales in my company in my first year. I am far from satisfied being anything but number one. Number one every year, that's what I expect. Number one on all the company records. I have a plan to carry it out it, too. All I'm missing is a motivated assistant. He or she will get rich as I do."

"Yeah, right? You talk big now, but when it comes down to it, you men are all the same. You'll keep what's yours and walk away."

"Since you have it all figured out, I'll just keep looking, then. You're one who pays close attention, so make sure you remember the opportunity you might have had if you hadn't been so hardheaded." He started down the hall, spinning around after a few steps. "For what it's worth, I agree with you about this speaker." He pivoted again and left the hotel.

TWO WEEKS LATER, after another fruitful day trip to Jonesboro, Easton sat alone in the office on a Friday evening, shuffling through his mail. He was most interested in any resumes that had arrived during the week. There were seven. He stopped with the cover letter of four of them, scanned the next two, and threw them in the trash. The seventh garnered his attention because of how thin the packet was, as if the sender had forgotten to enclose the enclosures. Inside the envelope, Easton found a sheet torn from a hotel note pad: *Maybe I do give a crap what you think. Call me. If you remember my name, we'll talk.* A phone number followed. As fast as he could will his fingers to move, he punched the digits.

"Sherrill."

"Easton."

"When can you start?"

"Easy, cowboy. You don't get me that easily. I'll give you one hour to tell me how you will make me rich and not treat me like you're any better than me."

"Meet me in thirty minutes at the restaurant next to the hotel where we met two weeks ago."

"I'm not ready."

"You come to work with me, you'd better be. Six other resumes filled my inbox today, with more coming all the time."

"And if any of them were worth a plug nickel, you'd be on the phone with them instead of me."

"Thirty minutes."

"Geez, I'll be there."

Sherrill made it with a minute to spare. With wrinkled dress, spotty makeup, and her auburn hair pulled up in a ponytail, she slid into the booth across from Easton. He snickered. "Look, you gave me thirty minutes. It's a ten-minute drive, and I'm always early. You want somebody who will spend the other nineteen minutes primping or checking your company's financials?"

The rest of the interview involved barbs flying back and forth across the table as the two jockeyed for position in a business relationship they both considered a formality by that point. When the check arrived and Easton asked the server to split it, Sherrill nodded. "Well played, boss."

"That'll be the last time you call me that. We're going to work together, move in the same direction, dominate this sales force together. I show up at the office early, spend most of the day working as many clients as I can visit, and leave well after most of the other salesmen have gone home. I need you to be working just as hard to get out ahead of my schedule and handle my paperwork. You've been to enough self-improvement seminars to know that twenty percent of what you do accounts for eighty percent of your profit. I'm good at selling. The less time I spend on scheduling and paperwork, the more time I have to spend in front of clients. Get me in a room with a client, and I *will* discover something in our product line they need and close the sale. I'll train you to do the rest. You won't stop there, though. You will find other ways to make me more productive, and you'll outwork everybody here except me."

"And in return?"

"You'll get to choose your own title, within reason. It won't be *secretary* or *assistant*. It will be whatever you need it to be to move the needle with our current and future clients. Compel them to trust you as their go-to person for anything that doesn't require a face-to-face with me."

"You said you would make us rich."

"*We* will make us rich."

"I'm listening."

"Seventy-five thousand a year, plus benefits."

"Not interested."

"Good. Thirty thousand and twenty percent of my commissions on new sales." Easton had done the math and figured she would be hard pressed to earn the amount of his first offer in her first year.

"Forty thousand and fifteen percent of every dime you make." Sherrill could do math, too, and had assessed the potential of the market. "My income tied to yours—plus a decent secretary's pay," she said with the slightest of grins.

"You have a year, tops, to prove yourself."

"You've got six months."

"Show up Monday morning ready to work."

SHE WAS WAITING at the door of his office when he arrived at 6:45. "Thought you started early?"

It took Sherrill Riggs the better part of a month to learn Easton's routine, two months to make it more efficient, and six months before she controlled his entire schedule. Neither could outwork the other, and their production shot past anything Mid-South Med had ever seen from its sales force. Neither showed a hint of slowing down.

When one of the salesman's secretaries heard the rumor that Easton's assistant had made over a hundred thousand dollars in her first year on the job, she went to her boss to renegotiate her own pay. "Shadow her for one day from beginning to end, and then we'll talk," he had told her. She called in sick the following day, worn out from a sixteen-hour day, and never mentioned a raise again.

As far as Easton was concerned, the company Christmas party was a waste of time and money except for the announcement of that year's top five in sales. After a full year with Sherrill on board, his number almost doubled that of the guy in second place. When Easton handed Sherill her bonus check in private while everybody else was getting snockered, he told her, "Your total package would rank fifth in the Mid-South office. Nobody but us needs to know that."

"Fifth place," she repeated. "That'll do for my first year. Not bad for an executive coordinator."

He grinned, enjoying the light back-and-forth that their success had earned. "*Executive coordinator*, huh? It's about time you told me."

Sherrill chuckled. She had used the title with clients almost from the beginning. It had the ring that motivated the decision-makers to take her calls. Once they were on the line, she didn't accept *no* for an answer. When Easton followed up in person, it wasn't a matter of the sale but how much more he would convince the customer to spend. The handwritten notes and thoughtful gifts Sherrill sent as part of her routine caused their clients to be more eager than ever to schedule time with him.

"You going to get a drink?" she asked.

"I don't drink," he said. "Never have. I don't want anything clouding my thinking."

"You're kidding." She was genuinely flabbergasted. "All those client meetings, dinners, and all? You mean to tell me you've never taken a drink?"

"Oh, I'll take one, even act like I'm drinking it sometimes. I always keep the edge, though."

"I bet you drank during your college days, didn't you? You college athlete types consider themselves invincible."

"Not a drop. This work ethic didn't just drop from the sky."

"If I didn't know better, I'd think you were one of those Jesus freaks."

"Never been accused of that."

"Wow, you learn something new every day. I don't guess I know much about you personally. Do you even have a personal life?"

"Not much to speak of. You?"

"Too busy."

"I'd just as soon keep it that way."

"Same."

14

"Boss, I need a few minutes of your valuable time the next time you're in the office," Sherrill's voice message announced.

"You control my schedule, so name the time," his message responded. And stop calling me *boss.*"

I cleared out an hour before your lunch appointment today, she texted after her call with an doctor in Corinth.

Time is money for both of us.

It's that important.

For the first time in as long as he could remember, Sterling had trouble focusing on his two sales calls that morning. He and Sherrill had been in lockstep almost since she partnered with him. His commission idea for her position had been a stroke of brilliance. She didn't gripe about a raise because she was so busy creating her own bumps in pay. He could call her anytime he required anything, but she stayed a step ahead of him. *This can't be about money. I'll bet she makes more than any other assistant in the city already, maybe by a long shot. Sure hope she's not sick or pregnant. Does Sherrill even have a personal life?* His cluelessness carried with it the slightest tinge of guilt.

"IS THIS ABOUT MONEY?" Sterling asked before he had closed the door to his office. "If it is, name your number, and we'll make this a real short meeting."

"I gave my life to Jesus on Sunday."

Sterling sat speechless, which was no insignificant event.

"O-kay."

"Easton, I need you to realize I will evaluate every part of my life. I don't know what that means, but understand that whatever the Lord leads me to do, I will do it."

"Are you moving to Africa?"

"I don't have plans to that effect, but if God calls me to Africa, I won't hesitate. My *yes* is on the table."

"Is this your resignation?"

"No, Easton, no. I'm just informing you…"

"What then? Tell me what happened."

"Okay, here goes. I have been going to this church out near where I live."

"The one that's the size of a college campus?"

"No, a smaller church about a mile north of there."

"You don't say."

"It started about a month ago when my mom was in town from Houston. She requested we go to church while she was here, and I choose not to rock the boat with her. We had been to that church you're talking about when she had visited before, but I had a notion I should take her somewhere else this time. I can't explain it, but I can tell you God had me where he needed me to be that Sunday morning. I have been back every week since, and this Sunday, I committed my life to Jesus."

"Let me make sure I understand you. You're not quitting? You're not asking for a raise?"

"No."

"So, other than church, nothing has changed."

"*I* am changed, Easton, that's what has changed. Don't you care?"

"You understand what I care about, Sherrill, the same as always—to win. The reason I'm the best salesman in the history of this company is that it's not about the money for me. I don't need it or have time to spend it. Money is the scoreboard, and more money says *I win*. Now, I'm glad you've had whatever experience it was you had, but I don't prefer to train anybody else to do what you do."

"Easton, are you listening to me at all? I *am not* resigning."

"Sounds like you're setting it up."

"Never mind, then, *Mister* Sterling." She had used that tone and that name for him twice before. It cautioned him to retreat.

"What?"

"I figured the most important event in my life might interest you. Guess I was wrong."

"So you attended church and enjoyed it."

"No, Easton, I gave my life to Jesus. He took my sin and made me clean, and I'm going to heaven when I die. I don't carry the weight of guilt and shame anymore. I'm free."

"What should you feel guilty about? You're as straight a shooter as anybody. Unless you've been leading a double life, which I think I would know."

"Nope. No double life, no hidden secrets, just forgiven. I just wanted you to hear it from me. It might not be significant to you, but it matters to me."

"Okay, so you've told me. Let's get back to work."

SHERRILL RETURNED TO WORK, as efficient and reliable as ever, but something about her changed over the succeeding months that Sterling couldn't pinpoint. She seemed softer, almost pretty, which he chided himself for noticing. She still bossed him around in her usual manner, preparing him for where he needed to go, but she started throwing out little phrases like *be safe* and *take care of yourself*. He might have shrugged them off, but he noticed. She also didn't dive into her commission check with her usual zeal. She spoke of the places she was giving it away, instead, like a children's home in Haiti and a pastor's training center in Zambia—or was it Zimbabwe—and how communities would be *blessed* by her giving. He didn't know how she spent her money before, but this was a departure from it, for sure.

A FULL YEAR passed before she invited him to church the first time.

Sherrill scheduled Easton to attend the Saturday round of the FedEx St. Jude Classic golf tournament with a group of local physicians with whom he was working on another piece of software. His flight to Tampa wouldn't leave until around five o'clock on Sunday evening. Sherrill texted early Saturday morning to remind him of the details and to ask if he needed a ride. As soon as he declined, his phone rang.

"Easton, I have a favor to ask of you."

"You need to take a day off? You realize you don't have to ask me; just make certain you take care of my schedule and paperwork."

"Easton, I want you to meet me at church tomorrow morning."

He froze. "I'm not so sure about that. With my trip coming up..."

"I know your schedule. You'll be here. Come on, Easton, come to church with me tomorrow."

The kindness in her tone prompted him to entertain the idea. Instead of answering, he changed the subject, asking her to phone his brother to schedule a meeting about placing their mother in a nursing home. Their mother's recovery had not advanced enough for her to live alone, and her insurance coverage for hospital rehab was about to run out. She was dumbstruck by the change of direction.

"Are you seriously asking me to arrange a family meeting for you?"

"Why not? You schedule the rest of my life."

"Somebody needs a wife."

"No time for a wife."

"You are a piece of work."

"Thanks."

"It wasn't a compliment."

"Consider individuals we recognize for exceptional accomplishments throughout history. What do they have in common?"

"They were all single?"

"No, but most of them achieved what they did because they had a singular focus. It's the reason I hired you. We haven't just broken records in this company, Sherill, we've *shattered* them."

"I don't see my name on any of those plaques."

"But you and I both recognize that this good salesman became a great one when I brought you on board. I'll deny ever saying that," he joked, though it didn't hit its mark. "The money's not even the point, other than it serves as the scoreboard that lets me win, lets us win. I just want to be at the top of that sales board every single quarter, every year."

"What are we winning, Easton? The day I gave my life to Christ, the pastor asked us to imagine working our entire lives to climb the ladder of success, only to discover we had propped our ladders against the wrong wall. There was no question in my mind he was talking about me."

"But what makes you sure the preacher's ladder, as you say, is the right one?"

"Consider the top of your ladder, Easton. How could you be any more number one than you already are?

None of the other salespeople even care about competing with you anymore."

"They recognize when they're beaten."

"They realize the cost of your level of accomplishment is beyond what they're willing to pay."

"Look, Sherrill, when I started playing competitive ball not too long after I started walking, all I ever heard was that I needed to pay the price for success. My dad and my coaches said I had to work harder than the competition—values that served me well. I was an All-American baseball player, and if they had All-American salesmen, I'd be first team."

"Sure you would, but for what purpose? What's your end goal?"

"To be the best."

"The best what? Baseball player? You did that, and it didn't satisfy you. You own the top of the company sales charts, and it's not satisfying you."

"I'm satisfied with my life. Do you ever see me miserable?"

"No, but..."

"But nothing. I'm made for this."

"Are you? At what expense?"

"What do you mean?"

"This might make you uncomfortable, but I'm about to jump into your personal business."

"Nothing new there. You're as personal as it gets for me. Shoot."

"When your dad died, you took one day off, and then you flew out to an appointment the night of his funeral."

"He was as dead and buried as he could get. Sorry, I realize that sounds cold, but that was an important meeting. We have made a lot of money from that relationship."

"How important do you believe it was to your mom that you stayed with her and helped her through her grief?"

"Who paid for the funeral and the burial plot? Who paid for the hotel rooms and food for the out-of-town family?"

"I did. With your money, of course."

"Touché. Ronnie and Grace stayed with Mom the whole time, though, see? We all played our roles."

"But you could have taken some time for your mother. Don't you understand your family wants to spend time with you?"

"I have sent them places they could have never afforded to go. Mom always wanted to go to Europe, and she took three of her friends *for three weeks* the summer before her stroke. And I get how hard it is for Ronnie's and Grace's families to do anything with all those kids of theirs, so I make their vacations possible."

"Yes, Easton, you are generous to them. You direct me to spend money on them all the time, but I'm going to just state it: You are buying your way out of genuine relationships with them. I know they enjoy the trips because they send thank you cards you don't bother to read. Don't you think all those nieces and nephews of yours would love for Uncle Easton to go on one of those fancy trips with them?"

"Given the choice, they would probably prefer the trips over Uncle Easton."

"But don't you understand, it need not be either/or with you. You possess the wherewithal to pay for grand experiences *and* the freedom to take time off to appreciate them with your family. I don't understand why you won't."

"Sherrill, I'm proud of what I've built with this company. The devices we make help many people, and the software packages we're creating are helping doctors perform their jobs better. Yes, it's about the scoreboard with me, but we're still doing phenomenal things here."

"Phenomenal things will continue to happen when you take a week's vacation, too. Take your entire clan to the beach and do all the fun stuff with them and take them to eat at the best restaurants."

"Set it up if you believe that's what they would want."

"No, Easton, *go with them.*"

"Who will take care of Mom?"

"I'm sure she will live in the best assisted care facility money can buy as soon as her hospital stay is over."

"Paid for by whom?"

"You."

"Me."

"You're still avoiding the question."

"I don't even remember the question."

"Why don't you go *with your family* to the beach this summer?"

"What about my clients? I made my mark in this business by always being available. That's why they do business with me."

"How many of your clients take some time off from their patients during the year?"

"That's their business. I should be available to my clients. End of story."

"No, a heart attack will be the end of your story if you don't learn to relax."

"Doctor says my ticker's as strong as any he's seen."

"Yeah, three years ago when you went for your last so-called regular physical."

"Last year." Sherrill raised an eyebrow at him. "Okay, three years. But I am as strong as ever."

"I promise your clients will understand if you're out of pocket for a week. I can take care of your clients. They talk to me more than they do to you, anyway."

"Ah, there's your angle—going to slip in and grab some of my sales, are you? Have I ever told you how I got my start as a salesman here?"

"At least two hundred times. Wait..."

"No."

"That's it, isn't it?"

"I don't understand what you're talking about."

"You believe if you step away for a week—even a day or two—someone will take advantage of you like you did Barry Needham."

"That's crazy."

"You still feel guilty about that."

"I sent him that money, with interest."

"You had me send it."

"Whatever. Same thing."

"Not the same. You still owe that man an apology and you know it."

"I owe him no such thing. I sent him way more than anybody else would have. He would have done it to another salesman in a heartbeat."

"I understand you now, Easton Sterling."

STERLING HAD REPLAYED that conversation dozens of times since then. *Am I as heartless as Sherrill says?* He found it more difficult to look her in the eye as he saw her life changing. She was still doing the same outstanding job she had always done, but he didn't have twenty-four/seven access to her like he had always had. She didn't make that an option for next weekend, either, now that he thought about it. *Easton, I'll be at a women's retreat with my church next weekend. I won't have my business phone with me, so don't bother calling. I won't answer. If you need something, leave a message and I'll get back to you Sunday night after church.* Sherrill had a personal phone? That indicated a personal life, a strange new dynamic in their relationship.

This week, Sherrill had been insistent that he spend Thanksgiving with his family, maybe spend some unhurried time with his mom at the assisted living home. He had mumbled an excuse about his family already having plans, one that convinced neither of them. When he had instructed Sherrill to get his mother a room there, she argued that the name of the place made it seem like he was putting his mom out to pasture. Ronnie and Grace went by there several times a week, and he even stopped by last week. She was doing better, he could tell, but her admonishment to spend Thanksgiving with his family had about as much effect as Sherrill's. Only... he wasn't as convinced of his own importance as he had been before Sherrill's... what did she call it again... salvation?

15

The light poles of the baseball stadium caught Easton's attention as he drove past the university campus. He made a sudden turn onto the abandoned campus main drive and drove through its tree-lined streets until he reached the baseball field. Unconsciously, he parked on the right side of the stadium and walked through an unlocked gate. In another town at another stadium, his thoughts may have veered toward how outstanding he had once been at this game. He might have thought about the call from his coach: "Sterling, you're an All-American. First team."

But not today. Not here. His life turned on this field.

He pitched his best that Friday night in the first game of a three-game series to determine the conference championship. His school had never claimed a conference championship, but if their lanky lefty delivered one more win, they would clinch at least a share of the title. Even then, the moment never overwhelmed him. He might pitch at less than his best in a mostly empty stadium, but when the lights came on for a Friday night conference game in front of a packed crowd, Easton reached the height of his game. The hecklers attempted to get in his head, like the guy here who droned *Throw it in the dirt!*.

Hey, big fella, see how you like this slider in the dirt. Batter after batter reminded himself not to chase it, but each one couldn't resist.

The scouts nearly filled an entire section. *If you boys don't have a top five pick, you might as well stay home,* he taunted them in his mind as he continued to throw up zeroes on the scoreboard. In the bottom of the seventh inning, with the game still scoreless, his elbow barked on a slider that ended the inning with his thirteenth strikeout of the night. He refused to acknowledge the pain, though. The conference record for strikeouts was fifteen, and he planned to walk away with that record that night.

After his team scored a run in the top of the eighth inning, Sterling picked up strikeouts fourteen and fifteen on that slider. The scouts that night described the slider with phrases like *filthy, stinky, downright devastating,* and *unhittable at any level.* He had allowed two hits, both to the same batter now striding to the plate. *Jumped a fastball first at bat,* Easton reminded himself. *Flared a changeup over the second baseman's head last time. Hasn't touched a breaking ball. Get ready for three hammers, big boy.*

Strike one broke over the outside corner. Strike two was a swing-and-miss curve over the inner half. *Slide piece coming right at your back foot, big boy. Let's see you try to hold up on this nastiness.* Easton shook off his catcher's signal for a fastball outside. When his catcher tapped his left leg for the location he wanted, Easton grinned at the batter, savoring the moment before his name would replace Blake Jackson's as the conference single-game strikeout king. He wound and fired but never saw the batter swing and miss. The ligament in his elbow snapped on the pitch, and Sterling crumpled to the ground in front of the mound.

THIS THANKSGIVING AFTERNOON was the first time since the injury that Easton had allowed himself to move any direction but forward. Without realizing how he arrived there, he found himself standing on the mound, hands in front of his chest, glaring at an invisible catcher's invisible middle finger, ring finger, and pinkie signaling slider. He nodded. An index finger pointed inside to the imaginary righthanded batter. Again, he nodded, then flashed a knowing grin to the batter. With no one within a quarter mile of the mound, Sterling stepped back with his right foot, pivoted sideways as he raised his right knee as high as he was able, and strode toward the plate. His once golden left arm worked in harmony with his lower body to once again deliver that slider that had killed a record and a career on the same pitch. This time, he watched the batter that wasn't there swing through the pitch as his catcher dove to block it and keep the ball in front. He taunted back to his favorite heckler: *Threw it in the dirt!* As the visiting crowd cheered in appreciation of a new conference record for strikeouts in a single game, he reached for a cap that wasn't there to show his appreciation, the way it should have happened.

Then Easton Sterling walked to the spot in front of the mound where he had fallen and sat down and cried. He allowed himself to ponder what might have been. Forget the money—he knew those figures. Only a handful of guys had ever gone straight to the big leagues without ever having played in the minors. Would he have added his name to that list? Probably not, but still, he would've outworked everybody else at that level, too. Three years, and he could have signed his first big contract. The one before the big one. A few years later, he could have turned his thoughts toward the Hall of Fame, where only a few pitchers from every generation landed. Plenty were talented enough, but few stayed healthy long enough to put up the numbers enshrinement required. Even with a Tommy John surgery already under his belt, he would have found a way somehow.

He never allowed himself to look back because the last thing he needed holding him back was regrets. He sensed it now, though, years worth of regret rushing in on him faster than his ability to process it. The disrespect he had shown his dad with no more opportunities to apologize. The neglect of his mom, along with the excuses to his sister and brother of paying for her care when, in reality, he didn't want the hassle. He felt guilty for how he had mocked Sherrill. Whatever it looked like to him, finding God was important to her, and he shouldn't have made light of it.

WHEN EASTON RETURNED to his rental, he tried to push his meltdown out of his mind by reverting to his usual road trip habits. He slowed his breathing to focus his mind and followed by increasing the volume of his eighties rock station in increments until the speakers were blaring. The technique gave him the eye of the tiger as he turned his attention toward tomorrow morning's meeting with the hospital execs. The ten-minute drive from the ballpark to the restaurant re-engaged his mind and emotions to his purpose for this trip. He pulled into the restaurant parking lot in his luxury SUV, singing, "Gonna be a man in motion, all I need is a pair of wings."

Easton gathered his leather satchel with his laptop and the papers that needed two signatures to ensure he would once again cinch a new company sales record for the year. He grabbed his tablet from the glove compartment and tapped his pocket to make sure his cell phone was there. He considered a twenty-dollar meal a wasted one. It was a rare occasion when he ate for less than several hundred of the company's dollars, making them thousands in the process. Might as well use the time to prepare for Saturday's meeting with the group of surgeons in Jackson who let him pay for the privilege of beating a former college athlete in golf. He could beat them by a dozen strokes on his worst day, but that was the cost of doing business. It was a high cost for Easton to lose in anything, but these doctors bought everything the company pushed in their direction. Tomorrow, he would ask for their endorsements on the new software he had helped develop, and they would deliver. He had signed countless baseballs and old photographs for their various benefits, so it was a mutually beneficial relationship. Plus, these guys often filled the dates on his schedule around the holidays when everyone else wanted to spend it with their families.

Families. I wonder what Mom is doing this evening. Did Ronnie or Grace pick her up and take her to eat Thanksgiving lunch at one of their houses? They probably invited me... I don't remember.

Easton had his hand on the twenty-dollar bill that assured his immediate seating, but the hostess seemed eager to seat him right away. As he leaned over to plug in his laptop to the wall receptacle, he made eye contact with the old man sitting in the corner. He wondered if the old fella recognized him from his playing days. Perhaps he attended the game where Easton's career ended. *Please don't let him tell me how great I was and what a shame it was that I got hurt.*

Easton ordered water and a grilled chicken salad and set up shop. His electronic gadgets scattered all over the table, he got down to business, ignorant to the looks he was getting from all over the room. He waved off biscuits and cornbread and opened up his file of potential new devices and software in which his company might invest. No new Mid-South Med product ever launched without Easton's having an extensive list of why every doctor in his territory had to have it. Many of those doctors considered Easton a stronger expert on their needs than they were. He didn't need his usual level of preparation, but he had a reputation to uphold. Now, another thought kept crossing his mind in Sherrill's voice as he anticipated needs, products, and pitches at least a year in advance: *At what cost, Sterling? Why don't you let me plan that vacation?*

The grilled chicken salad sat untouched long enough for Easton's server to circle back around and ask him if everything was okay with his order. "Fine," he mumbled, waving her away. Computing key figures on the software deal, he glanced up to see the old man's eyes dart away. He was standing now, and Easton braced for an autograph request and a story or two. He determined he would humor the old gentleman—he had to be in his eighties, but he seemed a sharp character. Easton sat up and drew in a deep breath as he approached, but he walked past Easton's table without so much as a nod. Easton's eyes followed him to the server, who evidently knew the old man and was giving him some positive news. His figures called him back, but he paused for a few bites of his salad before diving back into his future. *Is anybody going to notice me when I'm in my eighties? Will my brother and sister even still remember me?*

"Sir, is your salad okay?" Easton's server asked. "I can swap it out for something else if you'd like."

Easton forced a smile. "No, it's fine. I'm just busy tonight, I guess. Here, I'll reassure you." He sampled a tiny bite and smiled again. "See? All good."

"Just checking. Wouldn't want you not enjoying your meal on Thanksgiving."

Oh, yeah. Thanksgiving. Mom would have asked what I was thankful for a half dozen times by now. My health, my job, Sherill. I'm positive "friends and family" is the right answer, but who am I kidding? Sherrill is the closest thing to a friend I have, but I doubt she counts. What word was it she used to describe me last week—avarice? He opened the dictionary app on his phone.

AVARICE: *insatiable greed for riches; inordinate, miserly desire to gain and hoard wealth.*

WORD BY WORD, he analyzed the definition to refute Sherrill the next time she brought it up. And she would, too. One of her best professional qualities was her relentlessness. On the few occasions they talked about what there was of their personal lives, that same quality bordered on annoying. It sounded cliché, but she knew Easton better than he knew himself. This time, he would push back.

Insatiable: incapable of being satisfied. He dared not defend himself, though Sherrill had no room to talk. She was as driven as he was. It's what made them such a formidable team.

Greed: Excessive or rapacious desire, especially for wealth or possessions. He wasn't greedy for stuff, he would say, but she would remind him of the price of the clothes he had her buy. Is it true I pay five hundred bucks for a pair of pants, he wondered. Sure, money was the scoreboard, but was he fooling himself about the accompanying luxuries?

Riches: abundant and valuable possessions; wealth. He wouldn't argue that he enjoyed riches. But, then again, wasn't that Sherrill's point in the first place, that he had plenty of money but didn't enjoy what it provided?

Inordinate: not within proper or reasonable limits; immoderate; excessive. He didn't like the sound of inordinate. He took great care to control his schedule— after Sherrill forwarded it to him, at least—along with his personal habits and temperament. The ones looking up at his sales records were setting the so-called "reasonable limits." He didn't have the burden of a wife or children. Was it normal to think like that? Who wanted to be normal, anyway? He let his mind wander for a moment, imagining walking into his condo to a family. It wasn't that he opposed marriage —it seemed to work for Ronnie and Grace. He supposed that he might marry and have a family one day... if Sherrill put it on his calendar. *Inordinate.* Yeah, moving on.

Miserly: of, like or befitting a miser (a person who lives in wretched circumstances in order to save and hoard money). There. Easton Sterling's circumstances were hardly wretched. Neither were Sherrill's, thanks to him. He was about to close his case when his eyes wandered to a second definition for *miser: a stingy, avaricious person.* That word again. But, he thought, I'm not stingy. Sherrill makes plenty of money, for one. I'm not selling people anything they don't need. I tip well. I am not miserly. Better see it through, though. Next.

Desire: to wish or long for; crave; want. Guilty. So shoot me. The opposite of that is laziness, and I would rather people accuse me of desiring more than being lazy. He could define Sherrill with the same words.

Gain: to get (something desired), especially as a result of one's efforts. No argument. What do you want me to do, Sherrill, give it away? No, that probably wasn't the best approach since she had done that very thing.

Hoard: to accumulate for preservation, future use, etc., in a hidden or carefully guarded place. He wasn't guilty of hoarding. Not like Dad, who never discarded anything from his shop behind his house. After he died, Easton and Ronnie found dozens of coffee cans with every kind of bolt and screw imaginable, most of them left over from one project or another. Easton wasn't a hoarder like that. Sure, he maxed out his retirement investments, but that was just smart. No sense in giving it to the government. His money was in a carefully guarded place, but that place was called a bank, and it's where most sane people kept their money. Not in the bottoms of dozens of coffee cans filled with every kind of bolt and screw imaginable. Dad's money invested in good growth stock mutual funds would have made him a wealthy man with the freedom to do what "the man" never allowed him to do.

Wealth: a great quantity or store of money, valuable possessions, property, or other riches. It pleased him that wealth that made him "the man" his father never overcame. Was that where his quenchless desire had originated? Was he trying to win because his father didn't? He had never considered why he was so relentless in sports and sales, only why others weren't. Was he the oddball, after all? If he was, he wouldn't acknowledge it to Sherrill and admit she was right. Plus, he had ruled out *miserly* from the definition, so *avarice* didn't define him at all. Did it?

Perhaps Sherrill's point lay in the word *and*. *To gain and hoard wealth*. That was the change he had seen in her. She was making several times what her education and previous experience levels should have afforded her. She drove a nice car and dressed professionally enough, but he didn't see where she was spending any money otherwise. He assumed she hoarded it, at least before her change. Now, she wanted to give her money away. It was hard for Easton to imagine living somewhere in the world without running water. Sherrill was doing something about it, though, and the more she gave her money away, the happier she seemed. He couldn't argue with that, but why did she have to bring him into it?

Oh. He had asked. He didn't want another "new Sherrill" conversation, one that didn't focus on products and programs and sales and commissions. She was so different, though, and he wondered aloud what her smile was all about. She turned her phone around to show him a photo of an entire village gathered around a new well pumping its first water. The excitement of the people in the photo matched Sherrill's. He had to admit to himself the unbridled joy on their faces was attractive. He wouldn't admit it to her, though—couldn't have her losing her edge.

EASTON ATE a bite of lettuce and grilled chicken from time to time so his server didn't take offense. He wrapped up his projections and saved his file. *Maybe I'll call Ronnie and see how Mom's day went. He's more likely to answer my call than Grace. I really hope Mom had a pleasant day. As annoying as the "what are you thankful for" question has been through the years, I kind of miss it this year. Maybe I'll go by to see Mom before Christmas.*

His server checked on him one last time, making sure he didn't leave room for dessert. "Nope, I'm ready for the check."

"Oh, about that. Check with Laticia at the hostess station about your bill on your way out." The unusual order of operations threw Easton off track, but he decided not to pursue it. Packing up all his devices, he started for the hostess station. The old man stood there with a young lady who seemed to be simultaneously crying and laughing.

"Are you Laticia?" he asked. She nodded. "My server instructed me to see you for my check."

"Oh, yeah, about that..."

"There's not a problem, is there?"

"Oh, no sir, no problem at all. It's just that someone has taken care of your meal."

"What do you mean, 'taken care of'? I told my server the food was just fine. I just... well, I was busy with work and didn't feel like eating much. Is that an issue?"

"No, sir, you can eat what you want. No, we had

somebody in here earlier who paid for all you folks who were eating by yourselves."

"But I can afford to pay for my…"

"Wasn't about you paying. Ain't nobody gonna mistake you for a charity case, mister. They just wanted to pay for folks that may be a little lonely this Thanksgiving."

"Well, why don't you let me…"

"Sir, I'm just passing along what's already been done. They don't want any payback and no thanks necessary. Just accept the gift." She jerked her head to her left and added, "These folks here—they're sticking around to drink a cup of coffee and eat some pie. I know you said you weren't that hungry, but why don't you oblige 'em by sitting down with 'em for a spell."

"What the heck, I'll do it. As long as you let me pay for everybody."

"No, sir, this time it's on the house."

EASTON SAT at the de facto head of the table formed from two smaller ones. He felt like he should pass around product folders or at least some Mid-South Med swag. He was the outsider here; the others conversed readily with one another.

A forlorn-looking woman who looked to be in her late thirties, early forties looked in his direction and drew him in to their conversation. "So, Mr. Important, what's your story?"

The impromptu nickname set Easton aback. "Mr. Important?"

"You can't deny a table full of computer gizmos. And on Thanksgiving, no less. What's your story?"

Gizmos. Easton hadn't heard that word in forever, but his mom was resistant to the computer era and used it to describe pretty much anything electronic. It caused him to smile... and to tell his story to a group of strangers. All of it. He didn't intend to share anything more than coffee and pie with them, but once he started, he didn't stop. These lonely strangers were engaged, too. He wished he had something to sell them.

When Easton relived his days as an All-American pitcher, he caught the old man's eye and a faint smile. *I was right. He remembers me.* They cringed when he told them the circumstances of his first sale. He thought he heard the pleasant-looking fellow in his sixties mutter "Ouch." He felt a jab to the conscience himself. His story gained momentum until he was in front of the pitcher's mound, crying his eyes out and not knowing why. He had told himself he would never tell anybody, not even Sherrill. That promise did not age well.

Ouch Man seemed empathetic. "Mr. Sterling..." he began.

"Easton."

"All right. Easton, if you don't mind my saying so, what you experienced this afternoon is some long overdue grief."

Easton laughed. "I'm sorry, I don't mean to be disrespectful, but I don't think it was grief. Nobody related to me has died since my dad."

Ouch Man pressed on in a firm but reassuring tone. "People grieve more than death. They grieve the loss of a family member or friend through death, for sure, and that's what we normally associate with the word *grief*. However, people grieve all kinds of things: loss of a pet, loss of a marriage, a friend's moving away, a job change —all kinds of things. Sounds like you're just getting around to mourning the loss of a dream."

"Yeah, I guess that makes sense. How are you so informed about grief?"

"Well, I am familiar with grief on two levels. I've been a pastor for nearly forty years, so I've counseled people through many issues, grief among them. On a personal level, though, I'm here by myself tonight because my wife passed away a few months ago. This year has been difficult, grieving through holidays without Janie Ruth for the first time."

"Sorry to hear that, Pastor." *Better change his name from* Ouch Man *to* Pastor *in my mind. He's a friendly sort for a preacher. The ones on TV seem angry all the time.* "You've got it worse than some silly baseball injury."

"That may be true, but you've been holding on longer. Grief will always find you, no matter how well you think you're holding it in. It sounds like you adjusted and moved on with a new career and a fresh dream, but if you never buried the old one, grief will find you."

"Yeah, I guess it did this afternoon. So I'm good now, right?"

Pastor couldn't hold back a laugh. "I'm afraid not, although I wish it was that easy. It would make the counseling side of my job easier if it was. No, grief has stages. The difficulty comes when we deal with the cost to the people surrounding you."

"That's how I roll, Pastor, head on."

"Good. It'll take a while for you to see how you may have hurt others by forging ahead without dealing with your past. You might not even realize…"

"If I can't figure it out, my assistant—excuse me, my executive coordinator—will tell me. She knows me better than I know myself. Now, if you all will excuse me, I need to touch base with her."

Hi, this is Sherrill Riggs, executive coordinator for Easton Sterling. I'm not available to take your call, but if you will leave a brief message, I'll call you back as quickly as possible.

Of course you're not available, Sherrill. Good for you, I guess.

"Sherrill, this is Easton. Hey, I need you to do something for me. I'll be in Harriston tomorrow and in Jackson on Saturday morning, but would you see if Ronnie and Grace and Mom want to do something together on Saturday night or Sunday afternoon?" After he clicked his phone to end the call, he considered how Sherrill would receive his message.

Hi, this is Sherrill Riggs, executive coordinator for Easton Sterling. I'm not available to take your call, but if you will leave a brief message, I'll call you back as quickly as possible.

"Hey, Sherrill, this is Easton again. When I mentioned doing something with Ronnie, Grace, and

Mom, I meant with me, too. I realize that's not usually the case, so I wanted to be clear. And I understand you said today was off limits. You can call them tomorrow. That's all. Bye."

Hi, this is Sherrill Riggs, executive coordinator for Easton Sterling. I'm not available to take your call, but if you will leave a brief message, I'll call you back as quickly as possible.

"Me again. Hey, look, start making some plans for that beach vacation for the entire family for the summer after the kids get out of school. Not tonight, though, because today is off limits." There, he had said it before he reconsidered. He turned to return to the table and downed a bite of pecan pie.

Hi, this is Sherrill Riggs, executive coordinator for Easton Sterling. I'm not available to take your call... "Hey, who is this, and why do you have Easton Sterling's phone?" his executive coordinator demanded.

"Sorry, Sherrill, I know you said no calls today. I wasn't expecting you to answer."

"What's going on, Easton? Have aliens abducted you?" *She was joking, wasn't she?*

"I have some people waiting on me at the moment, but I have something else I want to ask you."

"Shoot."

"Can I... would you mind..."

"Spit it out, Sterling."

"Would you mind if I met you for church on Sunday morning?"

AUSTEN

16

"That's three so far," Austen said. "Need a warmup on your coffee? How about a piece of sweet potato pie?"

"More coffee but no pie," Laticia said. "We nibbled on enough pie in the back of the restaurant today to last me a minute."

Austen filled their half-empty cups and waited for Laticia to continue.

"Okay, so we covered Pops, One Month Sober, and Mr. Important so far."

"Do Pastor Widower next."

"Oh girl, his story is interesting. Sad but good. When I told him somebody had paid for his meal—course, I didn't give you up—he looked ready to laugh and cry at the same time. It took him back some place. Army Mom walked up about that time, though…"

"Army Mom?"

"I'll tell you about her next. Anyway, Pastor Widower told his story after Mr. Important got back to the table from making his phone call—*calls*, actually—to that Sherrill girl."

PASTOR WIDOWER

17

"Sorry about that," Easton said, pulling out his chair. "Needed to make some overdue phone calls. Pastor, I'd like you to tell your story, if you don't mind."

Easton's disarming nature had engaged many a stressed-out doctor and hospital executive. He found that after they talked about their troubles for a few minutes, the sale he sought at the end of the conversation became an afterthought, the cost of counseling. This time, he had nothing to gain.

He wouldn't have tabbed this guy as a pastor. He was too thin, and the preachers on TV rarely were. In his worn jeans and untucked plaid shirt and worn work boots, he might have stepped off an old family farm. He didn't seem angry like the TV preachers, either.

"Well, you'll laugh when I tell you my first name, so let's get the wisecracks out of the way. My name is Calvin Hobbs."

"Nuh-uh!" One Month Sober said. "I read them to my son all the time. They're my favorite."

"Are they named after you?" Army Mom wondered.

"Oh, no, no, I came along well before them. Gives people something to talk about when they meet me, though."

"Are you a fan?" One Month Sober asked.

"Oh, sure. It was a sad day when the creator stopped making it. I have several of his collections. Reading that strip can be effective therapy after a trying day."

Mr. Important leaned over to Pops. "What are they talking about?"

"The comic strip *Calvin and Hobbes*," Pops answered. "Don't tell me you've never heard of it."

"I went straight from the sports page to the business section, I guess. No time for comics."

"Your loss. It's the funniest strip in all my time reading the paper, and I'm ninety-two years old."

"I'll check it out. You're ninety-two?"

"If I'm a day."

"I wouldn't have guessed over eighty." Pops smiled.

"As you can tell, my introduction takes longer than most and gets derailed almost every time," said Pastor Calvin Hobbs. "My parents didn't understand how they would make me a household name one day. I grew up over in north Alabama, but I went to school at the seminary in New Orleans and stayed near there after I graduated. I've been in the ministry for over forty years, always as a bi-vocational pastor."

"What does that mean?" Army Mom asked.

"I work a 'real' job besides pastoring because my congregations haven't had the budget for a full-time pastor. I prefer to stay in little churches. The Lord grows them as He sees fit, and some of them He causes to grow past my calling. I thank God for the growth, bless 'em, and move on to another small church that needs a pastor but can't afford one. I've done package delivery, full-time and substitute teaching, mechanic work, and officiated ball games. Our kids live across the globe now —from New Orleans to Salt Lake City to Haiti to southeast Asia. Two church planters, a missionary nurse, and an international Christian school teacher."

"I can tell you're proud of them," Pops said as Pastor Hobbs beamed. "What drew you to Harriston?"

"Safety," Pastor Hobbs answered. "Hurricane Katrina transplanted thousands of folks, preachers not the least among them, because of the seminary in New Orleans. Those pastors live in towns and cities all over the South now. Katrina flipped a lot of lives upside down.

"We didn't have a church building left after the storm or people left to fill it. My wife, Janie Ruth, and I started looking for where to help. This area took quite a hit, but it wasn't destroyed like New Orleans and the coast. Harriston was a place people from Louisiana would move, so I found a church out in the country who needed a pastor and prepared for their arrival. I found plenty of roof work to do to help make ends meet in the meantime.

"We loved it here because there was plenty to do with hurricane cleanup. Our little church grew by taking in some New Orleans and Baton Rouge transplants. We missed our children, though. The Thanksgiving table would be empty without them. All four came home this past Christmas, which was good because it turned out to be Janie Ruth's last one with us."

Pastor Hobbs paused for a long sip of coffee. "Ah, that's excellent, Ms. Laticia." He continued, "The holidays are the hardest without her. She hosted a Valentine's Day brunch for our widow ladies and gave them flowers and chocolate. She took pride in handing out red, white and blue ribbons at the town Fourth of July parade and again on Veteran's Day. In our current church, two old boys served in Korea and a young couple both did tours in Iraq. I'm telling you, she made over them so much that you would have the thought the four of them alone were responsible for her freedom. She dressed up for the kids coming around for Halloween trick or treat—nothing scary, mind you. She wouldn't have forgiven herself if she had frightened one of the little ones. Thanksgiving was her thing, though, and I missed her especially bad today."

"Why today?" One Month Sober asked.

"Well, young lady, the first Thanksgiving we lived here after Katrina, we didn't have two nickels to rub together. It was just going to be Janie Ruth and me since none of the kids could come. I wasn't so sure we should splurge for our usual Thanksgiving meal, and I figured most of it would go to waste because you can only eat leftovers for so long. Janie Ruth told me she had brainstormed a novel idea for our Thanksgiving, and I told her I had an idea, too. My idea was to skip any Thanksgiving festivities and start decorating for Christmas. At least that way we wouldn't focus our minds on what was missing on Thanksgiving Day."

"No, sweetie, you first. If I like the sound of your idea, I won't even mention mine."

"Okay, here goes. I realize we don't have the money for a fancy Thanksgiving meal..."

Calvin smiled at her. "We think so much alike."

"So I suggest we buy three or four turkeys and invite whoever wants to join us for a Thanksgiving meal down in the fellowship hall. If everybody brings a little, nobody will be out much, and everyone can enjoy a meal together. Did you have the same idea?"

"Uh, sure, something similar to that."

"Maybe if this goes well, we can put together food boxes for people who might be hungry or hurting or even just lonely next year."

"I TOLD her I loved her idea," Pastor Hobbs continued, "and that's what we did. It became our congregation's favorite part of our year. Only, Janie Ruth wasn't there today. Our people missed her, no doubt, but they didn't feel the heart of our little mission missing like I did."

Pastor Hobbs stopped, not knowing how much more his table mates wanted to hear.

Pops spoke up. "Tell us about her, Calvin."

Pastor had become almost a first name to him. He compared it to how unchurched folks heard the name *Jesus Christ* and assumed *Christ* was a last name. He appreciated Pops' calling him by his given name and made a mental note to return the favor.

"I met Janie Ruth Brown when we were still toddlers. We lived in the country with only a few neighbors within ten or twelve miles. When her family moved into the Carter place next door, I was three and she was two. She was an only child, but even when we were children, she could see right through your circumstance to your soul. If something was wrong with you, she recognized it before you realized it yourself. I couldn't stand her.

"If I looked distraught about something, she'd come sit next to me on the school bus and pound me with questions. *Why are you unhappy? Did somebody do something to you? How can I help?* She worried the stew out of me. Half the time, I hadn't finished processing whether I even wanted to be upset. She'd pester me so I'd forget whatever I was fretting about and get mad at her instead.

"She came to our house to play all the time, too, like she had an open invitation. I'm sure my mama *had* given her such an invitation. Anyway, my little brother and I would be running around playing some game we'd made up, having a whale of a time, just the two of us. Never failed, Janie Ruth would pop up wherever we were and flick her curly brown hair to the side and say, 'Can *I* play?' Well, Tanner and I knew Daddy would tan our hides if we weren't nice to her, so we let her join in.

She could be quite a tomboy, so we didn't resent her for long, but we still always tried to avoid her first. I guess she became the younger sister we never had."

"When did that change?" One Month Sober asked. "When did you fall in love with her?"

"My second year of junior college. She had finished high school but wanted to stay home and work for a semester or two to save up money for college. Because her mama and daddy never did have much, they weren't able to send her. I had just come back to my dorm from a study group that turned into a game of cards when I got a phone call from my mama. She said that I needed to hurry home as quick as I could get there. My first thought was *oh no, something's happened to Daddy*. But then she said Tanner was in the hospital because he had overdosed on drugs, and that they didn't know if he would survive.

"I couldn't believe it. I had never known my brother to drink, much less mess with drugs. After I left for college and Janie Ruth started working full time, he didn't have anybody to hang out with, so he picked up with a dangerous crowd from school. They had gone to a party in the cornfields that night when one of his buddies pulls out some cocaine. Next thing they knew, Tanner was going into convulsions. Praise the Lord, they somehow got him back to town and to the emergency room.

"Anyway, it took me about an hour-and-a-half to get home, and I had conflicting thoughts running through my mind. I felt mad one minute and sad the next and guilty all the time for not looking out for my little brother. When I walked into the hospital, Mama and Daddy were back with Tanner, but Janie Ruth was there, too. She met me at the door and wrapped one arm around me and put her other hand on my chest and rested her head on the front of my shoulder. She didn't say a word. Amidst the thoughts and emotions I had running through my mind, I fell in love with her right then and there. I wanted her head resting on my shoulder for the rest of my life."

Army Mom had locked in to Pastor Hobbs's story, along with everyone else at the table. "What happened to your brother?"

"By the grace of God, Tanner pulled through that night. He was ashamed of what he had done to us and swore he would never touch that stuff again. As far as I know, he has kept his promise. He's still living on the home place with his wife and three kids. Mama and Daddy passed on a few years ago, but he's the one who took care of them when they'd get down. He almost killed himself that night, but it was ultimately a life-changing event for him. If he had continued in that direction, he might not be alive today, and he sure wouldn't be the fine Christian man he is."

"And you and Janie Ruth?" One Month Sober pressed. "When did you two marry?"

"The next day, the doctors informed us Tanner would live. Janie Ruth hadn't said more than two dozen words to me the whole time, just kept holding me like she did. When they told us he would make it, she squeezed my shoulder and patted my chest, but she didn't let go. As soon as we ventured off by ourselves, I looked at her and said, 'If folks didn't know any better, they'd think we were a couple.' She stared at me with her big blue eyes before she said, 'That'd be all right with me.' I married her three months later."

"Aww," replied the ladies in unison.

"We stayed in lockstep for almost forty years. I would have loved to have hit that big round number with her, but the Lord had other ideas. I can say this regarding my wife: she never changed during the entire time I knew her. Now, we took plenty of hits along our journey, but she remained steadfast in her love for God and people. I realize how cliché that sounds, but Janie Ruth Hobbs was somebody you could count on to be there when life was good. She celebrated like nobody's business when one of her friends enjoyed success. When somebody she loved reached their lowest point, though, my wife was at her best. Like she did the day I fell in love with her, she joined you in your pain. She just stopped talking and kind of absorbed your pain while she sat with you.

"Her way with people started with her daddy. People in our neck of the woods found it strange for somebody to move to our part of north Alabama without some kind of family ties to the region, and they didn't have any. Folks claim renegades have been hiding in Freedom Hills for years—Union sympathizers, moonshiners, criminals. They say Jesse James and his brother hid out there once upon a time. Word around the country store where folks gathered was Janie Ruth's daddy had been a part of a lynching down around Mobile, so they came to Freedom Hills to avoid the law.

"Janie Ruth never understood for sure why her family moved, but her daddy kept his head down and farmed his land and put together a meager living for them. I tell you what, though, she would stand up to him in a heartbeat if he ever said anything negative about one of her black friends. One time, she brought Pearlie Mae Jones home with her from town. When they walked in, her mama started fretting and her daddy spun around and walked out the back door to their barn. Well, Janie Ruth followed him back there, pulling Pearlie Mae every step of the way."

"Daddy, this is my friend Pearlie Mae. Pearlie Mae, say hello to my daddy, Mr. Alvis Brown."

"Nice to meet you, sir," Pearlie Mae said, extending her slender light brown arm. Mr. Brown feigned interest in a bolt lying on his worktable.

"Daddy, Pearlie Mae is trying to shake your hand." Alvis Brown reluctantly took it, but a tentative handshake didn't satisfy his daughter. "Daddy, Pearlie Mae said 'nice to meet you.' You should return her greeting."

When Alvis hesitated, Pearlie Mae broke the awkward silence. "Mr. Brown, you sure have raised a fine daughter in Janie Ruth. She's about the best friend I've ever had. I don't even care what my people say about being friends with a white girl. Did she tell you she's helping me read better?"

Something fundamental and generational inside of Alvis Brown snapped right there. He turned to face Pearlie Mae Jones. "I thank you, young lady, for saying what you did about my baby girl. We're mighty proud of her. If you girls need a place to work on your reading, you're welcome here."

"You can imagine her mama's shock when the three of them walked back into the house," Pastor Hobbs said, shaking his head. "Janie Ruth told me her daddy stared back at her mama and said, 'Well, Margaret, don't just stand there. Get these girls some milk and cookies. They've got work to do.' That was my wife's manner. She could dissolve the nasty deep inside people like nobody I've ever seen. It was a gift, for sure."

"She sounds like a veritable angel," Easton said.

"No, not an angel, much better. Angels don't make the choice to follow Jesus. Janie Ruth followed Him at six years old and never looked back. That's not to say we didn't have our moments, though. When I didn't move fast enough to decide something or complete a project, she sometimes persisted to the point of nagging.

"One day, I reached my limit of her going on so. I stood up and walked toward the back door. She told me to get my backside back in there because she hadn't finished with me. I stopped but didn't go back to the den. She started back in on whatever her grievance was, so I headed for the door again. She became even more upset with me. 'Calvin, I am not finished talking to you yet. What's your hurry to go outside?'

"I told her I was going to get the ladder. She didn't pay much attention to what I said and started scolding me for walking out on her. When it finally stuck that I had answered her question, she stopped right in the middle of her scolding and asked me, 'Why are you going to get the ladder?'

"I told her my Bible said it is better to live on the corner of a roof than with a contentious and nagging wife. Well, she burst out laughing. She realized she had gone a bit too far, and that ended our spat. We made up, and all was well. I can't tell you how many anxious young wives she helped through those first rocky years of marriage with that story. When we counseled young couples, though, I'd also be sure to tell the husband how it worked both ways. See, Janie Ruth sometimes threatened to get the cattle prod if I didn't take responsibility for something. I'd laugh and get right to it."

"And that works for y'all?" asked the woman at the end of the table opposite Mr. Important.

"It *worked* for us."

"I'm sorry, I forgot. I haven't slept much in the last couple of days. My husband had a most inconvenient heart attack, and he's recovering across the highway at the hospital."

"No, it's okay. When I mention Janie Ruth, I sometimes talk as if she's still here." He patted his heart. "Many young couples have a delightful time while they're dating, and they are sure they want to spend the rest of their lives with that young man or young woman. When they get married, they think life turns serious all of a sudden. They're right in many ways, but a couple who leaves their humor in the dating stage…" He stopped, looking around the table at a group of people who had eaten Thanksgiving dinner alone. He didn't know what hurts they might have brought to this table and didn't want to risk going further.

Breaking the silence, Army Mom said, "You make it sound so easy. My experience didn't look like yours, but thinking back, my husband and I let every petty argument explode into a big fight. If he had threatened to get a ladder, I would have encouraged him to climb to the top so I could knock it out from under him."

"Ouch," Easton said.

"Sorry, I guess we didn't let the humor of our dating days carry over into our marriage. Might be why it didn't survive. I wish I understood then what I know now. But, hey, I got two exceptional kids from that nightmare."

"I'm glad," Pastor Hobbs said. "I love my kids, too, and I can't wait to see them at Christmas. They will be here with me for a full week this year."

"I'm glad," Army Mom said. "You'll miss your wife the most then."

"No, it's actually Thanksgiving when I'll miss her most every year. The year Janie Ruth had the idea for serving our community on Thanksgiving, I not only considered skipping Thanksgiving but also stepping down from the ministry. Remember, we had just lost everything to Katrina. We had moved to a town where we didn't know anybody, and the kids couldn't come here for Thanksgiving. The church didn't pay much, and the prospect of rebuilding our finances exhausted me.

"I had ventured out and met some folks with the church, but nobody was coming to check on us. Not counting today, that was the loneliest I have ever felt. We couldn't afford a fancy Thanksgiving meal, and it was just going to be the two of us, anyway. So I was ready to mail in Thanksgiving and start looking forward to Christmas. I agreed with Janie Ruth's idea for a community Thanksgiving lunch because I didn't have the energy to argue about it with her. I think she sensed how discouraged I had become, but like I already said, she stayed quiet when somebody close to her hurt. She was just, you know, *there*.

"Fast forward to Thanksgiving Day, and folks started showing up early to our church potluck. Turns out they wanted to meet us but didn't want to disturb us while we were still getting settled. The first folks Janie and I met that day were the Staplefords. Their best friends had moved away a month or two earlier, and they were feeling lonely themselves. They set up a tailgate at the high school football games in the fall on Friday nights, and when football season ended, they played Rook on

Friday nights. Roger and Vicki are close in age to Janie Ruth and me, and we love to play Rook, so they invited us to join them. They've become our closest friends. We vacationed together and did mission trips together, and there's no telling how many glasses of lemonade we shared with them. Friday nights aren't the same anymore, I can tell you. Plus, Roger owns a construction company. When he discovered I do roofing, he put me right to work.

"Some folks at our first church Thanksgiving meal had things much tougher than we did, and we connected with them. Through what I call the power of everybody, we helped them get back on their feet. Our day encouraged me all the way around, and Janie Ruth stayed lit up like the Fourth of July throughout the day. When we arrived home late in the afternoon after visiting and cleaning up, Janie Ruth grew quiet again. I talked and talked about everybody I had met and my roofing job with Roger and the potential I saw for our little church. She let me talk on and on. When we lay down in bed that night, she reached over and patted me on the chest in that way of hers. She said, 'Calvin, the Lord knows when we need encouragement, and He delivers it, pressed down, shaken together, and running over.' And then she went to sleep. I've never considered leaving the ministry again."

19

Everyone was quiet for fifteen seconds, waiting for someone to break the silence and broach the topic on everyone's minds. Mr. Important asked, "What happened to her, Pastor?"

Pastor Hobbs said nothing, his quivering lip speaking for him for a solid minute. At a volume those on the other end of the table strained to hear, he answered, "A man shot her at the mission house here in town." Laticia and the lonesome six gasped. He continued, even softer, "We served there together every Thursday night. We helped serve the meal, and then she took dessert to the men's tables while I prepared to preach a brief message, our usual routine. The regulars —they appreciated us and trusted us and nicknamed us *Mr. Pastor* and *Ms. Pastor*. They tried to welcome any new folks like it wasn't charity they were receiving, but love.

"Well, one week in October, the forecast called for

nasty weather on Friday night, so the high school moved their football game to Thursday. The coaches counted on me to do their pre-game devotional, which I had been doing since the first season after we moved out there. Janie Ruth—she decided that the football team needed me most, and the men at the mission needed her most, so she drove to town by herself. One coach who goes to our church and several of the boys in the youth group come by our house after the home games for pie and coffee or a soda. She planned to leave early from the mission to make sure she was back at our house in time for them.

"We didn't realize it until they talked to the police, but three regulars had a verbal altercation with a first-timer to the mission earlier that night. When he was going through the serving line, Janie Ruth didn't give him as much spaghetti as I reckon he wanted, so he said, 'Gimme more, white lady.' She smiled and filled his plate with as much as it would hold, the same as she would have for anybody who asked for a bigger helping. Well, the boys in line gave him a hard time about 'disrespecting Ms. Pastor' when he sat at their table. He didn't say anything back to them, just ate his spaghetti and left, so they forgot about him.

"When the men filed into the little chapel for the message, Janie Ruth slipped out the rear door through the kitchen to get home before Coach Barnes and the boys arrived at our house. The troublemaker was waiting out back. I'm not sure if they exchanged words —I'm guessing not because if he had gotten to know Janie Ruth the least bit..."

Pastor Hobbs sucked in a deliberate breath and exhaled before he spoke. "He had a gun, and he shot her in the stomach. The men in the shelter rushed to her, and someone called 911 right away. They did everything possible to keep her alive, but she had bled too much by the time the paramedics arrived. The head of the mission called my cell phone, and I drove like a madman straight to the hospital. They pronounced her dead before I arrived."

"Oh, Pastor, I am so sorry," One Month Sober said, wiping tears from her eyes.

"There, now, it's okay, young lady. I know where my sweetheart is, and it's only a matter of a few short years, if not sooner, before I'm with her again. The apostle Paul wrote in his letter to the Philippians that to live is Christ and to die is gain. Now, I understand what he meant was that he would remain with God forever. That's my primary hope, too, but I'll say when I lost my Janie Ruth from this earth, heaven became much sweeter for me."

Army Mom blurted, "But you didn't even get to say goodbye."

"That's true. Before she died, I would have loved to whisper *so long for just a while* in her ear, but I am content that we had left nothing else unsaid."

"Well, I don't understand how you can be so calm. I would have found him and given him what he had coming to him. Eye for an eye—isn't that what the Bible says?"

"It also says he who forgives much, loves much."

"No way I would forgive that sorry—" She stopped

the expletive on the tip of her tongue but not the thought.

"I'm not talking about my forgiving him, although I have. When I consider how God forgave us and the price He paid to do it, I see little choice. If I let what that man did to Janie Ruth instill bitterness in me, hate wins again and again. Some times are harder than others, I'll be honest with you, but I am determined that love will win. That's the way my wife lived, and it's the best way for me to honor her memory."

"I can tell this is one of the tough days," Pops said. Bless you, Pastor, for making that choice. I've seen hate destroy many a decent man from the inside out."

"Today has been a sad day, but serving was healthy for me. Janie Ruth just loved blessing other folks on Thanksgiving."

"How can you keep following a God who would take such a kind woman?" Army Mom demanded. "It's not fair for that... that man who killed your wife to live while somebody like her doesn't. It's just not, and you won't convince me otherwise."

"Ma'am, God is not responsible for explaining Himself to me. When I gave my life to Him, I compare it to the vows Janie Ruth and I exchanged: *for better or worse, for richer or poorer, in sickness and health*. His ways are higher than my ways, and His thoughts are higher than my thoughts. When I decided to forgive Charles, I resolved to see him as a person and not for what he did at his worst moment. Forgiveness has created doors for me to communicate the goodness of the Lord that I never could have opened otherwise. I mean, just look around this table. Are you interested in hearing a story that ends with hate? No, ma'am, we see plenty of hate in this world. If my precious wife's memory will mean something, I must go through the 'for worse' part now to learn how God will use me.

"The day after Janie Ruth's funeral, I went to see Charles in jail to look at him face to face and let him hear that I forgive him. I'm not saying it was easy, but I sensed the Lord was leading me to do it for her sake. To be honest with you, I was in the fog of the early stages of grief, maybe still in shock. Either way, it seemed like God was carrying me to that jail and that the words were coming out, but I wasn't saying them. I'm not a strong enough man to forgive what he did to our family. But the God who sent His Son to die for the sins of the world lives inside of me, and He is plenty powerful."

Inconvenient Heart Attack raised her hand to intervene. "What did your kids think about it?"

"As you would imagine, it devastated our children when their mother died, but we helped carry each other through those awful first few days without her."

"I mean, were they all right with your forgiving that man... Charles?"

"They weren't any more okay with it than I was. Here's what I mean: It's not anyone's natural inclination to forgive like God called me to do, but each of my kids has a relationship with the Lord, and they agreed it's what I should do. Plus, Janie Ruth and I had ingrained in our children the need to forgive since they were old enough to take each other's toys. Do you have kids, ma'am?"

"Yes, four—two boys, grown and out of the house, and two girls who will finish college soon."

"Chances are, you taught them to say *I'm sorry* when they did something wrong, when they wronged somebody else." Inconvenient Heart Attack nodded. "The process we trained our children to follow was to name what they had done, apologize for it, and tell the offended one he or she would try not to do it again. We taught the offended one to say *I forgive you* and to the best of their ability, release the offense. Now, I will concede that those words seem mechanical, but it creates the habit of repentance and forgiveness. It's a process I needed to model besides teaching it to my children."

Army Mom shook her head. "Yeah, but you did nothing wrong. That man did. It's his place to ask your forgiveness."

"You're right. It is. But I have seen too often how that works out. If the apology doesn't come, and I live my life waiting for one, my offense turns into bitterness. I carry around the poison of what I let an offense to do me. This is difficult, for sure. I've just counseled enough people who have carried bitterness for years, for decades, that I didn't want to still be carrying that venom later. It would spill out on others around me."

"But so soon after he killed your wife?" Army Mom pressed. "He should have to live with it."

"I figured the longer I waited, the greater the chance I would never go see him at all. Waiting wouldn't bring Janie Ruth back. And he *does* have to deal with the physical, emotional, and spiritual consequences of his actions. I'm not minimizing those. Forgiveness in this case was as important for me as for him, so I arranged a visit. I told him who I was and that I forgave him. I didn't stay long, but I said what I needed to say."

"How did he respond?" asked Inconvenient Heart Attack.

"When I had said my piece, he lowered his head and mumbled something to himself. I called for the guard after that and left him to deal with God—who I hope has mercy on his soul. I wasn't looking for any specific response. I trust the justice system of this state to take its course, but I hope Charles asks God's forgiveness. I could never wish another human being to hell."

"You're a better person than I am," said Army Mom. "Did you not think one evil thought toward him today?"

"No, I can honestly say I didn't. I don't know Charles's story, so I leave open the possibility that if I did, I might understand what led him to do what he did that night. Then again, I might not. Doesn't matter. I acknowledge the senselessness of it—at least from a human perspective—but today was more about the emptiness of Janie Ruth not being there on *her* day. I'll confess I asked God *why* several times, but that was my loneliness talking. I read somewhere that grief is love trying to escape, so I guess I felt an impressive amount of love today, in a way. Opening the doors to our little church's kitchen and fellowship hall without Janie Ruth was difficult, but she would be happy I did.

"I started perking up once people started arriving. The cooks showed up shortly after me. They must have sensed my sadness because they made sure I had something to do. The ones who volunteered to fill the trays came next, and several sought me out to tell me how Janie Ruth had invited them to come their first time. Over the years, most of our regulars rearranged what had been their Thanksgiving traditions to serve their neighbors who might have fallen on hard times. By the time the delivery folks arrived and we gathered to pray over the food and those who would receive it, my soul was full. I choked up when I tried to pray, and one of our deacons stepped up and led it for me. That alone was a big encouragement.

"Well, when delivery started, the room emptied, but many of our people found me and wished me a happy Thanksgiving before they headed out. It has been mine and Janie Ruth's practice to wash the pots and pans so that the cooks could deliver meals or go home to their family Thanksgiving. Several people stayed and cleaned the pots and pans before I made it to the kitchen this year, but I told them to save the utensils for me. Washing the dishes always helped Janie Ruth and me wind down from such a hectic morning. For me this year, it was therapeutic, plus I didn't have any place to be. I received several invites from church families for Thanksgiving lunch, but I had one last delivery to make."

"What was that?" Easton asked.

"I took a dozen lunches by the jail and told them to be sure Charles received one. He's still here, waiting on his trial. He'll spend this Thanksgiving and perhaps the rest of his Thanksgivings away from his family, if he has any. Once I dropped off those plates, I went home and enjoyed a nap. I guess I slept longer than I had planned, and when I woke up, I was hungry for the first time all day. I didn't think I'd have a taste for turkey and dressing today, but that's what I wanted. So here I am. I hope to hear your stories of what brought you here, too."

"Tell us more about her, Pastor," Pops said. "I remember seeing something about the shooting in the newspaper. People they interviewed spoke so well of your wife. Y'all had her funeral in a school gym, if I recall."

"That's right," Pastor Hobbs said, brightening at the recollection of his wife. "Our church wasn't big enough. Her funeral was a walk down memory lane, I can tell you that. We had friends and family from north Alabama, and we had our seminary buddies from all over who came. There were so many preachers there that if every one of them talked, we'd still be sitting in that service today."

Everybody around the table laughed.

"Janie Ruth and I had served in more than a dozen tiny churches through the years, but the total number of people we served adds up after a while. At least a handful of friends from every single church where we'd pastored showed up for Janie Ruth's funeral. And like fine country church folks, they didn't come empty-handed. I mean to tell you, there was enough chicken and deviled eggs and potato salad for a year's worth of family night fellowship suppers."

20

"People packed out the gym for Janie Ruth's celebration service—that's a much better term than *funeral* to describe what it was. Her best friend spoke first. Marge was a godsend to my wife. Let me give you a little backstory. When Janie Ruth and I married, I had enough scholarship money coming in to finish junior college, but we planned ahead and saved for me to finish my bachelor's degree. With her working full time and me working part time, I finished my undergraduate degree without having to take on any debt. When the master's program at the seminary accepted me, I didn't qualify for as much financial aid as I had before, but I landed one decent scholarship. A few days before my graduation, Janie Ruth came to me with the idea of her going to college."

"Calvin, I wonder if you might take a break from your studies to discuss something important to me."

Calvin welcomed the break. With his last round of undergraduate finals coming up and his scholarship offer to seminary having arrived last week, he was finding study laborious. His emotions longed to break into celebration mode, like a man in dire need of a vacation working his last week before a trip to the beach. Not that a beach vacation showed up on his and Janie Ruth's radar—or any other vacation. They had enjoyed two days in Gatlinburg for their honeymoon, but they had been nose to the grindstone ever since.

Pushing his chair back from his desk and spinning it to meet his wife's gaze, Calvin asked, "Tell me about this thing that means so much to you."

"Well," she began, "I've been going over our finances, looking at what we have and what our expenses will be in New Orleans. We've been able to put back more that we had originally planned."

Sure they had. Calvin had worked afternoons detailing cars at the local Ford dealership for the last two years. This past year, he had served as the assistant youth director at a small church just outside of town. It didn't amount to much in pay or responsibility—the church only had a dozen students—but it helped their finances and gave Calvin valuable ministry experience. Perhaps it was the care that this little church gave their newlyweds that turned his heart toward serving his entire career with small, struggling churches. Their small, well-timed gifts gave Calvin and Janie Ruth an occasional date night or weekend getaway when they needed it most.

Calvin did his part to bring in as much income as possible. Janie Ruth's job as a teacher's assistant at one of the elementary schools in town provided a steady income and insurance. In part to help them save for seminary and in part because Calvin needed quiet time to study, she worked a few nights a week shelving books at the library. They would need every dime they could scrape together to pay for Calvin's seminary education. One thing they could ill afford was the debt a pastor's salary would not easily repay. Now that Calvin had won a scholarship, she presented her dream.

"When you factor your scholarship into what we've saved," she continued, "and if we assume we'll both keep working at least part-time while you're going through seminary..."

"What is it?" She had his full attention now. Was she hinting at a trip to the beach? He was all in if she was.

She took a deep breath and spat it out. "Calvin, I want to go to school to become an elementary school teacher." There, she had said it. His reaction was not what she had expected. A smile crept over his face until it became a broad grin. When he started laughing, her face fell, and a tear formed in her left eye.

"No, no, no, no," he broke in, touching her wrist. "Don't cry, don't cry, sweetheart. I'm not laughing at you, please don't think I'm laughing at you." She calmed. "It's just that when I was spending time with the Lord this past Saturday, He showed me something I think has been right before both of our faces. I couldn't tell you—I still *shouldn't* tell you."

"Tell me what?"

"Promise you will not rat me out for telling you? I'm serious, Janie Ruth, if you can't keep the best of secrets, don't let me tell you."

"Have you ever known me to tell anything you told me in private?"

"No, but this is important. Ms. Gregory at the school—"

"Marge Gregory. She's a fourth-grade teacher like Ms. Paulsen, the teacher I assist. Marge is a first-year teacher, so I help her, too, when I can. She's a wonderful friend."

"Yeah, that's her. Well… are you sure you want me to tell you?"

"I do now."

"Okay, she is making plans to throw you a big going-away bash, and she called me to ask for a list of your favorite things."

"What did you tell her?"

"I told her how much you loved the beach."

"Even though I've never been."

"I promise you we will get to the beach one day, sweetheart."

"And remove the joy from our ongoing banter about our 'one day' vacation? What is the connection between Marge's call and my going to school?"

"Okay, that phone call was on Friday evening a week ago when you were working at the library. I was spending time with God the next morning when he showed me plain as day that you should be an elementary school teacher like her. You care so much for the kids in your school, particularly the ones who might otherwise go unnoticed, and you give so much to the other teachers. I asked the Lord if I should tell you, and He assured me *He* would tell you. And boy, has He—making the dream come alive in your soul and then putting my scholarship in place to give us the financial flexibility to send you to school, too."

Janie Ruth slipped her arm around Calvin's shoulders, placed her hand on his chest, and rested her head on the crease between his shoulder and chest.

"What's wrong?"

"Nothing. I do this when my happiness is so complete that words won't express it." She lifted her head a few minutes later and said, "Marge is the first true best friend I've ever had. I love her." When Calvin feigned a pout, she added, "First female true best friend. And I love you, too."

———

"She and Marge remained best friends for the rest of their lives. Janie Ruth was Marge's matron of honor at her wedding. Her husband built houses between here and the coast with great success, but Marge is still teaching today just because she loves it. When we graduated on the same weekend, Tom and Marge came to both of our ceremonies. This time, I kept Marge's secret."

"What secret?" One Month Sober asked.

"Her favorite thing that she had never experienced."

"They sent you to the beach?"

"The four of us went to the beach together. Oh, Marge and Janie Ruth had such fun together, and Tom taught me to play golf. I didn't have the time or money to play before, but he brought another set of clubs for me to use, and we played every day. I loved it. I wasn't good at all, but we enjoyed chasing my ball over the entire course. They ended up buying a condo in Destin, and we went there with them almost every summer, even though we lived too far apart to visit often. Every year's beach trip was the reset button for us. Tom needed dates on the calendar that forced him to walk away from his work, or he might have worked all the time. Marge and Janie Ruth were both in between school years, and it gave them a chance to pick back up with their friendship. I would slip out early and spend time by the gulf, listening for the Lord's voice. More often than not, I came back with direction for my ministry for the next few months. Our kids grew up with their kids over those summers. Just a real special bond. When Marge spoke of Janie Ruth at her funeral, it was as though she was reflecting on a part of herself.

"After Marge spoke, Daniel Lindsay did. He was her principal at West Cary Elementary School for the last fourteen years of her career. He told story after story of how Janie Ruth invested in their students and the other teachers at the school. Y'all may not be familiar with West Cary, but they have won several awards in the last few years for how the kids' achievement has improved. Mr. Lindsey said Janie Ruth was the reason for that, but not because she implemented some educational reform program or infused the school with funding that they had always lacked. He said that her greatest contribution to West Cary was love that showed itself in a thousand little ways. He gave an example of the impact she made after school hours. I remember when the Lord birthed the idea in her head."

"Hey, dear."

"Hey, yourself. What's for supper? I'm starved."

"I thought tonight we might drive to town to eat."

"I just came from town. I would have picked up something." When Janie Ruth didn't answer, Calvin added, "But if you just need to skip cooking tonight and go to town, to town we shall go. What did you have in mind?"

"Oh, I don't care; you pick. I need to tell you about an idea that's been pressing on me."

They arrived at a local meat-and-three place that was one of their favorites, especially on Thursday nights when country fried steak was the featured special. They ordered water because Janie Ruth had not allowed restaurant drinks back into the budget. *By the time you take the price of sweet tea and add tax and tip to it, you're paying nearly four dollars for a drink that might cost a quarter. No, sir, I'll make you all the sweet tea you want at home, but it's water at restaurants for everybody on our bill.* She ordered her usual—the country-fried steak with mashed potatoes and gravy, boiled cabbage, and turnip greens. Calvin couldn't stand cabbage or turnip greens, so he ordered fried okra and purple hull peas along with his country fried steak and potatoes.

When their server had taken their order back to the kitchen, he drummed his fingers on the table, his mannerism that called their family meeting to order. "Tough day at school?"

"Yes. And no."

"From what are we escaping today?" Janie Ruth's occasional request to eat out hinted at a trying day when she lacked motivation to cook between school and Calvin's arrival. Since today was Thursday, he didn't mind the drive back to town for chicken fried steak.

"Nothing… and everything."

Calvin leaned backward on his side of the booth and drew a deep breath, his sign that she had the space she needed to elaborate.

"Calvin, these poor children are so behind in their studies. They're at least a grade level or two back. It's easy enough to teach most kids to read and do basic math, but it takes consistency and repetition. How can we catch them up when many of them are absent once or twice a week?" She didn't expect an answer but let the question hang between them for a moment before continuing. "It's a generational thing. If the parents were on board with their children's education, they would make coming to school a priority so their kids would receive the consistency and repetition they need. Then, they'd have the requisite skills for middle and high school, perhaps even college. Most of these students probably don't have a single family member who has ever graduated college.

"What if we gave the parents a vision for what their kids might become if they had a good high school education? What if we inspired their children to consider college or trade school? You and I both have experienced obtaining our college degrees with a dash of ingenuity and a tremendous amount of hard work. With the income of many of these families, they would qualify for grants, so higher education might be affordable—at least junior college. Say one of these kids goes into the logging industry, for example, like so many of their daddies. Would it hurt for a logger to have a bit of business sense—make a little more money and keep it and invest it?"

This time, she paused for a response. "No question," Calvin said. "And I know you well enough to understand that if you've identified a problem, then you have thought through solutions. What do you have in mind?"

"Well, I haven't even finished my first year at the school, so I informed the Lord of the obstacles in my way. I'm just one small person to face such enormous issues. I'm new, so I don't have relationships with any of the kids' parents. By the time we moved here, West Cary had already had their back-to-school open house, so I missed out on meeting the ones who came. The other teachers told me that few parents show up for our open house or the special programs they try to do. You remember our class Christmas party—if you and the Staplefords hadn't helped me with the food and the decorations, it wouldn't have happened."

"Like it didn't in most of the other classes."

"Right. The teachers are so beaten down that they don't have the energy to put together those extras these kids need to understand how much we teachers care about them. And Mr. Lindsey—he's an unselfish man who wants what's best for the kids, but he has considerable obstacles facing him. I wouldn't be surprised if he takes another job in a better situation first chance he gets.

"I laid all that before the Lord, but He is so faithful. I put my obstacles in front of Him—reminded Him how small I was and how little I could offer. And He showed me the one thing guaranteed to change the course of West Cary Elementary School."

Here it was. Calvin leaned forward and propped his forearms on the table. "And what, Ms. Hobbs, is that?"

"Hope."

A grin formed on first Calvin's and then on Janie Ruth's face. "The most powerful motivator on earth," he said as their server arrived with their meal. After thanking her, Calvin looked back across his plate. "How, pray tell, does Ms. Hobbs plan on delivering this hope to the administration, teachers, and students of West Cary Elementary School?"

"May I?" Janie Ruth asked, nodding toward the food and reaching for his hand.

"By all means."

"Heavenly Father, thank you for our food tonight and for providing our income that allows us to pay for it. Thank You for hope. I pray for You to bring hope to my school. I'm available, Lord. Bless our food and our bodies to Your service. In Jesus' name, amen."

"Amen. Now, let's hear this proposal of yours." Calvin cut heartily into his chicken fried steak as he awaited the plan he perceived his wife already had.

"I told the Lord to use whatever He wanted from me. When I reminded Him I didn't have much, He reminded me He didn't need much. So I started a list of the little that I had, hoping He would be clear in showing me what He wanted to use. I was halfway down a sheet of paper listing what I had to offer. I had listed where we've lived and where I've taught, my education, the online community of teachers where I get many of my ideas for the classroom, and such as that. I waited after each one, and the Lord kept whispering to keep going. After a while I felt I was writing the most insignificant items. When I wrote *two hours in the afternoon between the end of school and the time Calvin gets home,* it jumped back off the page at me. And that's when the ideas started coming, one after another. Before long I had a plan at four levels: parents, administration, teachers, and students."

"Do I need to learn to cook?"

"No, dear, you already work two jobs. During that hour each day between when you get home and when you start on your church work, I want you to relax. My asking you to give up your only time away from both jobs wouldn't do either of us any good."

"I'm not saying I wouldn't be willing to for something the Lord has led you to do," Calvin said, "but I like that hour each day, too. Some days, that's the only time I can count on when somebody's not frustrated with me. Now, take a few bites and lay out this grand strategy to bring hope to West Cary."

The next few minutes passed with brief conversation. When Janie Ruth had eaten her fill, she pulled a sheet of notebook paper from her purse. "The way I figure it," she began, "is that the culture won't change until the people in it do. My fourth graders are a product of the homes where they live. The teachers and administrators, I think, would go the extra mile to help these kids establish the skills they will need when they leave our school. They're salt-of-the-earth people trying in vain to push against a system that accepts mediocrity as its best. So if genuine progress is to happen, it starts with the parents."

"How will you make them see the value of education?"

"Visit them."

"All of them? If they won't show up to back-to-school night, how are you going to convince them to come in to meet with you?"

"I'm not. This is where the Lord has to take my five loaves and two fish and multiply them. I have two hours in the afternoons before you get home and five work days a week. I will visit the kids in our school where they live until I've talked to every one of their parents."

"Honey, that's quite an undertaking. Tell me again how many students are in your class. Twenty?"

"No, Calvin. I'm going to visit the parents of every kid in our school. It might take me a year or two, but the

Lord told me the road to West Cary's hope is through my visiting the parents. What He does is up to Him, but I'm determined to be obedient."

Calvin drew in a deep breath. He opened his mouth to speak, then thought better of it. He considered how outlandish it must have sounded to Janie Ruth when he had told her he sensed the Lord's calling to small churches that couldn't afford a full-time pastor's salary. When they had grown the first church to over 150 people in two years' time, he discovered the elder board wanted to double his meager salary and use him full time. He imagined Janie Ruth's angst when he told her he felt God was telling him their season in that church was finished. He had no right to throw a wet blanket on the overwhelming plan God was birthing in her.

"How can I help?"

Her face burst with pleasure. "Fold a few socks and wash a few dishes. Hold me when it gets difficult. Bring me here to eat and decompress on the toughest days."

"I can do that. Tell me—what are your plans for the kids, the teachers, and the administrators?"

"I will cast a vision for what change might look for our school, one person at a time. I am meeting with little Ida Jean Thurman's mother Friday afternoon after she finishes cleaning the cafeteria. Ida Jean loves to braid the other little girls' hair. One time, I said something to her about becoming a hair stylist one day. Can you believe she didn't know that was a legitimate occupation? She would be the happiest person in the world if she styled hair for a living. I want to cast a vision to Ms. Thurman to make sure Ida Jean gets the help she needs now so her dream has a chance of coming true. She might change her mind a hundred times regarding her future vocation by the time she finishes school, but a solid foundation will give her those options.

"I have an underlying motivation to get Ms. Thurman on board, too. She has worked in the cafeteria for years, and she knows which kids are coming to school hungry and which ones don't get enough to eat on the weekends. I was over at Roger and Vicki's yesterday while you were still at work, and I told them of my concern for the kids who can't learn because they haven't eaten. Roger told me to tell him or Vicki what I needed, and they would come alongside and provide it. When they saw how much that Christmas party meant to my students last semester, they wondered what else they might do. I'm hoping Ms. Thurman can help me formulate a plan to make sure we can move forward with our plans without insulting the dignity of the families who need help.

"Since talking to Ida Jean, I have been paying attention to the other kids in my class and what their dreams are. I have given them writing assignments about their dreams for the future so I can have conversations with students and parents like the one I had with Ida Jean. Every parent loves to believe that their children's teachers are taking a personal interest in them, so that's how I plan to connect. All I need is a few productive parent meetings to get the ball rolling. Then, I will leak what I'm doing to other teachers and hope they feel inspired to come alongside me and meet with the parents of their students, too. At the very least, they can encourage the students in their classes to dream so I will have something to work with when I meet with their parents myself.

"When two or three of us teachers have success stories, we can share them with Mr. Lindsay. I don't expect him to make it mandatory for teachers to do more than they already are. However, he might help us set up extra tutoring and other programs to push our kids to catch up to where they should be."

"You know good and well that won't satisfy you."

"Why not?"

"To *catch up*? You won't rest until they have *surpassed* everybody's expectations. And you'll get them there, too. It will be hard work."

"I'm ready."

"Are you sure?"

"Today, yes. I'm positive there will come a time when it becomes overwhelming, but the Lord will give me strength as I need it. He'll use you and the Staplefords to encourage me. He'll give me minor victories when I need them to keep going. If this was my plan, I might worry about having what it takes to carry it out. But it's not my plan, so I'm not worried. God will make it happen."

21

"God did it, too," Pastor Hobbs said, wiping a piece of sweet potato pie from the corner of his mouth. "He brought her vision to life. Because she worked so tirelessly to give those kids a better future, the parents caught her vision. The programs got off to a slow start, but as she predicted, the minor victories came when she needed them most. It took her three years to meet with every parent at the school, but she did it. Every grade started setting up tutoring after school two days a week, and then three. The kids showed up excited because the Staplefords made sure they had an ice cream break halfway through their sessions.

"At least a handful of kids in every grade were showing up for tutoring by the close of that first school year. It's a small school with only two or three classes per grade, so convincing even a few students to come to tutoring is enormous. The fourth grade after-school program was drawing over half of the kids in the entire grade by the end of the year. It was happening one conversation with parents at a time, but Janie Ruth stuck to it. She had a difficult run-in or two with folks who didn't understand what she was trying to do, accused her of coming in here with fancy outside ways to change their kids. She won them over in time, but it took much hard work from her and a few country-fried steak dinners with me.

"Roger and Vicki Stapleford dedicated themselves to Janie Ruth's vision. Every week, Roger made sure the after-school kids had their ice cream treats, and he took off work early on Wednesdays to hand out the ice cream himself. Vicki was there volunteering, too, bouncing from room to room to encourage the teachers and ask them what supplies they lacked. The teachers learned that if they told Vicki, they could count on having what they needed by the next week."

"Tell us what she did for the kids who came to school hungry," Pops asked.

Pastor Hobbs laughed. "Janie Ruth concocted a sneaky solution for that. Ida Jean Thurman's mama hopped on board from the get go, but the poor families in our school had more pride than they had needs. She and Janie Ruth put their heads together and came up with a new volunteer program in the mornings. They invited the kids on the free and reduced lunch program —and others they identified whose families were going through a tough spell. As far as the kids understood, though, their responsibility was to help the teachers in the morning before school by doing simple jobs like cleaning their boards. To pick up their chore list for the day, they met in the cafeteria, where Ms. Thurman had a warm sausage and biscuit or cinnamon roll for them to eat, compliments of Stapleford Construction. Then, they did their jobs and went to class with a full stomach."

"And a full heart, too, I bet," Army Mom said. "There were times I wish someone had done that for my kids."

"Janie Ruth didn't stop there. As she acquainted herself with the kids and their families, she started this little club. Ms. Thurman identified the needy kids every year, and Janie Ruth had their teachers invite them to be a part of the Change It Now Club. They did fundraisers every other weekend for field trips they took once a month. The fundraisers might be a pancake breakfast one week or a catfish lunch one time or a spaghetti supper another time. The community responded, but the sponsors always managed a surplus after they had served every person who bought a plate. Janie Ruth would huff and start filling plates for the kids to take home, with their family's dignity still in hand. As usual, Roger was paying for the food, so the club always managed a profit. I'm not sure the families the Change It Now Club benefitted ever figured out what Janie Ruth and her cohorts were up to, but they ate many a meal because of them. They took neat field trips, too, only two hours away from home, at most, but several of those kids had never been outside Cary County."

"How long before their grades started improving?" Inconvenient Heart Attack asked.

"They saw a slight jump on their standardized test scores the first year after they started the after-school program and a bigger jump the second year. By the third year, most students below grade level in reading and math were taking part in everything the teachers created for them to do. They were having fun, and it became its own little ecosystem. The one thing Janie Ruth kept in front of everybody was hope, the dream of what could be if everybody was to do their part. They bought in, too, starting with the administrators dreaming that their little school so near failing at one time would one day be an A-plus school. They're not there yet, but they're getting closer every year. Janie Ruth gave the teachers hope that they would one day see what a difference their little extra effort was making. Getting rich is never why teachers choose the business, but I can't tell you what an encouragement it was for them not to have to spend their own money on school supplies. Janie Ruth recognized that, and she caused Vicki Stapleford to dream about what a few dollars and a few trips to the store every month could make.

"And boy, did she make those students dream. She introduced them to careers they didn't even know existed, just spending one-on-one time with them to ask them what they liked to do. Kids came to her classroom before school, during break, during lunch, and after school just because she cared enough to ask about their interests. She gave them possibilities to think and dream about. I've got to tell you, though, her biggest impact was with those parents. It's amazing what people will do for a teacher who cares for their kids. Those folks sent us fresh fruits and vegetables in the spring and fall, enough that Janie Ruth canned enough to get us through the winter. They sent us deer backstrap and tenderloin and jerky and sausage—enough to fill our outside deep freeze every single winter.

"The third year of the program, West Cary scored in the top half of the state on the math test. Improving reading skills proved to be more difficult, but one year's fifth grade class scored in the top five in the state on the language test. That was about the time several of the least involved parents requested to meet with Mr. Lindsay regarding Janie Ruth's program. They didn't bother to tell Mr. Lindsay the issues they had with Janie Ruth and the others, but he gave her a heads up about the meeting the day before they came to see him. I remember we had country-fried steak that night. We needed a refresher that God started this thing and that it was His to do what He wanted with it.

"Well, the next morning she was on pins and needles during lunchtime when they were meeting with Mr. Lindsay. When their meeting was over, he came straight to Janie Ruth's class and motioned her out in the hall. She said he sputtered to get his words out because he was so excited, but those parents inquired about the possibility of starting a remedial program for adults. These parents had not finished high school and wanted to get their graduate equivalency diplomas, but they needed a path. How do you like that?"

"So did they? Get their GED's, that is?" asked Inconvenient Heart Attack.

"They sure did. Two teachers and several others from our church who had gone back to get their GED's took on the project and made it happen. When the parents not only got on board with their kids' education but started investing in their own, that's when the school's performance improved by leaps and bounds.

"It took four years, but the school moved from the bottom quarter on overall state scores to the top half. People took notice. Another four years, and they jumped into the top quarter, and they've been there ever since. The local superintendent of schools was well aware of the transformation because Mr. Lindsay kept bringing it up in their meetings. The state superintendent spent three days observing the school and its after-school programs, and a writer for a national teaching journal wrote an article called 'The West Cary Miracle.' As principal, Mr. Lindsay received most of the credit for the turnaround. He wasn't fond of the spotlight, and he tried to deflect it to the people who truly made it happen, but the writer had already crafted his narrative. The year after they published that article, Mr. Lindsay won Principal of the Year for the state.

"Mr. Lindsay set the record straight at Janie Ruth's funeral, though. He talked longer than he wanted, but he identified the proper hero behind the so-called West Cary Miracle. He made sure they realized it wasn't a miracle that took place at his school but a tremendous vision from a godly teacher and a mix of ingenuity and old-fashioned elbow grease. When he finished speaking, folks stood and cheered so long I wasn't sure they would stop. I tell you, I loved my wife with all my heart for so many years, but I've never been more proud of her than I was at that moment. I'll tell you this, too: I'll never eat another piece of country-fried steak without remembering how God transformed an entire school through her."

"Gosh, I'd hate to follow that," Army Mom said. "Who spoke after that?"

"The girl who did her hair for her funeral," Pastor Hobbs said.

Puzzled looks gave way to understanding. "Ida Jean Thurman," Pops said. "I remember reading it in the paper."

"Ida Jean Thurman-Jones now, licensed cosmetologist and owner of an eight-chair shop. She is also the chairperson of the newly created Janie Ruth Hobbs Scholarship Foundation for students who would be the first in their families to attend college. Ida Jean told her story and announced the foundation at the funeral. She walked away that day with several thousand dollars to get her started, and she has had no problem adding more. Mr. Lindsay promised the Change It Now Club at West Cary would host events to help with the scholarship fund. And they did, too. They hosted what they called an Eat for College day. They cooked pancakes for breakfast, fried fish for lunch, and grilled burgers and hot dogs for supper—all in the same day. People bought food and made donations throughout the day, and by the time they wrapped it up, they had raised over ten thousand dollars for Janie Ruth's scholarships. I didn't know that until Ida Jean announced it at the funeral. It was quite a way to lead into my message that day."

"You preached your own wife's funeral?" an astonished Army Mom asked.

"I did."

"Always wondered who preached a preacher's wife's funeral," Pops said to no one in particular.

"Not her husband, most times, maybe a pastor friend of theirs or another staff member in a bigger church. I needed to do it, so I did. It was a struggle at times, but Roger and Vicki were there on the front row helping me hold it together. I told them we could have another good cry afterward, but I needed to hold my emotions in check to tell the story God told to this world through my Janie Ruth. Several times, I almost broke down, but I'd look at Roger, and he'd nod and make a fist, his way of telling me to power through it. I'm so glad I held it together between the Staplefords' strength and the power of God. Most people at Janie Ruth's celebration lived parts of her story with her—even sizable chunks of it—but through people's stories and my message, they saw a better picture of God's story through her. The preacher might stand up at a funeral and say some words, but it's the person's life that preaches a funeral. Janie Ruth did an outstanding job of preaching hers."

"Sounds every bit the celebration you wanted it to be."

"It was, but it has left a hole in the deepest part of my being that I can't seem to fill. I'm trusting God will give me strength when I need it, especially this first year, but sometimes the sadness hurts so bad I don't think I can stand it another minute."

"I felt the same way after my Catherine passed," Pops said. "Still do some days."

"How long has it been?"

"Better than twenty years now."

"What do you do—I mean, how do you make it?"

"I walk to her place to have a chat with her when I need to hear her voice."

"You mentioned that earlier. How does that work?"

"I just start telling her about my day. Sometimes, I take my chair if I expect I'll be awhile. We did these daily talks long enough that I can guess what she will say without her having to say it. I've done this so often, her voice is still strong inside my head. I think that's what keeps me going."

"Let me make sure I'm hearing you right—you visit with her in the cemetery?"

"Sure do."

"How often do you go?"

"Oh, I try not to make a nuisance of myself, so just a few times a week. Went twice today, though. My son spends a lot of time with me, but he's sick, so I spent quality time with my sweetie today."

"And that works for you?"

"Sure does."

"I might just have to try that."

"You just imagine her sitting there with her arm around you with her head on your chest, just like she did when she was here."

"That's right, I won't even have to remember her

voice, although I don't want to lose the sound of it in my head. I wasn't sure why I came here tonight, just hoped the turkey and dressing might fill part of this hole in my heart while it filled my empty stomach." Pastor Hobbs extended his hand to shake Pops'. "Thank you, sir."

ARMY MOM

22

"Who's next?" asked Easton Sterling.

"I'm interested in your story," Pastor Hobbs said, pointing across the table to Army Mom.

"Me? No, my story can't compare to yours."

Easton could tell he would have to use his best sales charm to get her talking. "It's not about whose story is better than another's. Look around the table. We came in as individuals for reasons as unique as we are. We just want you to tell us your story, that's all."

Army Mom hemmed and hawed around about her uninteresting story, but Pops helped Easton close the deal. "Young lady, I want to hear about your life. I can tell by your T-shirt, you're a proud parent and that your child is in the Army. I, for one, appreciate his or her service." She softened as the others nodded. Pops added, "Plus, at my age, if the conversation trails off very much, I'm liable to doze off." She smiled at that.

"Okay, I wouldn't want that. I'm not sure where to start."

"Do you have a name?" Easton asked.

"Of course."

"Start there."

"Okay, that's easy enough. My name is Paula Gull, like a seagull. I'm here alone tonight because I'm a single mom. Thanksgiving is important for us, but this year my daughter and son are away from home on Thanksgiving for the first time." She stopped as if that would satisfy the curiosity of the table.

"Away? Away how?" Inconvenient Heart Attack asked.

"Lisa is my oldest. She's in her third year of college. She's out of town this weekend. David got a pass to come home last Thanksgiving, but he's in Iraq this year." Paula shook, trying in vain to hold her emotions in check.

Inconvenient Heart Attack reached over to touch her hand, but Paula recoiled, defiantly collecting herself.

She's going to be a tough nut to crack, Easton realized. "Must have been an important trip to miss Thanksgiving with her mama."

"Huh?"

"You said your daughter was out of town?"

"Oh, yeah. She is meeting her boyfriend's family for the first time. He's from down in the Florida panhandle."

"Have you met him?" Easton asked.

"Oh, yeah, he's over at our apartment several nights

a week for supper. He and my daughter go to school together."

"Like him?"

"*Love* him. Jake's a good boy with manners, unlike my ex-husband. We can't even convince him to get himself a drink or a snack without asking, even though we've told him a million times to make himself at home. If I've had a tough day and go to bed early, he'll excuse himself, even if he and Lisa are in the middle of a movie. I'll tell him it's okay to finish their show, but he'll come up with some excuse like needing to study for a test or something like that. His last name is Noble, and I'm always telling Lisa he lives up to his name. She did well, that's for sure, but I'm a little worried about her this weekend."

"Why is that?"

"Well, his family is a lot better off than ours. They're not rich, to hear him tell it, but his parents are still together for one thing. His dad runs an appliance company, and his mom is the manager of a crafts store. I have worked hard to keep food on the table for my two kids, but we don't match up with a family like Jake's. I hope they don't look down on her. Lisa is smart as a whip, and she had her college paid for with good grades and a high ACT score. She has to do some community service as part of her scholarships, but that's right up her alley, anyway. I mean, she knows how to handle herself with the better off crowd, but I worry about her."

"Any chance of a wedding soon?" Inconvenient Heart Attack asked.

"They'll probably get married when they finish

school. They're both in accounting—that's where they met, in one of their classes. It wouldn't surprise me if they got married right after graduation next December. If they keep it small and private like I have advised her, there's a better chance they get through it without my ex-husband finding out about it. He would ruin it for them, trust me. He ruins everything he touches."

"How long were y'all married?"

"Two."

"Two years?"

"No, *too* dad gum long." She allowed herself a smile at the success of her pat answer to the question she had answered more often than she cared to count. The other faces bade her go on. "So, I'll take you guys back to the beginning of my stupid. I'm always telling my kids if I could go back and give my younger self any advice, it would be this: Don't touch a drop of alcohol until you've said *I do*. I met Brandon Gull at Jimmy's Bar & Grill over on College Street. He was on about his fourth identity by that time. He had tried star athlete in middle school, but he couldn't get along with the coach long enough to finish a season. In high school he was a preppie. His freshman year of college, he tried frat boy, but he didn't go to class and got kicked out of school. Then, he switched his identity to country boy, but he got his truck repossessed and had to drive a little hatchback that used to belong to his great-aunt."

"Nothing'll shut down a redneck reputation quite like a hatchback," Pastor Widower quipped.

"I didn't find out all this stuff until after I married him. Stupid me. When I met him, he was going through a hippie stage, I guess you'd say. He was all about saving the world, talking about joining the Peace Corps and all that jazz. I was seventeen, underage, and rebelling against all things high school. I dropped out after my junior year and got my GED that summer. He was twenty-one, mysterious, and willing to buy the pitchers of beer we consumed as we fell in—whatever that was I fell into. Seemed like love back then and a cesspool shortly thereafter.

"I had landed a full-time job as a dispatcher for a small over-the-road truck outfit by the summer before my senior year would have started. Since I didn't see myself going back to school, I started saving my money right off. I also figured my parents were going to flip out when I told them, maybe even kick me out of the house. Well, it was as bad as I expected. I imagine they thought their threat of exposing me to the real world would change my mind about quitting school. By the time they got home from work the next day, I had rented a small house not far from where I worked—cash deposits— and moved all my stuff out.

"Jimmy's Bar & Grill was about halfway between my house and work. Sometimes, when the weather was nice, I walked to work—it was less than a mile away. Some of my coworkers asked me to go by Jimmy's with them after work one day, and I went. They had no idea I hadn't even turned eighteen yet, but nobody carded me. By the time I met Brandon, I had been with my friends enough times that nobody was going to check my ID. He was walking in as we were all walking out one night. He says, 'Hey, Cute Thang' and I said, 'Hey, yourself.' I wouldn't say I was drunk, but I wouldn't say that I was sober, either, since I fell for a dorky line like that. I didn't exactly fall for it then, but he stayed on my mind later that night, and I looked for him the next day when I stopped in by myself after work.

"Sure enough, he walks in when I was halfway through my second beer. I was a little nervous because I knew why I was there drinking alone. Brandon saw me when he walked in, but he played it cool and acted like he didn't noticed me. When he walked by me the second time, I said, 'Hey, yourself.' He studied me for a few seconds like he was trying to recognize me—played it real cool—before he flashed recognition from the day before. I would see right through that today, but I was seventeen and stupid and needy and already a little tipsy.

"I'll save the details from the rest of the night because I imagine Pastor doesn't care to listen to my worldliness. Suffice it to say, he spent the night at my house. I should have noticed he wanted to go to my house instead of his. He was crashing on a friend's couch at the time, I later discovered. When he wore out his welcome at one place, he would move on to another or sleep in his hatchback for a while. He had this certain charm about him that made you believe he was just unlucky, that one good break would change everything.

"He would tell me about a dream he had of opening his own mechanic shop. At his shop, he would only hire honest mechanics who wouldn't keep trying things to fix your car and charging you for it. He had it all figured out. I naturally assumed he was a mechanic, but that man had never turned a wrench. He was just mad because he took his truck to the shop, thinking it needed a tune-up and unable to afford the fuel pump it did need. When the shop finished the work, he couldn't pay. He told them he would pay a certain amount every week—which he wouldn't have, and they knew it—but they kept his truck. They eventually turned him over to a collection agency, but he had no plans to pay them a dime. Besides, he had his great-aunt's hatchback by then. Soon, he was borrowing my car whenever I was at work and using my gas."

Paula stopped, looked around the table, and chuckled. "I realize how this sounds. I talk about him like the loser he is, but it's me that sounds gullible and stupid and…"

One Month Sober reached across and put her hand on Paula's. Paula tried to recoil, but she held firm and looked Paula square in the eyes. "I understand you think you've cornered the market on stupid, but you haven't." Nodding in Pops's direction without taking her eyes off Paula, she said, "If it hadn't been for that sweet man down there, I'd be about halfway through a bottle right now. I'm a month sober and proud of it, but tonight is a big test. I told Pops my story, and I'm going to make it through now. It didn't change the stupid from my past, but it helped me get through today." Looking around the table, her eyes pleading, she added, "I don't see judgment at this table tonight. I believe you're safe to tell the rest of your story without having to beat yourself up while you do it."

Paula swallowed hard and nodded and then

breathed an inaudible thank you. After a deep breath, she continued. "So it kept going like this for several months. I was doing well at work—got a raise and started getting benefits. A job came open for a forklift driver, and I put in a word for Brandon, and he got the job. I let him move in after his hatchback gave out on him. It wasn't worth getting fixed, and he needed a couple more months to save up for a decent ride. He slept on the couch most nights, but we were doing a lot of drinking after work, so I wasn't in the best frame of mind when he asked me to marry him one night. I'm telling y'all, he was cute, and I was stupid, so I said yes.

"We drove to the justice of the peace to get married on the last Friday in June. I hadn't even been out on my own a year yet, hadn't met his parents, and hadn't talked to mine in several months—certainly hadn't told them about him. We got married at the JP's office and headed south to beat the traffic. Brandon booked a room at a casino in Biloxi, and we checked in and then had a nice dinner. That night was the beginning of the end for us, a disaster of epic proportions."

23

"You ready?"

"For some you-know-what?"

"For some casino action. Then that."

"Brandon, I can't go to the casino."

"Why not? I withdrew a thousand dollars for us to see what we can do."

"You did what?!? You didn't talk to me before taking that much money out of *our* account."

"Come on, Paula, chill. This is our honeymoon. Let's live a little."

"Well, if risking our hard-earned money is what you call living a little, you can do it by yourself. They won't let me through the door."

"Why not?"

In her best broadcast voice, she imitated the disclaimer near the end of the casino ads on the radio: "You must be twenty-one to gamble."

"You're kidding."

"No, it's a state law. Everybody knows that."

"No, I mean you're not twenty-one? How old are you?"

"I'm eighteen." Paula's heart sank with the words. Her age never seemed important enough to mention until now. If she had ever told Brandon before, he didn't remember it.

"*Eighteen!?!*"

"You heard me."

"But how did you… Jimmy's… why didn't you…"

"I started working at seventeen, and one day my coworkers invited me to Jimmy's after work. They didn't realize how old I was. I guess the bartenders at Jimmy's assumed I was the same age as the regulars I came in with, so nobody ever checked my ID."

"Including me."

"I suppose so. I figured you were cute, and you paid attention to me, so I decided not to mention it. One thing led to another, and here we stand."

"Well, why don't you walk into the casino like you walked into Jimmy's."

"Brandon, this ain't no Jimmy's off-the-radar dive. You realize what big trouble they'll be in if they get caught letting underage kids gamble? *Kids.* There, she had said it. She had run from it since she left home. Run from it by being responsible and getting a steady job. Run from it by working hard and getting along with her coworkers. Run from it by paying her rent and her bills on time. Run from it by keeping her car clean and getting the oil changed and having the tires rotated every other oil change. Run from it by hanging out at the bar where they shouldn't have allowed her. Run from it by marrying Brandon without telling a soul. But she couldn't run from being a kid at a casino for adults.

"Tell you what. You take a hundred bucks and play for an hour. I'll go to the room, freshen up, and change into something I bought special for tonight." She never expected him to pull a big bill from the envelope in his pocket, then another, and hand her the rest.

"Two hundred."

"Brandon, you're not serious," Paula said to his back as he walked away.

An hour later, he returned to their room with a bottle of champagne and proposed a toast to his angry eighteen-year-old wife. Two glasses later, they consummated their marriage. She dozed off, and he walked back downstairs with $800.

"MAD AS A HORNET describes how I felt when I woke up and he had left me alone again. I checked to see if my envelope with what amounted to *my* $800 was still in my purse. It wasn't. If I had understood the process of annulment, I would have hopped in my car right then and left his sorry butt in Biloxi. By the time he came back to Harriston, I would have thrown his stuff on the porch, changed the locks on my doors, and ridded myself of him by Monday morning. Instead, the worst thing you can imagine happened."

"He cheated on you, didn't he?" One Month Sober guessed. "On your wedding day, too?"

"Worse."

"What can be worse than that?"

"He stayed at the casino all night and left you alone?" Inconvenient Heart Attack tried.

"Nope, worse."

"He won big," Pops said without a hint of doubt.

Paula nodded. "We have a winner... ooh, no pun intended."

"How did you know?" One Month Sober asked Pops.

"Well, for one, she was desperate enough to leave him. If she was still stewing when they returned to Harriston, she would have found out how to end it. For another, they had two children together, so I figured they stayed married long enough for that. I got to asking myself what he might have done to get her to stay with him after bumbling his honeymoon so bad to that point. I realized he must have hit some big money and made some accompanying big promises." Pops turned to Paula. "Am I close?"

"He won four hundred bucks at the blackjack table and then hit it big on a slot machine. I was laying in bed trying my best to look asleep when he walked in after midnight. He flipped on the light, crawled across the bed, and held over $5,000 in front of my face. He apologized for how our attempt at a honeymoon had turned out and asked me what I thought of spending a week at the beach later in the summer. I'm not sure he could have found another route to forgiveness, but he found one that worked. So I rolled over, told him how great that sounded, and kissed my future goodbye."

"Did you at least enjoy your trip to the beach?" Easton asked.

"He never took her to the beach," Inconvenient Heart Attack deadpanned.

"What do you mean? She said…"

"No, she's right," Paula said. "As soon as we got home, Brandon found this 'unbelievable deal' on a truck he wanted and bought it without ever talking to me about it. He said we'd save up for the next couple of months to go on our trip, but it was a deal he couldn't refuse."

One Month Sober nodded. "And he kept spending y'all's money as if it was his."

"More than a year passed with my heart still set on a trip to Florida—it's not that far, for crying out loud. Brandon had a nice truck and a bass boat by then. I still had my same little car with the miles piling up on it because we never drove anywhere but the lake in his truck. Unless he wanted to show me off, I never rode in it. I tell you, he lived the perfect country song for a while."

One Month Sober laughed out loud. Inconvenient Heart Attack snickered and said, "In an old school country song, he would have lost it all."

"We're not to the second verse yet. The bass boat was *our* first anniversary present. He said we didn't spend enough time together, so the boat would be a perfect way for us to bond. The day he bought it, he told me I ought to pack a picnic basket, and we would spend that Saturday at the lake together, the two of us. The two of us went, all right, but his buddies and their wives and girlfriends met us there. He knew I didn't care for them, but that didn't matter to him. It gave him an excuse to fish and drink beer with his buddies. The other girls were too catty for me, so I kept my mouth shut while they ripped first one person, then another. Their own husbands took the brunt of it. I was miserable and fed up with Brandon."

Paula whipped around to Pastor Widower. "We're quite the case study, huh, Pastor? You ever counseled anybody as messed up as us?"

Pastor Widower smiled. "First, understand that pastors must hold counseling conversations in the strictest of confidence. If they weren't, nobody would trust us with their deepest problems. But while I'm not at liberty to reveal any specifics, I daresay I'm not as naïve as you might believe I am."

"Humph. I'm just getting started."

Pastor Widower unfurled his hand toward the center of the table. "By all means, please continue."

"So, you're thinking the lake episode should have been the last straw. You might be correct except for... Pops?"

"You were pregnant."

"Old timer, you're mighty sharp."

Pops grinned. "You live as long as I have, you learn a thing or two if you're paying attention."

"Well, you're right. I was pregnant, over three weeks late, so I had taken a pregnancy test that very morning. I considered our lake day to be the perfect day to tell him the news. I was naïve enough to believe Brandon wanted to use the bass boat to spend more time with me. I packed a bottle of sparkling grape juice in the picnic basket and planned to pull it out with our lunch. Knowing he would ask why I brought the non-alcoholic stuff, I would tell him I shouldn't drink alcohol for the next nine months. Oh, I had this whole goofy speech practiced and ready.

"By the time the guys returned from fishing to where the other girls and me were hanging out near the dock, they were already three sheets to the wind. They plopped down on the blanket I had spread out for Brandon and me. Brandon said, 'Feed this hungry fisherman, woman!' He reached into our picnic basket to grab a sandwich and pulled out the sparkling grape juice. He couldn't leave well enough alone. He says, 'Oh, yeah, Paula can't drink the genuine stuff anymore. She was old enough at seventeen, but after she snagged me, she told me she was only a kid.' I jumped up and told him I'd be in the truck. An hour later—*an hour later*—he came to the truck and told me I needed to grow up and quit pouting."

"Bless your heart," Inconvenient Heart Attack said, venturing her hand to empathize with Paula. This time, Paula didn't refuse it. "When did you tell him?"

"Two weeks later, maybe three. I stewed on it for a while. When he started taking days off work to go fishing, it became obvious he had no plans to save any vacation to take me to the beach, but it was okay. I couldn't stand the idea of him and me alone together for an entire week. After I thought on it, I considered he might be right about my being immature. So I swallowed my pride and decided I should tell him he was going to be a daddy.

"I remember it was on a Saturday. He left before sunup, headed for the lake. I spent the day cleaning up our place, making it look and smell nice. If I say so myself, I cooked a wonderful meal. I set out our only matching dishes and even put candles on the table. I was ready to light them as soon as I heard his truck pull into the yard."

"And he stood you up somehow," Mr. Important offered.

"I'll be honest, I had imagined every scenario how he would destroy my best intentions yet again. Late at the lake. Too drunk to drive. Over at a friend's house. Headed to Jimmy's. A burger on the way home. A snide remark about the house being clean the minute he walked in the door."

"But he pulled something unexpected."

"Sort of. Surprise, surprise—he arrived home before dinnertime, even called to tell me he was on his way. He was sober, too. He noticed everything I had set up and stood there with his mouth open. I suggested he get cleaned up right quick and come see what I had fixed for him. When he came back into our little dining nook, I had the food on the plates: spaghetti with a touch of habanero sauce just like he likes it, green beans, and garlic breadsticks. I had an apple pie cooling on the stove, too.

"I had been rehearsing ways to break the news to him, but I didn't end up using any of them. He sat in his chair, took one bite of spaghetti, and looked up as if he would ask why I made all those preparations for him. His mouth was still full, though, so I jumped in and said 'I'm pregnant!' He was dumbstruck at first. He started asking the dumb new father questions like if the baby was a boy or girl, which, of course, I didn't know yet. We had a most enjoyable meal. After that, we cuddled up on the couch and watched a movie. He kept reaching over and rubbing my belly.

"It was all I could do to stay awake until the end of the movie. I was slap worn out from cleaning and cooking and from the mental exhaustion of not knowing how he would respond. I said I was going to bed. His phone rang, so I told him to take it and I would see him in the morning. I heard Brandon's side of the conversation, and I thought nothing of it then, but it stuck with me. It made more sense a little farther down the road.

HELLO.

OH, hey, Bubba.

NO.

NO, I didn't.

• • •

I'M NOT GOING TO.

No, no, no, Bubba, listen to me: I'm not going to. Bubba, I'm going to be a daddy.

THAT'S RIGHT, Paula's pregnant.

TAKE THAT BACK. Of course it's mine.

YEAH, I'm happy, real happy.

YEAH, well, it takes one to know one.

No, I'm going to stay home with Paula. Might even go get up and go to church tomorrow.

YOU'RE WEIRD. Night, Bubba. I'll talk to you tomorrow.

24

P aula turned to Pastor Hobbs. "Look, I was hard on you, and I'm sorry. I haven't always been calloused about life and... God. After I closed my eyes that night, thinking our baby meant a fresh start for Brandon and me, I felt close to God, like He was giving me a break. I imagined Brandon's distancing himself from that toxic group of friends of his, showing up to work every day, all that jazz. Can you believe I was so dang naïve I thought we might wake up on Sunday morning and go to church? I woke up by 8:30 the next morning, excited. I even cooked breakfast."

"And he didn't get up," Pastor Hobbs said.

"Just grunted when I shook him."

"That scenario plays out every Sunday morning all over the world. One spouse has good intentions to make a change, but the other spouse's inaction cancels them out. Sorry, go ahead with your story."

"It's okay. It's not as if I was living a Christian life to

that point in my life, either. But I figured the time was ripe for some changes since I would be a mother soon. Anyway, as awkward as I imagined walking into a church with Brandon would be, I sure didn't want to walk into a strange church by myself. I won't lie, I got mad at God, and I guess I've been mad at Him ever since that morning. I'm just being honest. Saying it loud, though—sounds like more of my stupid choices than anything God ever did to me. Hang on, though, it gets worse.

"Brandon didn't go to church with me, and he didn't cut down much on his fishing like he said, but he went with me to my doctor visits. I didn't ask, and he couldn't afford any more time off from work, but I was glad he came with me. I felt sorry for the girls in the waiting room by themselves. Brandon wanted a boy, but when we found out we were having a girl, he seemed fine with that, too. When Lisa was born, he handed out those 'It's a Girl' cigars to whoever would take one— didn't matter if he knew them or not. Heck, he waved down the garbage man and gave him one.

"He became Mr. Helpful for the first few days after we got home from the hospital, but I reckon his demons came calling again. He started spending more time at Jimmy's bar carousing with his friends. When Lisa was six months old, Brandon got a DUI on his way home. We live less than a mile from Jimmy's. He could have walked home. After I bailed him out, I lectured him up one side and down the other: *What were you thinking? What kind of example are you setting for your daughter? You have more than just yourself to think about.* After I'd go off on him, I'd apologize for piling on and make up with him. During one of those make-up sessions…"

Paula blushed as she caught Pastor Widower's eye.

"… you became pregnant again," he finished. "Pastors don't spend every day in a cave praying, like you might think. I have four kids of my own, and I understand how they came to exist, believe it or not."

"I'm sorry. I've just never been this close to a pastor. I'm a little nervous, I guess."

"It's okay, I don't think I've never been this near a truck dispatcher."

"Former truck dispatcher. We'll get to that part next."

Pastor Hobbs motioned for her to continue.

"I picked up a pregnancy test on the way home from work one day after dropping Brandon off at Jimmy's and picking up Lisa from daycare. As I expected, it was positive. I pulled out the candles again—first time since my first pregnancy announcement—and prepared a special dinner. Well, Brandon came staggering through the door in worse shape that usual. He saw the candles on the table and the first slurred words out of his mouth were, 'Don't tell me you got yourself pregnant again.'"

Paula waved off the signs of sympathy around the table and continued. "Oh, it gets worse. We went to bed mad, which we had been doing more and more often. We woke for work the next morning, and he declared he wasn't going. Before lunch, the owner of the company called me into his office and told me he was sorry, but he was going to fire Brandon for not showing up for work. He had used all his vacation and sick days for the year. I fell apart right there in the boss's office and begged him for one more chance, for him to take the day from my sick days. I told him I had just found out I was pregnant again, and we needed the money.

"Mr. Dobbins said that he would give Brandon one more chance, one *final* chance, and that he would take the day from my vacation days since I needed my sick days. Looking back, I understand his generosity. At the time, though, I thought taking it from me was harsh since I might need my days later in the year. The other girls in the office had complained about doing my work during maternity leave, and he wasn't excited to go through that hassle again.

"When I told Brandon Mr. Dobbins' ultimatum, he straightened up for a month, but I made the mistake of telling Brandon I gave up one of my vacation days for him. Not a week after that, he told his boss on the loading dock that he felt sick and needed to go home at lunch. When our paychecks came out at the end of that week, I noticed another half day taken from my vacation. I didn't care about the days because I wasn't going anywhere, but I should have seen the writing on the wall—it wasn't just Brandon's job on the line.

"Brandon waited three weeks before another 'sickness' sent him home early. I had a doctor visit two days later, and he got mad when they told him he didn't have any time off left to go with me. He told them to do whatever they wanted, but he was going with his wife on her doctor visit. Six months into my pregnancy, Brandon used up the last of *my* vacation days, and they let him go. He let me have it something fierce when I walked in the door after work."

"He hit you?" Inconvenient Heart Attack interrupted, her face flashing red.

"No, that's one thing he never did—hit me. He just gave me a tongue lashing for my brilliant idea for us to work for the same company. He blamed me for not convincing Mr. Dobbins to cut him some slack. When he I told him I saved him from being fired months earlier, he yelled at me to shut up and started packing a duffel bag. I asked him if he planned to walk out on his pregnant wife and his kids. He shouted from the porch that he just needed to get away and clear his head. Before he escaped my shouting range, I called him a loser and a quitter and other names I won't repeat. He threw his bag in that stupid truck and spun his tires for good measure on his way up the street. I haven't laid eyes on him since.

"To make matters worse, I was up so late arguing with him that I slept right through my alarm the next day. I woke up two hours late to Lisa's crying in the other room. I called into work to tell them I would be there as soon as I dropped off Lisa at her daycare. The girl who answered the phone seemed unusually nice to me and told me to take my time. I was in such a rush that I didn't pay much attention to her manner, but I should have detected something by how sweet she was."

"Y'ALL, I am so sorry I'm late. Brandon and I had a big fight, and he took off on us last night. I didn't get to bed until after three o'clock, but my mind kept racing. I guess I dozed off and slept right through my alarm."

"No problem," Veronica said from the desk next to Paula's. "We covered the phones for you... again. Oh, Mr. Dobbins came by this morning and asked for you. He said to send you over to his office when you got here."

Veronica smiled sweetly, and Paula's stomach soured. *No, no, no, I can't lose this job now!*

Paula's entire life seemed exposed on her walk across the lot to Mr. Dobbins's office adjacent the dock. She caught a glance from the trailer mechanic sitting up high patching the roof on trailer #132. A diesel mechanic working on truck #18 took notice but re-engaged in his work under the hood. Several dockhands gathered around a stack of empty pallets for their break stared at her all the way to the dock steps before they turned their attention back to their chatter.

Paula took a deep breath and knocked on the open door.

"Come in, Paula," Mr. Dobbins said. "Close the door behind you." He motioned her to take a seat across from his desk without rising from his chair.

"Mr. Dobbins, I—" He raised his hand as a firm stop sign.

"Paula, I realize this is just about the worst timing on your end, but I must put the company first and let you go. I hope you agree that we have been more than flexible with you over the last few months, but I must put a stop to it today. It's not fair to the other employees covering yours and your husband's work."

"Please, Mr. Dobbins, Brandon left me last night, and I'm six months pregnant. I can't get another job." When his face didn't soften, she reached for all she had left. "So close to Christmas…"

"Paula, you were an exemplary employee during your first year with us. The drivers loved you. So did the girls in the office… until we hired Brandon. It was a terrible idea for us to hire your husband, but we figured if he worked as hard as you, we should make the move. I take the blame for not vetting him as I should have. However, it doesn't change the fact that your job performance has gone downhill since he came to work here."

"But he's not here anymore. I'm not sure I will ever see him again."

"I can't take that chance, Paula. The timing stinks, and I understand, so we put together what I hope you will see as a generous severance package. Since you are being terminated for job performance, the company is not obligated to offer you a severance. But we are a family business, and we want to show you we care in these extenuating circumstances. We will give you three months' pay, which means you'll be able to stay on our insurance through your delivery. We will also give you your year-end bonus, which should help you through another month while you try to find another job."

"I REALIZE NOW the severance package was more than generous and that Mr. Dobbins did everything in his power to help me. But at barely twenty years old, I locked in on being a single mom of two crying babies. I should have thanked him for the opportunity and his generosity. If I had apologized for the position I put him in, he would have given me a good reference for another job or maybe hired me back after he saw Brandon had left for good. But I signed the paper, snatched the check, and marched my pregnant self out of there.

"I drove home and wanted to stop at Jimmy's along the way to drown my sorrows, but I didn't. I almost forgot to pick up Lisa from daycare. Well, at least that was one expense I could cut from the budget. Before I drove to get her, though, I stopped by my bank and deposited my severance check in a new account, one I determined Brandon would never discover, even if he came back. We had a couple thousand in our account, and I asked to move that over into my account, but Brandon had beaten me to some of it. He took six hundred dollars, which is the most my bank allows you to withdraw from the ATM in a day. I moved what he left over to my account before he took any more of it.

"While I drove to pick up Lisa, I concocted a plan to put the money he took back and then some in our budget. I had worked it out in my head how we could survive until after David's birth. I needed a decent job a few months after he was born, but we might make it without having to take public assistance. With a little hope dangling like a carrot in front of me, I determined to make it as a single mom, to possess the grit it would take for me and my babies to survive. Then, we turned the corner on the street toward the house, and I saw the hole in the yard where the bass boat used to be."

Inconvenient Heart Attack and One Month Sober blessed Paula's heart at the same time. Mr. Important nodded, not shocked by the latest twist in her story. Pastor Widower asked her how she made it.

She straightened in her chair and coiled her fists. "Without a dime of government money."

"Did you and your parents reconcile?" he asked.

"Eventually, but that's not how we made it."

Pops suggested the group let Paula tell the rest of her story.

"Thank you, sir," she said with a nod toward Pops. "Without the cost of daycare, I stretched our money further. David was born in January. Meantime, I fell in love with being a mother. I determined to stay at home with him and Lisa. I had made connections in the trucking industry, so I called a few of them for ideas. One older lady I talked to did third party logistics."

One Month Sober interrupted, "What's that?"

"Best way I can describe it is like this: A trucker takes a load from somewhere else in the country—say, Chicago. He delivers the load and then heads back home. Well, that empty trailer's not making the company any money, and there are plenty of folks looking to send a load to wherever he's returning. Third party logistics negotiates a rate for the load and connects the two parties. With the right connections, you can make a hundred fifty, two hundred bucks in five minutes' time. Not all day and not whenever you want, of course, and other loads cause you to work harder to cover. That make sense?"

"I think so."

"We used third party logistics all the time at Dobbins. Well, this lady I was talking to had been doing logistics from home for several years as a transition toward retiring for good. I had to buy a cheap computer and the logistics software, but she let me take a few loads to make that money back during training. As far as anybody noticed, this lady worked from an office and was training a woman to take over for her when she called it a career. After I started flying solo from my house, the trick came in handling phone calls that came in at the same time one of my kids was throwing a tantrum, which didn't happen often. One thing I am most thankful for from those early years as a single mom is the discipline of my kids to stay quiet when I was talking on the phone.

"The few times the kids acted up, I'd tell the dispatchers my sitter was sick, and I had to bring my kids to the office today. They understood—folks with kids of their own usually do—and said nothing else about it. The lady who gave me her business told me I could do the job from home in my pajamas. She spoke the truth, but it was more a matter of *having* to go to work in my pajamas. The loads started showing up online at five or five-thirty, and there were other third-party companies competing for the same loads. If I picked up several loads from anywhere near here and headed to the Midwest, I could guarantee a productive day. Once I made sure the driver picked up the load, somewhere between nine o'clock and noon, I had time to clean up and enjoy my afternoons with Lisa and David. I even kicked some business over to Dobbins to work on repairing that bridge.

"That job kept food on the table for several years. Once the kids started school, I started driving a school bus for the health insurance. I kept the logistics gig for several years, a few loads a week and more during the summer. I loved being a mom... I love *being* a mom, but my children are grown up now. It wasn't easy to raise them by myself, but they were easy to raise, if that makes sense. I grew up so much after Brandon bailed on us, started taking responsibility for the terrible choices I made to put myself into such a tough position."

One Month Sober asked, "So, I remember you said you haven't ever seen Brandon again. What about your children?"

"When he left, he left for good. He never called, and I'd just as soon keep it that way. I want nothing from him, don't care that he ever sends the kids a dime. We're okay without him. I swallowed my pride and showed up at my parents' house unannounced on a Sunday afternoon and introduced them to their grandchildren. I don't believe Mom and Dad have ever fully forgiven me for rebelling against them the way I did, but that didn't keep them from being super grandparents. Lisa and David spent at least one night a week there for most of their childhood."

"So, if you've never seen or heard from Brandon again," One Month Sober pressed, "does that mean you are technically still married?"

Paula stared into the distance and sighed. "Ever heard of a common law marriage?"

"Yeah, when a couple lives together so long that the law recognizes them as married."

"Well, I guess you might say we have a common law divorce. While we might not possess signed documents to prove it, we are as practically divorced as two people can be."

25

"That's quite a story, Paula," Pastor Widower said. "You said Thanksgiving was a big day for you and your kids. Tell us why."

"Early in Lisa and David's childhood, Thanksgiving was just another day. When Lisa started school, she learned the history of the holiday and heard her classmates talk about the meals they ate with their families. She asked if our family could eat a meal like that. A restaurant near us sells Thanksgiving dinners—frozen turkey and dressing and the works—so I started buying the food there and warming it up while we watched the parades. The kids believed I was cooking it all, and I was happy to take credit. For me, Thanksgiving became a time to celebrate what we have overcome. By the time they got to high school, Lisa was an honor roll student, and David was big into ROTC. His grades weren't stellar, but he was ready to get out on his own and learn new skills, so he planned on joining the Army right out of high school. My kids didn't have many social connections, but they each had a few solid friendships, and they had one another. Every Thanksgiving they reserved the entire day to spend with me.

"That has been our routine every Thanksgiving until today. The morning started off okay since the kids sleep late on holidays. I ate breakfast and drank my coffee and watched the parade on TV, like other years. Mid-morning every other Thanksgiving, I put the dressing in the oven, but there was no dressing this year. I tried to watch a movie, but I got to missing Lisa and David and couldn't pay attention, so I turned the movie off and went for a walk. A nap helped pass the time, but I was so lonely I couldn't stand it anymore. I needed to escape the isolation and do something, and I had forgotten to eat lunch, so I came here to at least eat a traditional meal today."

"Same here," said Pops. "How did we forget to eat lunch on Thanksgiving of all days?"

"Different this year. Threw me out of my routine, I guess."

One Month Sober said, "Tell us more about your daughter and her boyfriend."

"Lisa and Jake are accounting majors and math nerds. They were once in a study group that soon became a group of two and stayed that way. They'll be in the den studying, and sometimes I laugh out loud at their little accounting humor."

"Such as?"

"Oh, last week they were quizzing each other on terms for a test they had coming up. Instead of counting right and wrong answers, they were calling right answers *debits* and wrong answers *credits*. Silly stuff like that. You can tell he comes from excellent stock and knows how to treat a young lady with respect. Lisa would kick him to the curb in a heartbeat if he treated her any other way. We've had good heart-to-heart talks concerning the mistakes I made with her daddy and how she can avoid the hard times I've had.

"I wish my son was here to hang around Jake and learn from his example. I'm proud of him, and he's a fine young man, but I know he inherited Brandon's genes. I'll admit that's a mama's fear talking. I wish I had seen how lazy and selfish Brandon was back then. If there's one thing David is not, though, it's lazy. My dad taught him how to mow grass and trim and clean up and started paying him to help him mow his yard when he was nine years old. He saved his birthday and Christmas money for two years to buy a good push mower and started cutting yards for older people who lived within walking distance of us. By the end of that summer, he was cutting three or four yards. One of his customers offered to let him use his string trimmer and blower on his other yards for doing his yard for free once a month. David realized what a generous arrange-ment that was and took him up on it while he saved to buy his own equipment. At the end of the summer, Mr. DuPont told him if he would clean up his leaves during the winter, he could keep the string trimmer and blower.

"Since David owned the equipment he needed, he started offering deals up and down our street. He ended up with nine yards the next year. On mowing days, he started around ten in the morning because as he often told me, 'Mom, you don't cut wet grass.' It took him until the middle of the afternoon to get through them, and he'd swap out the mower for the trimmer and start working through the yards again. An hour or two later, he swapped out the trimmer for the blower, and when he finished, he made the rounds one more time to collect. I worried about him on the hot, humid summer days—if he was getting enough water—but I discovered his customers brought him water and lemonade and sports drinks throughout the day.

"He'd work those yards in the spring and summer and rake their leaves in the fall and winter. When he turned sixteen, he paid $5,000 cash for his first truck and found a deal on a nice trailer for a thousand more. He doubled up on his equipment and expanded his coverage to within a mile or so of our house. He had plenty of referrals by then, so he hired several younger kids to help him out. I asked him why he didn't hire his buddies, and he said they wouldn't be trainable because their parents had given them too much. He was looking for hungry junior employees who could keep the business going while he was in the army.

"That's the first he ever said to me regarding joining the army after his business took off, and that set me back, I'll tell you. I assumed he wouldn't leave if the yard business became lucrative enough. His plan was to put in two or three years in the service and let them pay for college while he kept his business going. He says now that the army has helped him learn discipline, but he developed discipline before he enlisted. I mean, while he's off serving his country, his workers are bringing over two thousand dollars a week from his yards. He pays them well, but still, I'm putting a thousand a week in his account."

Mr. Important leaned across the table and handed her a card. "I don't believe you have any worries as far as your son being like your ex-husband. When his time is up, you tell him to call me. He need not wait until he finishes college, either. He seems a natural-born salesman, and I'd like to help him in whatever direction he goes. From what you've told us, you did an incredible job raising him. And your daughter, too."

"Thank you. I just... I hope David comes home so I can give him this card. If y'all have never had a child in the military, you don't understand that there's always a chance it's your son's picture on the evening news with his flag-covered coffin. I love my country, and I'm proud that my son put his life on the line to protect our freedoms. But I'd rather welcome him back home in one piece, picking back up where he left off with his life. Those military benefits like sending him to college when he gets back don't help him one bit if he's dead. I'm sorry, I realize that sounds blunt, but that's the reality of being an army mom."

"Was it just the benefits that caused him to join?" Mr. Important asked.

"Oh, no. Now, he knows what he's got coming to him, and he plans to take full advantage of his so-called free education, but that's not why he enlisted. He started doing ROTC in high school, which started him in that direction."

"What motivated him to join ROTC in the first place?"

"My ex-husband."

"But you said…"

"Let me explain. Brandon has had no interaction with the kids, but he has been a cautionary tale to David since he was little, perhaps to an extreme. David's biggest fear has always been that if he relaxes for even a day, he will start sliding down a slippery slope toward becoming his father. He can hardly sit still long enough to watch a movie. When he was younger, he would get a toy for Christmas or his birthday, and within a week, he had it taken apart to see how it worked. More often than not, he put it back together, but it was maddening as a mom. Now, I can see that his curiosity in trying to figure out how things work is one of his greatest strengths. Not just with toys and lawn equipment and cars, but also in figuring out how life works.

"When I was helping him put together his class schedule for his sophomore year, he told me he wanted to join the ROTC at his school. When I asked him why, he said to teach him discipline. David was athletic, but we couldn't afford for him to play sports when he was growing up, so he didn't play. But he noticed that the high school athletes were more disciplined than they were when they were in middle school because of weightlifting and long practices and such as that. He wanted something like sports to push him beyond what he was capable of, and he believed ROTC would. It did, to a degree, but it also propelled him to be a leader. Sergeant Addison told me David was the most dedicated and teachable student in their program. He pushed David hard to pass that down to the younger kids, which David did. Even though I wasn't a big fan of his getting involved with ROTC at first, he sold me on it, too. He was proud to be a soldier-in-training, and he was ready to get to boot camp the summer after he graduated.

"That's a long answer to a quick question, but I'm proud of my son. I just want him to come home alive and free of PTSD and addiction and the other things soldiers sometimes bring back with them. We both went into this—him as a soldier and me as a military mom—with eyes wide open. We still talk once a week when he is able. He still struggles sometimes with a fear of turning out like his dad he has never known, but I try to encourage him that I don't see it in him and never have."

Pastor Widower raised his hand and spoke. "I'll echo what Easton said earlier. From what you've told us about both of your children, you've done just fine."

Paula nodded. She was on the verge of tears as she saw the smiles around the table. "Y'all don't understand what that means to me. You push so long and so hard to get them through and raise them right, and they're grown and gone before you know it. I've had my nose down so long trying to get my kids through childhood and through school that I've never stopped and reflected on who I am becoming. Honestly, as proud as I am of them, I'm scared."

"Scared of what?"

"Scared of me without them. If Lisa marries Jake and David picks back up with his business or starts a career selling whatever Mr. Important here sells, I'll be alone within a few years. I haven't been alone since I was seventeen, and I've already told you how that turned out."

"You've become a more mature person since then," said Inconvenient Heart Attack. "You won't make the same mistakes again, will you?"

"Won't I?"

"I don't expect so and neither does anybody else at this table." She looked right and left for confirmation, which she received.

"I'd like to believe you're right. My kids have been my accountability all these years, though. What happens when they're not here anymore?" She tapped her heart. "There's such an emptiness here. If one weekend causes me to react this way, what shortcuts will I take to keep from feeling this way again?"

"Have you not dated during your time as a single mom?" One Month Sober asked.

"No."

"Not a single date?"

"Not one. Guys asked me out a few times, but I couldn't risk jeopardizing my relationship with my children. They needed me to be present, not caught up with some guy." Paula's eyes met the stares from around the table. "You're right," she answered their unspoken comment. "It wasn't about them as much as it was about me."

"Haven't you felt the loneliness of not having a partner to walk with you through life?" Inconvenient Heart Attack asked.

"I don't allow myself to get caught up in that. If I don't think about it, I'm not forced to deal with it. Even though David has been gone for months at a time, Lisa is home when she's not in class. She told Jake she preferred to hang out at our house instead of anywhere else most of the time. I make them go out on dates to give them time by themselves, but as I told you guys before, they are both math nerds more comfortable at home.

"Lisa has mentioned I ought to consider dating again, but I don't let that talk get very far. She's my best friend, but that topic still sounds weird for me and my daughter. Plus, I would have to deal with tracking Brandon down and getting his signature on a divorce certificate. Honestly, it's strange to be sitting here talking to a group of near strangers about my lack of a love life. So why aren't the rest of you besides Carol in a relationship?" Paula grinned with they squirmed at the topic's being turned on them.

"Waiting on Mr. Right," One Month Sober said.

"Catherine wouldn't approve," Pops said.

"Too soon after Janie Ruth's death," Pastor Widower said. "I'm not ruling it out but not looking, either. Janie Ruth made me promise to marry again if the Lord took her and brought somebody else to me. We promised that if either of us survived the other and remarried, our graves would still be next to one another."

Laticia chuckled, reminding the group she was still taking in every word they said.

"And you, Miss Friendly?" Paula asked.

Laticia smiled. "I might have a little something getting started. We're just talking, but you never know."

"Mr. Important?" Paula asked. "You can't tell me a good looking athlete like you isn't involved with at least one woman?"

Easton blushed, the first time he ever remembered doing so. "I guess I'm one of those people who gets so locked in to whatever I'm doing that I don't focus on much else. It was baseball in college—I mean, I had a girlfriend, but she would tell you I was married to baseball for as much attention as I gave her. Reflecting on it now, I feel embarrassed. I tried going on a few dates later on, but I couldn't pay attention. Gosh, that sounds awful, doesn't it?" He flashed a sheepish grin and added, "Maybe I should get Sherrill to schedule a date for me."

"Yeah, and what *about* her?" Paula pressed. "She sounds as available as you are."

"Sherrill? Oh no, I don't view her that way."

"And why not?" Paula was clearly having fun turning the focus away from her own personal life. "Is she good looking?"

The heat surged through Mr. Important's face and ears. "I don't know."

"Oh, come on, pretty boy, you mean to tell me you haven't noticed how the only woman you spend any significant time with looks?"

"We text and talk on the phone, so I'm not looking at her. Besides, we were talking about you."

"No, we need to sort this out, don't we folks?"

"Well, is she pretty?" Pastor Widower asked.

"Not you, too," Mr. Important retorted. "Paula already asked that."

"But you didn't answer," Paula said. "Come on, sweetie, it's an easy question: Is Sherrill pretty?"

"Sure, I suppose. There, you happy?"

"That wasn't so hard, now was it, cupcake?"

"What's with the pet names? You working on your flirt game?"

"Nah, just seeing how red we can turn you." Everyone at the table burst out laughing.

Laticia asked, "Mr. Sterling, should I turn the air conditioning on for you?"

"The thing is," Easton replied, ignoring the laughter, "I have noticed a change in her since she—"

"Since she what?" Paula asked, realizing he was serious.

"Since she gave her life to God or whatever." Turning to Pastor Widower, he continued, "I don't even know if that's the right terminology."

"That's one way to say it. She gave her life to Jesus, to God. She got saved, or followed Jesus. Those work, too. What changes have you seen in her?"

"It's difficult to describe, other than she doesn't smart talk me as much as she once did. Just boss and assistant stuff—we have this relationship where we can be very frank with one another without having to worry about hurting the other one's feelings. Lately, though, she has been—*kinder* is an appropriate word. She used to be all business all the time, which was fine by me, but now, she mentions other topics. She seems more interesting, I guess is the way to describe what I mean. But I never…"

"Sounds like you'd better before somebody else comes along and scoops her up for his own," Paula said.

"Nah, she's not interested in me like that."

"You never know. You didn't believe you could be interested in her like that five minutes ago, but we've got you wondering now, don't we?"

"I plead the Fifth," Easton said as the heat swelled again. "Let's talk about you again, Miss Flirt."

"I can't even imagine speaking like that to somebody anywhere else. I was just messing with you."

"Oh, come on, sugar, you can dish it out but you can't take it?"

It was Paula's turn to flush. "I don't even understand what made me do that. Too much sweet potato pie?"

"If you're trying to pick up a senior citizen, that might be a better approach."

"Hey, I'm still sitting here wide awake," Pops intervened.

"Sorry."

"Oh, you're fine." He winked at Laticia. "Tell 'em, girl."

"Y'all need any—I mean *any*—advice on how to flirt, Pops here has got you covered. He's the best, I don't care what age."

Pops crossed his arms triumphantly. "Secret is, you've got to be absolutely harmless. Neither of you is in any danger of that soon, so the king keeps his crown. Call me up in fifty years, though, and we'll talk."

Paula folded her arms across her middle and sank back against her chair. "I'm not sure I've ever had a moment in adulthood where I have sat back and enjoyed life without having my kids with me. Thanks, everybody. For real, I've never been able to tell my complete story from start to finish."

Turning to Inconvenient Heart Attack, Paula said, "Your turn."

INCONVENIENT HEART ATTACK

26

"Hi, everyone, my name is Carol. Did you realize that the highest rates of heart attacks are at Thanksgiving and Christmas?" Inconvenient Heart Attack started.

"Yes, I did," Pastor Widower replied. "I'm guessing that's related to why you're here tonight."

"Irv—that's my husband—didn't want to ruin Thanksgiving or Christmas for the family. We should have been gathered around our dining room table this afternoon. Irv and I are close to being empty nesters, but our two children who have graduated our home live within a twenty-minute drive of us. Sunday lunch at our house is standard, but we make special occasions of getting together for Thanksgiving and Christmas, too. Anyway, I'm all over the place—sorry, but I needed to set up why my husband did what he did—or, better said, didn't do.

"Irv started having some discomfort about two

weeks ago. He chalked it up to some spicy food, but it didn't go away. Then, he started getting short of breath doing ordinary things around the house. Last week, he said something about getting the boys to help him get the Christmas decorations down from the attic, and he's always done that by himself. When I told him it sounded like a heart issue and he needed to go see a doctor, he put me off. He said he'd go after the holidays, but it wasn't a convenient time for heart problems. Well, Tuesday night, Irv suffered a most inconvenient heart attack that almost ruined every holiday from now on."

"Is he okay?" Army Mom asked, feeling more than a little ashamed for rejecting Carol's earlier attempts to comfort her. *When will I learn not to judge people without walking a mile or two in their shoes?*

"Yes, he will be. We weren't so positive on Tuesday night, though." She pulled a tissue from her purse and dabbed the corners of her eyes. "We had just had a good-natured argument that we repeat every year. I wanted to watch a Christmas movie, and he said I had to wait until after Thanksgiving. We weren't mad, mind you. After we clean up the supper dishes every night, we sit down in our recliners to watch TV for a little while. I usually let him pick what we watch as long as he turns it on *Wheel of Fortune* first.

"There's a little table in between the recliners where we keep the remote. Around this time of year, I'll grab the remote before he does and say something about finding a Christmas movie. He'll say, 'Oh no, you don't. No Christmas until after Thanksgiving.' Then, he'll go on a little mini-rant about how 'they' have commercialized Christmas and 'they' aren't taking Thanksgiving from our family. After he's finished his speech, we'll sit for a little while before I reach over and hand him the remote. We've done that same thing since the kids started hanging out with their friends more than they hang out with us. Well, Tuesday night, Irv said his spiel, and I waited for a minute and reached over to hand him the remote. He didn't take it at first, so I gave him a little longer, but he still didn't reach for it, so I looked over at him and recognized something was wrong.

"His head had slumped forward, and he was already starting to turn blue. I called 9-1-1 right off and tried to sit him up. I patted his cheek and told him help was on the way and begged him not to leave me. We live two blocks away from a fire station, which is a nuisance more often than not, but it saved Irv's life. Thank goodness, the EMT's arrived in about three minutes, and they revived him and got him to the hospital within twenty minutes. They stabilized him, and he had heart surgery on Wednesday morning—five bypasses. The doctor told us if the EMTs hadn't gotten to him when they did, I'd be planning a funeral instead of sitting in the waiting room.

"Irv took five or six steps late this afternoon—first time he's been out of the bed since the surgery. It wore him down, so he'll be out for a while. His afternoon nurse told me he'd be sleeping long enough for me to come over here and get something to eat. Since I had eaten nothing but vending machine food since Tuesday night, fried chicken, green beans, and hash brown casserole sounded appetizing. Irv's diet will require some major changes after this, and I guess mine will change with his. I figured I'd enjoy some fried food one last time without the guilt that he can't eat it."

"How long before he'll go home?" Pastor asked.

"Another couple of days, depending on how his rehab goes. Irv's, well, heartbroken that he caused everybody to miss Thanksgiving. He considers his heart attack inconvenient for everybody. He's the only patient in the cardiac unit over there, and he's getting the best care. They say it's unusual to have just one patient on Thanksgiving, so I might return and find some company on Irv's floor. They've been so good to check on us, but I guess being their one patient brings those privileges. They even let us sleep for a few hours at night before they come in to prod and poke him.

"I sat here listening to all your stories and determined that we've lived a normal life by comparison. Well, except how we brought our kids into the family in the first place, Irv and me." She paused and looked around the table. *Am I rambling? I understand I'm sleep deprived and probably not making a lick of sense.* They all looked interested, though, so she continued.

"Irv and I grew up in the same community up in north Mississippi. We graduated in the same class, and we were friends, but we never even dreamed of dating—at least I didn't. We ended up going to college down here in south Mississippi, and sometimes I would ride home with him. It made no sense for both of us to drive four hours each way by ourselves. Since we were both business majors, we wound up in several classes and study groups together. One night, our group of about fifteen thinned out a little after 10:30, and I said something out loud about having too much caffeine in me to sleep. I wondered if anybody wanted to go with me to the midnight showing of *The Rocky Horror Picture Show* on the lawn behind the student union. Our student activities group always showed *Rocky Horror* during the week of Halloween when we were in college, and I had never been. I figured several from our group would take me up on it, but only Irv did. Bless his heart, he didn't want me to appear rejected in front of our friends.

"He had been to see the show during our freshman year, so he told me we needed a quick shopping trip before the movie started. I thought it insane to be out buying rice and squirt guns and a deck of cards and newspapers and toilet paper. A college student on a budget shouldn't plop down twenty bucks on a bunch of stuff that wouldn't last more than the next couple of hours. I remember telling Irv the cashier would consider us half slap crazy, but he said she might surprise me. When our turn in line came, the girl rang our stuff up and said that she hoped we enjoyed the show. I looked at Irv and he winked at me. It was totally appropriate at that moment, but something in me saw something in him I had never seen, a playfulness that I guess took a while to show itself.

"I assumed we arrived to the union in plenty of time at 11:30, maybe even awkwardly early, but the lawn filled up fast behind us. We found a spot in the middle of the setup, a location Irv considered an ideal place to both see the movie and take part in it. He coached me through the important parts like covering your head with newspaper so we didn't get 'rained' on. When the time came to throw our rice and our rolls of toilet paper, he made sure I was ready.

"I can't remember ever having a more unexpected fun time than I did that night. By the end of the show, the caffeine that had kept me awake had long worn off, but adrenaline had taken over. Irv got a kick out of watching me enjoying myself so much. After the movie finished, the student association that sponsored the event asked for volunteers to help clean up the lawn. Almost everybody returned to their dorms to sleep before classes the next day. I told Irv I wanted to help because I felt sorry for the students who had to clean up and then wake up for class a few hours later, even though we did, too. He didn't want me walking back to my dorm by myself, so he stayed and walked with me since it was the middle of the morning.

"We helped for around thirty minutes, and I rattled on the entire time about what fun I had. Irv kept laughing at me. He didn't realize what he was getting into when he introduced me to *Rocky Horror*. Or perhaps he did. Anyway, my dorm wasn't far, so I was still all bubbly when we got there. He said, 'Well, here we are.' I threw my arms around him and kissed him right on the mouth. I hadn't planned it. I hadn't even thought about it. It just—I don't know—*happened*. I remember him saying, 'Well, all right...' but I was already spinning around to walk inside. When I glanced back to wave goodbye, he was still standing there with his mouth open, trying to figure out what had just happened. I kept walking toward the elevator, as happy as I had ever been in my life."

Carol saw that the others at the table all wore smiles. One Month Sober laughed and extended her hands toward Mr. Important and Army Mom. "It appears we've been approaching relationships all wrong."

"It's not the recommended path to love, I'll give you that, but, hey, celebrated our thirty-second anniversary this summer."

"What happened the next day after you kissed him? I mean, how did you know…"

"Here's the deal: I *didn't* know anything. I didn't *think* anything. I just did it. And I promise, I hadn't had a drop to drink."

"Well, what happened next?" One Month Sober pressed.

"When I woke up the next morning, I wondered *what on earth have I done*? I couldn't pay attention during my economics class, but I was glad it was a class Irv didn't have with me. I started going through all the ways he might respond, but I couldn't figure out how I felt, much less how he did. I decided I needed to apologize. He had a class in another building right after my class, so I returned to my dorm to rehearse what I wanted to say, thinking I had time for that. When I walked in the lobby, there stood Irv, holding a bunch of flowers. He said something goofy like, 'Remember, you started this.' And, well, we've never looked back. We dated through the rest of college and got married a week after we graduated."

"And then you had kids," Pastor Widower said.

"And then we had kids. That's the fascinating part of our story."

"With how you and your husband started dating and all, I think it has been interesting already," One Month Sober offered.

"Ours was a storybook romance, I guess you could say, looking back on it now. We were married at the church back home, a typical old-fashioned wedding with lots of bridesmaids and groomsmen and candles and flowers. Like I had envisioned since I was a young girl, I wore a long, flowing white gown, and my dad walked me down the aisle. Irv's dad was his best man, and he was so handsome—Irv, that is. He started losing his hair about three or four years later, but it didn't matter because I didn't fall in love with his hair. It's funny when someone who didn't know us when we married looks at one of our wedding photos. One of Irv's buddies even told me it must have been a photo from my first wedding, so that's what we say when we anybody notices our wedding photos for the first time.

"After the ceremony, we stayed overnight in Tupelo and drove to Destin for a week for our honeymoon. We spent the week after our beach trip packing to move to Mobile. Irv had landed an accounting job at a food services company, and I pursued my real estate license. It was the way you draw it up for your young adult life: college, love, graduation, marriage, fresh jobs in an unknown city we couldn't wait to explore. I got in with a reputable agency at a time of a boom in real estate in the Mobile suburbs, and Irv's company promoted him twice in his first five years there. We built our savings account for the next chapter in our boring, I-hate-you life.

"The problem was, I wasn't getting pregnant." She giggled at what she would say next. "It wasn't for a lack of trying. That part was fun. But one year of failure to get pregnant turned into a second and a third. We made appointments with various doctors, and both of us went through all sorts of tests. None of them told us why we weren't getting pregnant. So we changed our eating habits, our exercise habits, our sleeping habits—seemed like we flipped our lives upside down trying to figure out how to have a baby. We kept a close eye on my cycle so much that Irv would take a long lunch sometimes—" She blushed. "Sorry, that's more information than you want to hear and more than I've ever shared with a group of almost strangers, for sure."

Laticia chimed in. "Honey, y'all are like family by now, don't you think? You're safe to go on with your story."

"Well, anyway, we kept trying and kept getting tested and kept not getting pregnant. We looked at fertility treatments and would have pursued them, but about that time, we had a guest speaker at church one Sunday night. She and her husband might as well have been telling our story, how they tried for years to have children. They talked about the strain it put on their marriage. Irv and I had not paid attention to the stress that had crept into our relationship, but it was there, nonetheless. He had said nothing to me, but he told me later that he went through feelings of being less than a real man because he couldn't give me children. It didn't help that he was approaching his thirties and balding fast. While he was blaming himself, I thought it was my fault and that I was letting him down.

"This lady and her husband ended up adopting siblings—a boy and a girl—when the children were sixteen months and three months old. She talked about the difficulties of their early years but told how they became a loving family. Their kids were a senior and junior in high school that year. When she finished her presentation, her husband and kids joined her on stage, and they looked like such a normal, content family. I looked up at Irv, and he squeezed my hand. That's when I believed that one day, that would be us standing on a stage somewhere, telling how the Lord had built our family through adoption. Irv and I had both grown up in loving two-parent homes, and we decided to give a poor child without parents a loving environment and save him or her from an awful life. We couldn't have been more naïve about how the adoption process works."

"I can see that," Pastor Widower said. "I have worked with quite a few families who want to live out the biblical mandate to 'help orphans in their distress.' Even though most of the families I counseled had honorable intentions, they didn't always count the cost."

"What do you mean by that?" Army Mom asked.

"Some believe they want to adopt because they see how somebody else's adoption turned out and then find it harder and more complicated than they ever dreamed. Same thing with foster care—perhaps more so. Understand, every case starts with something bad—often downright awful—happening to the child. Add to it foster parents in the system for the wrong reasons—"

"What do you mean by *wrong reasons*?" One Month Sober asked.

"Social workers pick up kids from foster parents sometimes, and those kids bring one or two sets of clothes, old and dirty and way too big or small. Those parents are in it for the check they get. It's obvious they are not using the money to care for their foster children. Sometimes, you can identify them from the beginning— the ones who go to the training and at the first opportunity for questions, they ask when their first check will arrive. They rarely get recommended as foster parents, but it might surprise you how many people abuse the system to make money on these poor children."

"No way," Easton said. "Why, when there are an endless number of other legitimate ways to make a living, would you stoop to taking advantage of foster kids? It seems like a crooked method of making not a lot of money."

"No question. Meanwhile, wonderful families who don't shortcut the process get grouped in with those in the system for their own gain. It can be one heartbreak after another for those who are trying to foster and adopt for noble reasons. And even those parents with right intentions are misguided when they believe they can be a child's savior. These are children we're talking about, not projects or charity cases. Most of the time, the issues come from a lack of understanding of everything adoption and foster care entail."

Carol jumped back in. "I can attest to that. When Irv and I drove home from church that night, we talked about our feelings, and we prayed about adopting. We sensed a peace about going in that direction, so we planned to call to an adoption agency the next day. I planned to shop for baby stuff the next weekend. We would transition the guest room in our house to a baby's room, and we'd be all set. Because the lady who spoke at church talked about how many kids there are waiting to be adopted, we figured we could be ready to take one of them within a month. We decided we wanted to adopt a baby that looked like us as much as possible. Oh, how incredibly stupid we sounded during that first meeting with the adoption agency."

27

"I'm not sure what we expected—maybe they had prospects in the back for us to choose from—I don't know. Anyway, we insisted on meeting with them as soon as possible. We called on Monday and set up an appointment for Friday afternoon that same week. I can only imagine how the social worker we met with perceived us. She was nice but firm. We discovered how long adoption took, the steps we needed to take to qualify, and how *expensive* it would be. I'm jumping ahead of myself a bit, but we understand enough now to realize the process filters out people in it for the wrong reasons.

"That first session set us back for a while, but we broke the news to our small group at church regarding our decision to adopt and recapped our meeting with the adoption agency. It turned out two sets of parents who had adopted in our group agreed to come alongside us and teach us how adoption really worked. The ways our guest speaker presented the adoption process made them cringe. Over the next two years it took our adoption to go through, they gave us the lowdown—the good, the bad, and the ugly. They came over and helped us prepare our home for children. Goodness gracious, the things you never consider in childproofing a house.

"Fast forward close to two years, and we had grown more and more impatient. We could no nothing else but wait for a phone call. That was the hardest part: waiting. As long as we had something to *do*—filling out the mountain of paperwork or making adjustments to our home or preparing for yet another interview—we sensed we were making progress. When nothing remained but to wait, Irv and I both became restless. I got sick from the stress—I mean, can you imagine a pregnancy lasting two years? I called it the morning sickness I never experienced. Our preparation period lasted much longer than a biological pregnancy, and there was no end in sight. I didn't dare see a doctor about my stress, though, because I didn't want to take any chances with pushing back the process any further.

"When I imagined I couldn't take it any longer, the phone rang. Irv had just walked in, and we sensed this was the call. I still remember the first words out of our social worker's mouth: 'Are you sitting?' I told her yes, and she asked what we thought of twins. My first notion was how adorable they were... when they belonged to someone else. It had been two years, though, and I didn't dare shoot myself in the foot by saying something stupid. The phone was on speaker so Irv could listen, and I saw the color drain from his face. We exchanged a glance that said *I'm scared, but let's hear her out.* I'll save you the details, but later that week, we met the cutest little African-American boy twins. It was a far cry from where we saw this adoption journey going in the beginning. By the time our path brought us to twins that looked nothing like us, we couldn't have been happier. We said yes, and Isaiah and Jeremiah soon became our forever children."

"Isaiah and Jeremiah," Pastor Widower echoed. "Count me a fan of those names."

"Well, that's far from the climax of our family's story. It was a significant change for Irv and me to have a child, much less two children at once, much less two black babies for whom we had not prepared family and friends. They were delightful babies, however, and they slept through the night soon after they came home with us. Even though adoption was expensive, we were in good enough financial shape for me to stay home full time, so I took a hiatus from the real estate business. Later, I planned to work from home for my agency to supplement Irv's income. But then we moved. Anybody want to guess why?"

"Mobile, so I'm guessing hurricane," Mr. Important suggested.

"Try again."

Pops raised his hand. "My sister lived in Mobile for a while back in the day, and lightning struck her house three separate times. Am I close?"

"Nope."

"Irv lost his job or got transferred," Army Mom guessed.

"No, thank goodness, as least not yet. I was jumping right into the fire with mom duties, so the last thing we needed was job issues."

One Month Sober shrugged her shoulders. "Speaking of fire, was that why you moved?"

"Nope. Pastor?"

"Unexpected visit from a social worker who found something that didn't check out? I've seen it happen. We came together as a church at the last minute to add a room to one of our deacons' houses before their adopted children came home once."

"No, we checked that list four or five times before our boys arrived. Laticia, you want to give it a shot?"

Laticia sat bolt upright. "Girl, you were pregnant, and y'all didn't have enough room!"

Army Mom exclaimed, "And your stress was real morning sickness!"

Carol smiled and nodded. "Pregnant, indeed. With twin girls."

"Oh. My. Word."

Carol reached for her phone sitting in the middle of the table and pulled up a family photo from her daughters' high school graduation. "We went from zero to four in less than a year. Is it possible for us to look more different?" Carol's dark flowing tresses contrasted with Irv's chrome dome while two identical dark-skinned brothers stood with their arms around two identical blonde-haired, blue-eyed sisters. "The all-American family, right?"

The diners passed the phone around the table. When it reached Pops, he said, "Bet y'all never get strange looks in public."

"You can't imagine the things people assume they have the freedom to share with us. For Irv and me, who grew up in such sheltered homes, it has been quite an education in the ugly side of mankind. But just like we knew no different childhoods from our own, our kids have known nothing but growing up with one another. It came as no surprise that they started asking questions early about how they looked identical to one sister or brother, but not at all like the others. They have always embraced how they came to be a part of our unique family, though."

One Month Sober laughed at an image. "I bet they made life difficult for their teachers. When I was in middle school, I dreamed of having a twin, especially in a class I didn't enjoy. That included most of them. I wondered what it would be like to swap places with my imaginary twin, whom I imagined loving the subjects I hated."

"Well, let me tell you about our kids and school. The boys were a grade ahead of the girls, and most people couldn't tell either set apart. When they started middle school, the boys graduated into full-fledged jokesters. They switched classes whenever they took a notion—Irv and I never encouraged that, just to be clear—and even took tests for one another. We punished them for it, though we discovered it when they ratted themselves out a year after it first happened; their teachers never knew. I asked the kids how they got away with it, and

Isaiah said, 'Mom, white people think all black folks look alike anyway, so they've got no shot with us.' They had heard that so often under people's breaths that Isaiah's matter-of-fact statement was funny and sad at the same time. The girls saw how much fun the boys had switching places, so they tried it, too.

"Their classmates who had known them since they started school could tell them apart, but most people just called them the Turner twins—"

"Oh, your sons are Isaiah and Jeremiah Turner?" Pops interrupted. "They played ball at the county school?"

"That's right."

"I thought their names sounded familiar. They were incredible ballplayers in high school. My son is a sportswriter, and I go with him to a lot of games, so I remember them playing football, basketball, and baseball. They were good in all three, too. I remember the night Isaiah dropped forty-three points on a talented team from Alabama in Gulfport's tournament... or was that Jeremiah?"

Carol grinned. "They claim they never switched places in sports—too difficult to switch jerseys. It's funny you mention that specific game, though. If you remember how many points Isaiah scored, you may also remember he picked up his third foul right before halftime. Jeremiah came out strong in the second half, so after the game Irv and I wondered aloud about a halftime switcheroo. Jeremiah pouted and asked us if we doubted his ability to take over a game. We said no and assumed they told us the truth. As we lay in bed that night, Irv said, 'You realize they never gave us a direct answer.' They still maintain they didn't take the chance of switching places in sports—too much to lose if they got caught.

"We enjoyed so much watching them play. Everybody else loved seeing our boys with numbers on their backs to tell them apart. Anyway, I told you people called them the Turner twins—when they started middle school and high school, they were the *only* Turner twins. The next year, we showed up to parent night and introduced ourselves to Kate and Beth's teachers as the parents of the Turner twins. They wrinkled their brows, wondering why we came back to visit after Isaiah and Jeremiah had moved on to the next grade. We informed them the girl Turner twins belonged to us, too. Several teachers blessed our hearts."

"Were your girls pranksters, too?" One Month Sober asked.

"Not by nature as much as proximity with Isaiah and Jeremiah. The boys challenged the girls to hijinks, and our daughters didn't back down. So, yeah, just when the teachers thought they had figured out which one was which, they pulled something to confuse them again."

"Like what?"

"Well, the girls took most of their classes together, so at least the teachers didn't have to worry about them switching places like the boys did—not that they ever figured out the boys' misdeeds. The girls didn't dress alike most days, so their teachers listened for one of their friends to call them by name, and then they called them either *Kate* or *Beth* with confidence. The girl twins tested how well their teachers recognized them by getting one of their classmates to call one of them by the *other twin's name* as they walked in the classroom."

"Did it fool them?"

Carol laughed and shook her head. "Every single time. Homecoming dress-up days were the worst for their poor teachers when the kids would dress alike. I remember the one that took the cake during the boys' senior year. There was one class—one of their science classes—where one teacher taught all four of the Turners in the same class. Bless her heart, the kids had gone to the guidance counselor the previous spring and begged her to give them the experience of having at least one class all together. Anyway, one of the dress-up days during homecoming week that year was Twins Day. Now, you might imagine Twins Day would have been a bummer for my kids, but they loved it. Isaiah and Kate dressed in blue jeans and matching T-shirts and tennis shoes. Jeremiah and Beth dressed in khakis, matching button-downs, and loafers. Everybody at school took pictures of them that day."

"Sounds as if their childhood was about as perfect as yours," Army Mom said.

"Oh, heavens no. We made lots of wonderful memories and we wouldn't trade the experience of raising our two sets of twins for the world, but people still said and did thoughtless things to them. Nothing overly cruel, just thoughtless and ignorant. Irv and I grew up going to school with black students. We attended class with them, played sports with them, took part in clubs with them, and all. I never considered that we—white students, I mean—excluded them from our study groups. I don't remember it being intentional. We hung out with other white classmates on weekends, and they hung out with other blacks. We didn't go on near as many overnight school trips as they seem to nowadays, but when we did, whites and blacks didn't stay in the same room. That's just the way it was, and we didn't stop to ask why. I wish I had.

"Before we adopted Jeremiah and Isaiah, I would have told you our society has made significant progress in racial relations. Now, I think that was my naïveté showing. After some of my boy twins' experiences, I've dialed back my optimism a few degrees. I try to see the best in others, but people can be thoughtless sometimes. I'll leave it at that unless you want specifics."

Mr. Important said, "Dang it, I do. I would pitch up and in to an opponent who insulted one of my black teammates as sure as I would one of my white team-mates." What kind of mess did your sons endure?"

"Some of it's the usual stuff: name calling on the playground, comments from football parents about a black kid's mental ability to play quarterback when Jeremiah threw an interception—stuff like that, mostly. Sometimes, other parents who didn't know us made prejudicial statements—nothing against the twins in particular—and later ask us who our son was." Carol chuckled. "'The twins,' we'd say. Everybody noticed the twins. You couldn't watch any of the sports they played more than a few minutes before you picked them out. Irv got a kick out of being the dad of the best athletes on the field or court because he loved sports but didn't play past Little League. By the time the boy Turner twins got to high school, they experienced few issues with the guys on the team. Being two of the top athletes in the area brings with it plenty of credibility in the high school culture. Most of their teammates spent time at our house, too, adding to our grocery budget.

"In making friends with the white guys, it didn't hurt that the boy twins had two gorgeous blonde twin sisters a grade behind them. Any boy who wanted a date with a girl Turner twin went through the boy Turner twins first. Irv never had to sit in the den cleaning his rifle when a boy showed up for a date with Kate or Beth since Isaiah and Jeremiah had already vetted him. Most boys struggle to ask a cute girl for a date in the first place. But having to go through Isaiah and Jeremiah—well, most of them counted the cost and pursued another girl. That was fine with Irv and me. Just like so many things with their high school years, we didn't learn the dating paradigm until later. I remember wondering out loud how girls as beautiful as ours did not get asked out more than they did, but one day Jeremiah cleared it up for me. Irv smiled and walked away, glad he didn't need to serve as the heavy when boys came calling for our daughters.

"In public, the way our kids hug each other so often seemed to be off-putting to some of our kids' classmates, teachers, and principals. Irv and I are both from families that showed their love through hugs, so we're a hugging family—more than many people are comfortable with, at least in our case. When the four of them were toddlers, most folks found their loving on each other adorable. When the boys started becoming adolescents, some individuals felt the freedom to speak up about it, in particular when they met us through our daughters. The thing is, nobody who bothered to come near our family ever had an issue."

28

"Is one of those yours?" one of the freshman parents asked.

After helping Beth and Kate carry their gear into the high school gym, Carol watched their practice from a distance. She promised herself she would leave before being mistaken as a helicopter mom. As the squad ran through their first routine, Carol was oblivious to a younger woman approaching through the side door. When she noticed, it was too late. Rachel Lambert was chatty, and Carol couldn't escape.

"Two of them are mine," she answered.

"Sisters?"

Carol swallowed her first answer. She would save it to tell Irv later. Instead, she nodded.

"What grade?" Rachel pressed.

"Juniors."

"Oh, they're in the same grade. Are they twins?"

A lengthy pause. "Yes, identical, the two blonde-haired girls. Yours?"

"Whitley Anne is a freshman this year. She was head cheerleader in middle school, and she cheers on a competitive team that came in third in nationals last year. Do your girls do competitive cheer?"

"Uh, no, they just enjoy cheering for the school teams."

Rachel filled in Carol on her daughter's experience and expertise in the cheerleading realm, but Carol's mind ventured toward an escape route. She found it when Whitley Anne bobbled while climbing a pyramid. "No, no, no, you've got to keep your focus," Rachel scolded under her breath as though her thoughts were hardwired to her daughter's. As soon as Carol saw her lean forward to move closer to the second attempt at the pyramid, she excused herself and made her way to her car. Rachel wouldn't notice her absence, she was sure. A week later, she wished she had stuck around to relate more of her family history.

WHEN CAROL DROPPED off Beth and Kate at practice, she noticed the cheerleaders gathering on the track in front of the home side of the football stadium. Friday night lights were a mere two weeks away, and Carol was looking forward to it. With her window down to enjoy an unseasonable breeze, she heard whistles from the football practice field and musical notes from the band's fall routine drifting over the hill. She imagined the sights, sounds, and smells of the last few Friday nights of her sons' senior year.

With nothing in particular to do until a mid-morning meeting, Carol parked and strolled to the shade of an oak tree on the hill beyond the south end zone. She stood close enough to check out the girls' routines and far enough away, she hoped, to avoid interaction with the freshman cheerleader moms who attended every practice. After three routines, the girls took a break, and Carol turned to walk to her car and almost ran smack into Rachel Lambert.

"Oh, Carol, I'm glad I caught you. How are you *doing?*"

"I'm fine, just watching the girls for a while before a meeting this morning." *Take the hint... take the hint...*

Rachel did not take the hint.

"I am just loving Whitley Anne's being a part of the varsity cheer squad. Of course, she's used to calling the shots—she was the head cheerleader on the middle school team."

"Of course."

"I told her, I said, 'Now, Whitley Anne, wait your turn. Your ideas might be better than the older girls, but you need to give them time to get acquainted with you first.' Of course, I've been talking to the other freshman cheer moms, and we've come up with a few ideas to help the team bond."

"Of course."

"Well, so many of the older girls have never done competitive cheer like Whitley Anne and the others, so we thought we'd invite the girls over for a swim party.

That might give the older girls a chance to get to know the younger ones better and give the freshman girls more courage to speak up about their ideas."

"Their ideas?"

"Oh, we thought—that is, the girls thought entering more competitions might make us better prepared for the state cheer competition, even help us qualify for nationals. Of course, some of those competitions are out of state, and we would miss two Friday games."

"Of course. But miss football games for a cheer competition?"

"Sure, the squads at nationals do it. You've just got to prioritize. Plus, it gives the middle school girls a chance to cheer at high school games. I promise they'll get a kick out of that."

"*Prioritize,*" Carol repeated, dumbfounded.

"Of course. I'm glad you're on board, then. I'll get back with you on specifics of the swim party. If we can get the girls and parents together at one time..."

"You mean without their sponsor?"

"Well, yes, I guess so. If we approach the school administration with our ideas first... I mean, if they want parent participation..." Rachel walked away before Carol could counter. Carol followed for several steps before she lost her chance.

"I'm not so sure. My girls—"

Rachel wheeled around to face Carol again. "Oh, I almost forgot." She lowered her voice to a whisper. "Of course, I'm not one to speak ill of anybody else's daughter..."

Of course you're not. Carol later figured out a half-dozen ways she might have escaped the rest of the conversation running pell mell toward gossip that she habitually attempted to avoid. At the moment, though, she froze.

"One day after practice last week, the girls were gathering their poms in the gym when the football team walked through, going from the weight room to the field. Anyway, I'm positive it was one of your daughters I observed hugging..." Here she whispered, "... a *black* boy."

"Okay." *Let's see how far she will take this.*

"I'm not judging, but I thought I would bring it to your attention."

If you're not judging, why did you think it deserves my attention?

Carol pulled out her phone.

Rachel's fingers moved to her lips. "Oh, I hope I didn't get her in trouble."

"Why would she be in trouble?"

"I mean, you know..."

"No, Rachel, I don't. Is this boy in this picture the one who hugged her?" She turned her phone around to reveal a photo of Isaiah. Or it could have been Jeremiah, as far as anyone who didn't know the male Turner twins knew.

Rachel's face brightened. "Yes, I believe that's him. I mean, I can't be sure. They all look alike, you know, but I believe that's him."

Carol nodded. "Thought so."

"What are you going to do? Like I said, I'm not trying to stir up trouble, but I thought you should be aware. Since you have a picture of him on your phone, he's on your radar? I mean, if Whitley Anne... well, let's just say that we've had a talk regarding this very thing."

"Tell you what, Rachel, let me show you another photo to make *double* sure we're talking about the same boy." Carol handed the phone across with her family photo still facing herself. When Rachel turned the phone to look at Irv and Carol with their twin black sons and twin white daughters, the color drained from her face.

"But... I don't understand. Why are these boys...?"

"What you witnessed, Rachel, was Beth or Kate hugging Isaiah or Jeremiah—one of her *brothers*."

Rachel took a step back before extending her arm to return Carol's phone. "I'm so sorry. I didn't realize..." she retreated. Trying to regain control of the conversation, she offered, "So let me get this straight: You have twin sons—adopted, I assume—*and* twin daughters?"

"Obviously."

"I bet that's a remarkable story."

"It is."

"I would love to hear it."

"I love to tell our family's story, Rachel, but here's the thing: You pointed your racist comments toward *my son*."

"But I'm not a racist," Rachel insisted in full retreat mode. "I have black friends. Whitley Anne cheers with the black girls on the team. One of them even came to our house one time for a study group. I was trying to..."

"Let me stop you right there. I won't judge you for the attitude you brought into this conversation. It's far too common, and this is not our first encounter with it.

It's up to you what you do with it from here. I'll judge you by that."

———————

"WHOA, THAT'S STRONG," Army Mom said. "How did she act after that?"

"Avoided me like the plague. I mean, she poked a mama bear, so she was better off keeping her distance. Once you've talked about somebody's kids with such prejudice, there's not much coming back from that."

"Did you tell your kids?"

"No need. It ticked off Irv, but we decided it wouldn't serve much purpose to tell the kids. I talked with the girls to give them a heads up on how the freshman parents might try to hijack their team at the swim party. I was so proud of the seniors and juniors that year. They attended the party, but when one of the freshman parents started talking about competitions, one senior interrupted—with all due politeness, my girls said—and re-established their purpose of cheering for the school's teams. Then, they laid out their plans to encourage the guys on the football team throughout the season with little goodie bags and sticky notes of encouragement on game days. They said several of the younger girls came up to them later and thanked them. It seemed they were ready to live outside of mommy's shadow but couldn't figure out how to express them-selves. The older girls' leadership in that moment did more to bring that squad together than anything else they did. To my knowledge, none of the girls on the team ever heard about my conversation with Rachel Lambert."

One Month Sober touched Carol on the hand and said, "I'm sorry you had to go through that. I deal with prejudice around my extended family sometimes. It makes me cringe every time they make a comment, but I'm never sure whether speaking up will do more harm than good. Sounds like you were firm but polite in a suitable Southern way."

"Thank you. In some ways it was hard to determine what's right below the surface in people, but we discovered plenty of good in people, too. I think Irv had a harder time with it than I did. Several of our boy twins' fathers were real good to walk him through the unique challenges of having black sons, though. They went on a retreat together—the other fathers and sons, too—when our sons were near driving age. It's sad when you send your sons out there in a vehicle with so much trepidation over the color of their skin, besides the usual inexperienced driver angst. You just hope that teaching them to be respectful is enough.

"One time when all our kids were home last year, we discussed our driving records. The kids have lived in this same general area most of their lives and driven the same streets. Irv taught each of them to drive within a year of each other, so they received the same instruction. I've ridden with each of them, too, and our kids are careful drivers, at least with me in the car. The boys shared a car in high school, and so did the girls. We bought two four-door sedans, two years old—no bright colors or fancy rims or tinted windows or loud stereo systems. There's not a dime's worth of difference between them. I had to step up my real estate game while they were in high school, but we bought each of them a car for college. Again, minor variations among the cars—nothing that should draw attention to the drivers. That was the most consistent advice we received for our sons."

"Did it work?" Easton asked.

"When we talked last year, each of the kids had been driving for around ten years. Officers had pulled over Isaiah twelve times in those ten years. Six were in high school after he had left a white friend's house in a white neighborhood. I understand police are trained to spot things out of the ordinary, but six times in two years? Four times, he had to step out of the car while they shone their flashlights around the interior of the car. He didn't get a ticket any of those times, but he has received three speeding tickets for less than ten miles per hour over the speed limit over the years.

"He was stopped twice on the same day for a broken taillight. The first officer let him go with a warning and the second one gave him a ticket. He was driving to the auto parts store to buy a light when the second officer stopped him. Irv asked if he told the policeman about the warning, but Jeremiah didn't want to take the chance of antagonizing him. The last ticket was for rolling through a stop sign. I had warned him the day before regarding that, so that one was on him. So, twelve stops and four tickets. You can chalk up some of those stops to normal driving, but you can't convince me the stops in the same white neighborhood were fair.

"Jeremiah has been pulled over ten times. Officers searched his car twice for no reason other than looking out of place in a white neighborhood late at night. One of his best friends, a white teammate, lives there. Jeremiah has two tickets, one for four miles per hour over the speed limit and one for six over, both by the same officer in that neighborhood, two years apart. He wondered if he should ditch the friendship, but he's too loyal a friend for that. Both of my sons remained self-controlled and polite to the officers, and for the most part, the officers returned their behavior with professionalism and courtesy. Isaiah and Jeremiah have told me they feel guilty until proven innocent, though.

"Now, I have always had great respect and admiration for policemen and firemen and other emergency personnel who work so hard to keep us safe. I still do, but they stopped two young black men who are safe drivers and kind people twenty-two times in ten years. How often are other young black men, ones who didn't get the training my sons did, stopped for little more than their skin color? What happens if they push back even a little when they get stopped for no other reason than their skin color? I can't even imagine what goes through their mothers' hearts."

"You said all of your kids compared their driving records," Pops said. "What about your daughters?"

"Kate was stopped once, as a 'courtesy'—that was the word the officer used—because one of her taillights was out. It was after a late-night study session while she was in college. He told her to get it fixed as soon as she could and to take care. No search. She thanked him and was on her way in less than five minutes. When she told the boy twins that part, they laughed at her and said that none of their stops ever lasted less than fifteen minutes. She asked me later if they were kidding, and I had to tell her I was afraid not.

"Beth is our lead foot. She has been pulled over for speeding on five occasions, every time for ten or more miles per hour over the speed limit. When she was seventeen, she was running late for a service project one of her clubs was doing and was caught going fifty in a thirty-five. The officer questioned why she was speeding, told her to slow it down the rest of the way, and let her go. Total stop time of less than five minutes. Less than a week later, the same officer pulled her over for going eighteen over the limit. He wrote her a ticket that time but handed her a card informing her of defensive driving school. She completed driving school and still has a clean record. They let her go with a warning the other times. She could use a ticket more than any of my other kids.

"The boys have been stopped twenty-two times with six tickets, and the girls have been pulled over six times with one ticket wiped clean by driving school. With so many similar factors, you can't argue with those numbers. The kids pay their own insurance now, but when they were on ours, the insurance for the boys was twice what it was for the girls after tickets for Isaiah and Jeremiah. We had told each of them when they started driving that we would pay for their insurance, but that tickets and accidents that were their fault were on them. Sure enough, Jeremiah and Isaiah's insurance skyrocketed, but with the circumstances, Irv felt it might be piling on to follow through with our pledge. We said nothing to the boys, but I believe they understood and appreciated our not making an issue of it."

In the silence that followed, Easton drummed his fingers on the table. "I'm a salesman who drives an average of a thousand to fifteen hundred miles a week, many of them in a hurry to my next sales call. I can't tell you how many times an officer has pulled me over in those years, but I've deserved all seven or eight tickets and more. For me, it's the price of doing business. Most of the time, the officer tells me to slow it down, and I do... until he's out of sight."

"I didn't mean to get off on this kick about law enforcement," Carol said. "Trust me, I still respect the job they do, and I would put my sons' lives in the hands of the officers I know personally without a second thought. I just want my boys to get a fair shake in life. That's not the only part of life in which they can't escape their skin color. I mean, they're engaged in respectable careers. They give back to the communities where they live. Isaiah is a real estate agent like his mama, but once people look at his photo on a business card or on his agency's website, he gets pigeonholed as a black agent. He's a talented agent for his age, too. He shoots people straight, gives them expert advice, and goes the extra mile to find answers to their questions. Most of the people who list their houses with him are black or Hispanic, though. A few white friends from high school or college swear by him, but that's because they know him. He feels unfairly pigeonholed into a smaller segment of the market than his white counterparts, but he continues to give to the community and treat people like he wants to be treated. Perhaps one day, people will judge him by the content of his character and not the color of his skin.

"Jeremiah works at a decent-sized marketing firm in downtown Harriston. They do considerable contract work for the university. He married one of his colleagues there, a cute girl who happens to be white. They had been dating for a while before they introduced one another to their families. Jeremiah suggested they start with us since our family is integrated already. We fell in love with Rebecca right away and don't care what her skin color is. Her family took longer to warm up to Jeremiah. Remember that officer who gave him two tickets two years apart for just a few miles per hour over the speed limit?"

"Was it her daddy?" Laticia asked.

"Indeed. Our family never goes long without a healthy dose of irony. When Rebecca introduced Jeremiah to her dad, Jeremiah held out his hand, looked him square in the eye, and said, 'Nice to see you again, sir.'"

29

"Did Rebecca's father remember your son?" Laticia asked.

"Oh, yeah. He knew who Jeremiah was when he first pulled him over in the white neighborhood. Rebecca attended a rival school, and her brother played sports against our boy twins. Her dad shook Jeremiah's hand and apologized for the tickets. He explained that once a year, the mayor would order them to write tickets for anybody driving two miles per hour or more over the speed limit on that street, where the mayor just so happened to live. When his wife became fed up with the speeding on their street, she turned up the heat on him. The mayor transferred the pressure to the police chief, who assigned an officer to the mayor's street for three straight days. They hated it, but what were they supposed to do? He said Jeremiah fell victim to the wrath of Operation Appease Verlene—that's what they called their little speed trap off the record—twice in two years. If he had unpleasant feelings toward Jeremiah dating his daughter, I think his empathy for the tickets overrode it.

"After Jeremiah and Rebecca dated for a year, they planned a date at a fancy steakhouse to celebrate. Her dad pulled Jeremiah aside and slipped some money into his hand. My son is usually polite, but he counted the cash right there in front of his girlfriend's father. It amounted to $158, an odd amount. Before he asked—which I'm afraid he would have after counting it out in front of the man—her daddy told him it equaled the cost of the tickets. He wanted to make them right. Jeremiah thought about saying something regarding the uptick in insurance, but since he hadn't paid for that, he let it go and thanked him.

"Rebecca's mother was the harder sell. Like most mothers, I suppose, she had an idea about what her daughter's wedding would look like. She imagined Rebecca's groom *wearing* black but not *being* black. After Jeremiah and Rebecca dated about a year-and-a-half, they started talking marriage. Rebecca told him they might as well elope and let her mother deal with it when they came back as a married couple. I'm glad Jeremiah convinced her to give it some time. After a few more months, I guess her mother changed her mind. She pulled Jeremiah aside one day and told him if he was waiting on her permission before asking her daughter to marry him, he didn't have to wait any longer. Their wedding was beautiful, and the families get along fine.

Jeremiah kept a level head through all of it, but I hate how he has to work so hard to win people over sometimes."

"Is he good with his father-in-law?" Pastor Widower asked.

"Oh, yeah, they're two of a kind. Once they got past the business with the tickets, they've been thick as thieves. They go to ball games together all the time. Irv goes with them sometimes. They are both natural-born pranksters, good-natured stuff, but you better keep your head on a swivel when either of them is around. Jeremiah turned twenty-five right after they got married, and Rebecca cooked dinner for him and both families. She did burrito bowls with close to two dozen bowls of various fixings. Joe kept reminding us to save room for a special dessert. When we finished eating, Joe opened the freezer and pulled out an ice cream cake. When he turned around and showed it to us, we saw a big *25* in the middle, but there was smaller writing around it we couldn't read from across the room. We figured it said *Happy Birthday, Jeremiah,* or something like that. Oh, no. He brought the cake across the kitchen where we could read the words *I Can't Drive* above the twenty-five. That was the speed limit Jeremiah broke on the mayor's street. It made Jeremiah's day, I can tell you."

"What about your other son?" Army Mom asked. "Did he marry a white girl, too?"

"No, he married a beautiful woman of color that he met on a field trip to the civil rights museum near the capitol. She led a tour there for Isaiah's college group one day. They argue about who pursued whom, but they were pretty smitten with each other from the beginning. They talked on the phone every day any time Isaiah was down here on a break from college, and they would meet up halfway on to eat and visit for a while. She worked most Saturdays, but he brought her down to meet us on one of her days off on a Friday. He hadn't told her about his unique family dynamic at that point. That first weekend here was awkward, and she told him the following week she thought they should take a time-out. He came home for spring break the next weekend and moped to his room without even waving to me. I detected something was wrong, but I gave him a few minutes before I opened his door.

"He stared at me with that familiar look. He said, 'Mom, it's not fair. I've gone the extra mile with white folks my entire life so they can see the content of my character because I'm not white enough for them. Now, Aliyah wants to put the brakes on because I'm not black enough. Mom, I don't belong anywhere.' This topic was not unusual for us, but this discussion was one of the toughest. I couldn't figure out what to say to him. Irv and I wondered several times through the years if our sons wouldn't have been better off being adopted by a black family. But deep down, we knew the answer. If a black family had been available to adopt them, they would have gotten preference over us. We couldn't help being born white any more than they could help being born black.

"Isaiah moped around for the rest of that day and

the next. Irv and I felt helpless to encourage him, so we told him we loved him more than usual. He smiled back with his mouth, but not with his eyes. We were sitting at the dinner table that Saturday night watching Isaiah pick at his food when Aliyah texted him and asked to meet at their usual halfway place on Sunday. He responded *yes* a little quicker than I was comfortable with, to be honest with you. They talked, and she said he would be a hard sell to her family when they found out about us. She told Isaiah she couldn't stop thinking about him—and them—and she was ready to move forward if he would still have her. He wanted to pick back up dating her—again, quicker than I would have. Anyway, they met and talked and planned a visit to her family in the Delta for the next weekend.

"Her family took to him right away. He got out in the yard and played football with her brothers and cousins, where he more than held his own. He told Irv when he returned home that he ate the most disgusting things he had ever put in his mouth, but he didn't let on while he was there. Her mama liked him, which Aliyah said counted as the most important thing to accomplish through the first visit. Not long after that, they started talking about getting married. Isaiah wouldn't take that step without the two families—the *entire families* —meeting.

"As much as we might have enjoyed hosting Aliyah's folks down here for a weekend, she insisted we go there to meet her sizable extended family. Her idea was best, but our first impression didn't work out like she and Isaiah wanted since she hadn't warmed them we were white. From the time we arrived, her parents acted standoffish. Four or five of her cousins walked out as soon as Aliyah introduced us as Isaiah's parents. They didn't serve anything scary for lunch—they had a fish fry for us, or at least for the parents they expected. The minute Irv and I cornered Isaiah, we told him how uncomfortable they made us.

"Isaiah looked down at me with those melancholy eyes of his and said, 'Mom, that's how I feel in your world sometimes—like I don't belong.' I told him it wasn't about belonging, but I sensed they were talking about me and judging me. I almost said, 'because of the color of my skin,' but I stopped cold. He gave me an understanding hug and went, 'Mm hmm.' The weight of his life fell heavy on me then, living in a white world where he didn't fit in but not feeling comfortable in Aliyah's realm, either. Irv and I agreed to go back inside to find some common ground. We did, and the tension still existed, but we hung in there. I was glad we had booked a hotel room for the night. We left right after supper, which was phenomenal—Aliyah's uncle smoked some ribs, the best I have ever put in my mouth. Anyway, by the time we checked into the hotel, the day had exhausted me. Irv and I prayed the Lord would help us find a connection when we drove back for lunch the next day. Well, He answered in a fashion we wouldn't have dreamed.

"We ate breakfast at the hotel and checked out around eleven. Aliyah's mother had told us lunch would be ready at 11:30 and that it would upset the menfolks for us to be even a minute late. I think we upset the women because our visit made them miss church since we needed to leave by four o'clock. Well, when we got to the Burches' house, Irv discovered the reason for such a specific lunchtime. Every single man wore a Dallas Cowboys' jersey and hat. Irv informed me the Cowboys and Saints played at noon, and it looked like they would be watching. Irv had been moaning about missing the game all morning, so he was a happy camper. Problem is, Irv is a *huge* Saints fan!

"We sat down early to a delicious lunch—pork chops, potatoes and gravy, all sorts of vegetables—most of which we recognized, and all of which we ate. Everything quieted down after Aliyah's dad prayed over the food. I'm telling you, they flew to work on that food. About two minutes in, Aliyah's Uncle Deldrick said, 'White boy, you a football fan?' Irv's mouth was full, but he nodded. Aliyah scolded her uncle, but about that time, Irv blurted out, 'Who Dat!'

Let me tell you, that table just exploded, all those men laughing at Deldrick. Irv informed them he grew up a Cowboys' fan but would never forgive the current ownership for how they ousted Tom Landry, the longtime head coach of the team. Deldrick grinned back at Irv and said, 'You right, I give you dat.' Irv's color didn't matter after that.

"The men settled into the den to watch the ball game, and Aliyah's mother asked me if I was all into football. I told her I tolerated it, but I'd be just fine to help her clean up after lunch. I've noticed when I make such an offer with any of my friends, they won't hear of my clearing the dishes, much less cleaning them. Patrice set me up at the kitchen sink, and her and all the aunts brought me plates until I had washed them all.

"While I cleaned dishes, I heard the men in the next room watching the game. I'm telling you, my husband held his own as the lone Saints fan in the room. Now, remember, he is an accountant, and he has an accountant's demeanor for the most part. Irv came to that situation as a lifelong football fan, though, not to mention twenty years' experience as a sports dad. Jeremiah and Isaiah can get into games on TV, yelling at the screen and everything. So when those men started doing it, Irv joined in with them. He talked smack to those men, and they gave it right back to him. I called Irv crazy for antagonizing them every time the Saints did something good, but he understood what he was doing. I went outside to talk with the women—my interview, I guess —before halftime, but I walked back inside to go to the bathroom near the end of the game. The Saints won on a last-minute drive, but Irv didn't gloat too much. Funny thing, all the men started congratulating Irv as if he had helped the Saints win.

"Like I was saying, the women walked outside to drink a cup of coffee and sit under their enormous shade tree out back. When everybody was there, Patrice stared at me for a hot second and said, 'Now, tell us all about Isaiah.' So I told them stories from when we adopted him until the present. I shared pranks he had pulled, his devotion to his twin blonde sisters, and the dynamics of being a family that looks like ours. When I recounted how we prepared them to deal with racism and some hurtful things that have happened to them and to us by extension, those ladies said nothing. But they all started nodding as one. I told them how bad it hurt Isaiah when Aliyah called off their relationship and how that made him feel like he didn't belong in either world. Her mama and grandmother put their hands on my arm and said I didn't need to worry about that anymore. Far as I determined, everybody who stuck around to get acquainted with us parted as friends, and Isaiah proposed the next weekend."

One Month Sober smiled and asked, "Where did Isaiah and Aliyah go while y'all met with her family?"

"Oh, they took a drive to see the sights. They drove over to Money, where Emmett Till was murdered. She wanted to show him an abandoned schoolhouse, too, for some reason. Before they left, I asked him if he wanted to watch the game with his dad, but Aliyah said *no way* and pulled him out the door. We would have to sink or swim on our own. He told me later he thought we would be fine if they would give us a chance to show what we had under our skin. Aliyah told me she and Isaiah used the time to talk about alternatives to a big wedding with both families because she planned to marry my son either way. Turns out, she needn't have worried about it. They rented a venue near Jackson, and we met her family halfway, booked up half a hotel with both of our families and friends, and enjoyed a beautiful ceremony. One thing they saved a lot of money on was catering because Aliyah's uncles insisted on doing all the cooking. This venue featured a gigantic shade tree on the property—much like the one on the Burches' property—and they filled the shady spot with grills that morning and started cooking. Even some of Aliyah's cousins who walked out on us came. Jeremiah served as his brother's best man. It was one of the finest days of my life."

30

Pops sat bolt upright in his chair, alarming Laticia sitting next to him. "Mr. Jimmy Lee, you okay?"

"I'm fine, but I may have just connected some dots." Turning to Carol, he asked, "Did you have access to Isaiah and Jeremiah's background?"

"Not much of it. At the beginning of our adoptive journey, we imagined acting as if their former lives didn't exist. We figured the story of what brought them to us would cause them pain. Talk about sticking your head in the sand. The boys weren't far beyond talking age before they started questioning why our skin was white and the girls' was white and theirs was black. We had to tell them we adopted them, but we tried to focus on why we wanted them instead of why their mother didn't. Then, as they got older, we considered their family medical history, especially after the boys started playing sports. With as much natural talent as they showed at an early age, Irv wondered what athletes might have been in their biological family."

"I don't mean to pry..." Pops started.

"Oh, no, it's okay, I don't mind telling as much of their story as is mine to tell. When the boys graduated high school, they came to Irv and me to ask us about something important to them. We expected the topic, and if I'm honest, I had dreaded that day and hoped the life we provided them would suffice. Have I mentioned we were naïve? They started the conversation saying how grateful they were for us, so that made me feel better from the beginning. They wanted to understand their backstory and, if possible, to meet their biological parents. Bless their hearts, they begged us not to consider them ungrateful. I told them I would do everything in my power to get them the answers they wanted. And I did."

"Were you able to find out much?" Pops pressed.

"We knew their mother's name and not much more. She was a teenager when she got pregnant. The social worker told us off the record that the father had been here visiting family when they... you know... and she never told him she was pregnant. She lives in the county not too far from here, I discovered, so I contacted her and asked if she would meet with me. When she didn't respond to my letter for a month, I had almost given up on hearing from her. Then one day, she called. I told her I was reaching out to her because the boys were asking questions regarding their biological family. Although she didn't commit to meeting with me right away, she asked about the boys. She was glad they were living productive lives that she couldn't have provided for them. The longer we talked, the more she seemed to soften toward setting up a meeting. There was a problem, though: she had married, and she and her husband had three young children. She had told her husband about the twins and the adoption, but she hadn't told her kids. I told her to take her time because I didn't want to pressure her.

"Two weeks passed before she called again. After talking to her husband, they agreed she should meet with me, but they were waiting until after we talked to decide whether to say anything to their kids. We met at a coffee shop in town, and our conversation was awkward at first, to say the least."

"HI, EBONY. IT'S ME, CAROL."

"I remember you from your picture."

"I'm sorry, it has been over twenty years, and I didn't want to take for granted..."

"It's okay. When you give your twins away, you never forget the face of their new mother."

"Oh. Uh, do you want to order? It's on me."

"Thanks, but I'll get my own." She ordered a cup of Guatemalan blend.

"Anything to eat?"

"No, thanks."

Carol ordered a mocha latte and a raspberry scone. "Sure you don't want to try their scones? They're delicious."

"I'm good."

When their orders were ready, Carol led the way to a table in an area uninhabited by the light mid-morning café traffic. The coffee shop's nooks and crannies invited more private conversations. The two ladies sipped their coffees and made small talk for a few minutes.

Finally, Ebony said, "Tell me about your boys."

Carol recognized it as a rehearsed line, but it set her at ease to hear Ebony say it. She started with when she and Irv took Isaiah and Jeremiah home from the hospital and how they welcomed twin sisters less than a year later. She told the woman who had given birth to her twin boys how they succeeded in school, how they excelled at sports, and how they were positive influences in every area of their lives.

When Carol stopped to sip her coffee and take a bite, Ebony didn't fill the lapse in conversation right away. After a long pause, she offered, "Seems ironic, doesn't it, Ms. Carol, that a black girl named Ebony gave up her black twins to a white family to raise?" When Carol struggled to respond, she asked, "Did you and Mr. Irv ever wonder why I picked you? I had choices—all white couples, but choices."

"First, please call us Irv and Carol. We want to be friends as much as you are willing. To answer your question, we didn't find out until after the adoption that you had other options, and we have wondered all these years why you picked us."

"You and Mr. Irv—you and Irv, I mean—seemed genuine in your faith. You might not believe this about me, but I was an exemplary student in school. I had dreams of going to college. Until I became pregnant, I stayed active in my church—sang in the choir, taught Sunday school to second graders. I made a mistake going to the party where I—you know... I didn't tell anybody about this until I met Darrius—that's my husband now. I didn't give that boy permission to have sex with me. He was an older boy who seemed nice, and he looked good. We started talking and then he kissed me. I realize I shouldn't have, but I liked the attention, and I kissed him back. We ended up in one of the back bedrooms before I told him we shouldn't be there. I kept telling him to stop, but he kept telling me to relax, that it would be okay. Call me young and stupid, Ms. Carol— Carol, I mean—but I believed for the longest time it was my fault for kissing him back and letting it get that far. I should have told somebody, but I held that inside of me for ten years."

"Oh, Ebony," Carol said, reaching across the table to put her hand on Ebony's. Ebony didn't shrink back. "Did you..."

"I told Darrius that I didn't want to pursue charges, but I needed to tell somebody before it got the best of me."

"I'm sorry, I didn't know."

"When the adoption case worker showed me my choices, I told the lady I had made an unbelievable mistake, but I loved Jesus and wanted my sons to love Him, too. I told her nothing mattered more than that— color, financial situation, school district, none of that. She was a powerful woman of faith herself. She told me you guys had been waiting on a baby for two years and that you wanted a white baby in the beginning. But she believed God was softening your hearts toward maybe considering adopting a black child... or two. She said you checked off all the other boxes, too, but you were the least likely to raise the boys black, so to speak. I told her there would be all colors in heaven. I just wanted to make the best choice that would give my boys the best chance of getting there to reunite with me one day. Tell me, Carol, do my... do your sons love Jesus?"

Carol leaned forward and clasped her hands around Ebony's. "God has answered your prayers, Ebony. Isaiah and Jeremiah gave their lives to Christ on the same night at twelve years old. One night after church, they had questions about salvation, so Irv and I sat in their room for over two hours, reading Scripture and answering their questions. It might interest you to learn that the Scripture that helped them cross the line into salvation was one about God's adoption into sonship."

"Galatians four."

"That's the one."

Tears that had sat waiting in the corners of Ebony's eyes streamed down her face unrestrained. Just above a whisper, she said, "I've been praying that for them all these years."

"Well, God answered your prayers and then some. Isaiah and Jeremiah are not perfect, but they are exceptional kids—godly young men now. They are active in church and have such a heart for others. Isaiah led a group at our children's camp this past summer. Jeremiah would have, too, but he felt like God was leading him to go on a mission trip to Guatemala instead."

"I'm so glad to hear that." Daubing the remaining moisture from her eyes, Ebony gathered herself. "I'll be glad to tell you what you want to know about your boys."

"SHE GAVE me as much of their history as she remembered. She had written out a list of family members about four generations back on her side and any medical issues that any of them had. Isaiah and Jeremiah's father's first name was all she recalled about him. She never saw him again and didn't even know who invited him to the party where they met."

"I can relate," said One Month Sober.

Pops asked, "How did your conversation proceed from there?"

"Well, I asked Ebony if she would like to meet the boys she had birthed, now that they could meet her back. She surprised me by answering *no*. Even though she welcomed the opportunity, she didn't want to complicate life for Isaiah and Jeremiah nor the fresh start she had created with her husband and their children. I pushed her a little, but the circumstances around her pregnancy were too painful. She said when all her kids grew up and were a little better equipped to handle that news, then we would revisit the idea."

"Was that all?" Pops asked.

"No, there was one other thing. When we reached what I figured was the end of our conversation, she told me how much it meant to her that we continued to use the names she had given the boys. I'll be honest, I don't remember anybody ever telling us we could change their names. I just expected their names were, well, *their names*. We liked *Isaiah* and *Jeremiah* anyway—they were good biblical names and seemed to fit the twins. I asked Ebony if she had named them after the Old Testament prophets, but she named them after her grandfathers. She said *Isaiah* was her paternal grandfather's middle name. Even though he didn't go by it, she felt it paired well with her maternal grandfather, who went by *Jeremiah*.

"Ebony told me her grandfather died a year before she gave birth to the twins. When she was five, he led her to Jesus and taught her how to read and study the Bible. She was heartbroken when he died, but she said she couldn't imagine having to tell him about getting pregnant out of wedlock. 'Oh, he would have forgiven me and kept on loving me,' she said, 'but it would have messed me up something terrible to have to tell him.'

"Her grandfather used to coach kids in baseball, basketball, and football. There's a plaque with his name on it down at Taylor Park. He started off coaching kids in the black community, but some of his own people got upset with him when he started integrating the teams. She hinted that something else happened after that right before he died, but she wasn't specific."

Pops said, "They got mad at him for going to a white church that had never allowed black people before."

"So you're familiar with her grandfather's story?"

"Ms. Carol, your son is named after Jeremiah Johnson. He was my best friend from when we were five years old until the day he died. Remember I told y'all I started asking my racist father to take my friend Jeremiah to church when we were little boys? That was him. Even though it took the better part of his life, Jeremiah and I eventually walked through those doors together. The Lord took him home through a car accident the next Thursday, but nobody who ever met him has been the same since. Try as you might, you won't find a more integrated church in the city than ours. It's all because of Jeremiah... my Jeremiah, I'll call him. I think about him every single day, and I would love the chance to meet your son and tell him all about his namesake."

Carol's head buried her head in her hands, but she nodded with force. After she came to herself, she pulled a pen and a business card from her purse and circled her phone number and email address. "I would appreciate that, and so would my Jeremiah."

"Let's make it happen soon," Pops said, pulling a business card of his own from his wallet and handing it to Carol.

LONESOME, PARTY OF SIX

31

"Wait a minute," Easton exclaimed. "You're ninety-two years old. Why do you carry business cards?"

Pops grinned. "Son, we're not so different, you and I. You offer business cards so people can stay connected with you for business. Me, I network to fish. People prefer to take fishing advice from an old codger like me than someone who's still trying to figure it out. I meet fishermen, offer them a pointer or two, hand them a card, and tell them to call me with questions. They call, and I answer."

"What do they give you in return?"

"It can get lonely living by myself as long as I have, so it provides me acquaintances to chat with and to tell Catherine about when I visit. Plus," he said with a wink, "my new friends beg me to come to their fishing spots to teach them my techniques in person. I've earned permission to fish in most bodies of water bigger than a puddle in this county. My game has been lacking the last few months, though. This is the first one of these I've passed out in quite a while, and I was wondering if I was losing my touch." Turning back to Carol, he continued, "Tell both of your sons there's an old man in town who would appreciate the opportunity to teach them what he knows about fishing. You and your husband are welcome to join us for some lessons, too."

Carol retreated into herself. "My husband, yeah," she moaned. "I've stayed away from Irv too long. I should go back. Laticia, as Irv would say, 'what's the damage?'"

"No check. Y'all are my guests," Laticia said. "Anyway, we would have thrown out this pie or sent it home with somebody, and coffee doesn't cost much. I'm just glad y'all got to talk and help one another."

At that, Carol brightened. "Let me express how pleased I am to be a part of Lonesome, Party of Six, tonight. Seems like we all wandered into an empty season. I hope it won't last much longer for any of us. I wonder if we might all meet together next year with our families and consider how different our worlds are by this time next year? Maybe just dessert and coffee at night so those of us who do family get-togethers next year don't have to rush off or miss it."

Laticia said, "I imagine I'll be here working again. If y'all want me to reserve the party room, I'll be glad to."

"Yes, ma'am, please," Easton said. "I'm coming the farthest, so let me lay out one condition."

"You name it, Mr. Important," said Laticia.

"You invite whoever paid for our meals. I'd love to pay back the favor."

"For sure," Carol added.

Paula said, "Please make him understand how valuable this was for me. You'll tell him for me, won't you, Laticia?"

"Sure will, later tonight, if I get the chance."

Wiping tears from her eyes, Tara said, "If it weren't for him... or her, I would have walked out that exit, driven straight to the liquor store, and gotten plastered before my sponsor made it back to town. Now, I'll tell her a God story instead. And Mr. Jimmy Lee, thank you again for stopping me to talk. I wouldn't have made it without you, either. I'll see you on Sunday at church, but I'll be back next year telling you all about my thirteen months sober."

"I'll be back, Lord willing," Pops said. "I'm looking forward to telling Catherine about all of you tomorrow. She would have loved to meet you in person. Y'all are agreeable people."

Pastor nodded. "Same with Janie Ruth. She might not have said much at all, but I imagined her arm around each one of you as you told your story, loving you through your obstacles. I imagined her arm around me and her hand on my chest, telling me without words that she crossed over so I could be here and empathize with you folks tonight."

The no longer lonesome six stared at one another for almost a minute without a word before Tara stood. "My sponsor is half-worried to death about me, so I'm going to head her way. Anybody want to watch me drive past the package store with not so much as a second thought?"

"You'll be fine," Jimmy Lee Yates said, standing to say goodbye. She hugged him one last time and planted a smooch on his cheek.

When the door closed behind her, Laticia burst out laughing. "Pops, I've never seen you go more than about ten minutes without flirting with a cute young lady like that. She got to ya, didn't she?"

Pops blushed, likely the first time he had done so in a decade or three. "She called me by my name, just like you did tonight. That's what I needed more than anything else and what I'll be giving thanks for tonight. Guess I've been guilty of feeling sorry for myself for the better part of this year. That girl thinks I helped her out, and I reckon I did, but she didn't know how bad I needed one person to see me as *Jimmy Lee* instead of *Pops* tonight. Laticia, you probably didn't, either. I reckon I can flirt on another occasion."

"I'm sorry, I shoulda called you..."

Jimmy Lee waved her off. "You can call me whichever you prefer. I don't mind anymore. You just understand that whatever any of you call me, I can hear you." The remaining diners laughed and waved goodnight.

"I'm heading back to my hubby now," Carol said. "He'll be waking up soon, and he'll want to hear all about what I had to eat. I'll have even more wonderful stories for him. He will be delighted about the connection I've found to our Jeremiah. It might put him to sleep again with all the medication they're giving him, but I can tell you for sure that he won't forget Pops' invitation to come fishing. Thank you all for listening." With a smile and a nod, she bade the remaining representatives of the group goodnight.

Paula moved toward the exit next. "Guess I'll head out, too. Laticia, thanks for taking fine care of us. Easton, it was a pleasure… honey," she added with a wink. "I hope your meeting goes well tomorrow. Pastor, thanks for listening and not judging. I don't believe it was God who let me down, but my own unwise choices that put me where I am. I figure if you can still love Him after what happened to your wife, then I should consider giving him another chance. Who knows, we might meet up again sometime, perhaps on a Sunday morning. I understand there's a little country church whose pastor might need a little encouraging from time to time, and I might be willing to assist him with that."

"Yes, ma'am, we'd be happy to welcome you. Please thank your son for his service next time you talk to him. And I hope your daughter's trip goes well and that your future new son-in-law makes your family deeper and richer. This lonely pastor is sure glad he found your listening ears tonight. Goodnight, Paula."

"Listen, I'm gonna get these dishes and start making my way outta here to visit a certain friend tonight," Laticia told Easton and Pastor Hobbs. "Gentlemen, it has been a pleasure."

Easton shook Laticia's hand from across the table, and Pastor Hobbs gave her a hug. They both wished her a goodnight and shuffled away as she reached for their plates.

Easton stopped. "Pastor, may I borrow a few more minutes of your time?"

"I have no particular place to be nor particular time to arrive. How can I help?"

"I called my assistant earlier and asked about meeting her for church on Sunday morning. After hearing myself lay out my story tonight and listening to everybody else's, I realized there are some things in my life I need to resolve. And I'm thinking, well, perhaps I shouldn't wait until I return home to make the most important change. If you don't mind sticking around, I'd like you to be the person who tells me how to get right with God and start down a new path."

Pastor Hobbs motioned toward the vacant chairs. "Laticia, would you mind pouring us one more cup of coffee?"

AUSTEN

32

The clock showed a quarter to five by the time Laticia finished recounting her evening. "Austen, girl, you probably didn't have all this in mind when you did what you did. I clean forgot to give the servers your tip for them, but I'll do that on Saturday when I work again. That was generous, girl. They'll be happy about your generosity, just like our lonesome friends."

"Two hundred dollars seemed a lot at the time, but the Lord was nudging me to do it. I'll tell you what—the return will be priceless. Consider by the time they come back next year, how different their lives could be. I mean, that Easton guy is a new believer. The sky's the limit for him."

"Mm hm, he's good looking, too, ain't he?"

Austen laughed. "Yeah, maybe. I can't conceive he hasn't been on a date since college. I'd be willing to help him break that streak... now that he's a Christian."

"Austen, girl, I'm gonna chalk that up to five o'clock in the morning and too much coffee."

"You're right. He must prove himself first."

"For at least a week." They both doubled over laughing.

"Stop, that's all I can stand," Austen wheezed, clutching her side. She took a deep breath and continued. "Pops' story is precious, especially the way he talks about his wife as if she lived down the street. I think I'll run into him somewhere around town and ask him for fishing advice."

"What do you know about fishing, girl?"

"I fished twice with Mick."

"Yeah, but fishing with a mouse don't count."

This time, Austen fell off the couch laughing. "Stop, I'm gonna pee!"

"All right, girl, track down Pops if you want, but don't tell him about fishing with a mouse."

"Yes, ma'am, but I need to meet him before... well, you know."

"Yeah, you're right, it'll be a sad day for this town when we lose him, but he ain't showing no signs of going nowhere anytime soon."

"I wish I could be there when he takes Jeremiah fishing and tells him about his grandfather. Just imagining it, I'm getting goose bumps."

"Oh, girl, me, too."

"I sure hope that girl he helped tonight stays sober. Even though hers is not my story, for sure, she sounds like somebody who could be my friend."

"You wanna meet her? I can tell you where she's gonna be this Sunday morning at church time."

"Sitting right beside Pops. I won't be that forward. I'm not looking for anything in return, and I don't want to seem like I'm creeping on them."

"Do what you do, girl, but nobody at that table would be anything but excited to meet you after tonight."

"What about Army Mom? What do you think the odds are she'll ever go to Pastor Hobbs's church?"

"She'll be there on Sunday morning if my guess is right. You can't ever tell, but she seemed legit."

"I hope so, for her and for him. I mean, I can't imagine anything more encouraging for a pastor than to meet somebody and invite them to church and then they come. Except for leading somebody to Jesus, of course. I hope she goes. Was she interested in Mr. Important for real?"

"Naw, she's too old for him. They were just meddling with each other. No matter what he says, he's got feelings for that Sherrill girl. It's gonna take Army Mom a while to figure things out with the potential son-in-law deal, but she'd be a nice catch for somebody. It wouldn't take but a little attention to herself."

"She might bring a date to next year's reunion."

"You, too."

"Me?"

"Yeah, girl, ain't like you damaged goods just because you dated a mouse."

"I can't see it happening for me. I don't want to date

for the sake of going out, but we're not getting any younger. Oh, Laticia, I'm sorry, I didn't mean..."

"Naw, girl, don't you go feeling sorry for me. This time next year, I'll finally have my degree. There's a chance I'll even have a husband to go with it."

"A husband? Are you and Robert that serious?"

"Might be, we sure might be." As Laticia filled her in on her relationship with her potential Mr. Right, the clocked moved toward six. She and Austen alternated between the giddy school girls they had been and the mature young adults they were becoming.

"Oh, that's great, Laticia," Austen said when her friend finished. "I guess I'll be the old maid of our class."

"Girl, please."

"Seriously, I wonder how much our lives will change by next Thanksgiving. I feel you and all these people I haven't even met are almost family now."

"Me, too, girl, me, too."

"Tell me more about Inconvenient Heart Attack. It's hard to make up a story as interesting as hers."

"She was real quiet at first, but that woman's got layers. She tried to convince us she didn't have much to say, but once she started..."

"Her sons and daughters were a couple years behind us in school. It makes me wish I had paid more attention to sports so I would remember when our school played theirs. It's funny, these stories happened right here in Harriston, but we were oblivious to them. Even part of Mr. Important's story happened here. When I think about Inconvenient Heart Attack's kids, I consider her sons played ball against our school for three or four years, and her daughters cheered on our sideline. I mean, I attended most of the football games, so chances are I was there when they played, but I didn't pay attention to the other side. I hope Mr. Irv is gong to be okay. He sounds fun like my dad."

"I hope he's gonna be all right, too. No kids need to be without their daddy or mama, especially around the holidays."

"Oh, Laticia, I'm sorry, that was insensitive of me."

"Girl, please, stop walking on eggshells around me. My life ain't the one I would have chosen, but in its own way, it fits me. I was blessed with unbelievable grandparents who raised me as their own daughter. Even though I miss them and think about them every day— my mama, too—I'm aware my life could have been so much worse if it hadn't been for them. It's all good, girl, all good."

"I'm sorry just the same. If tonight's experience has taught me anything, it is to walk around in somebody else's shoes before I assume I've got them figured out. I'm glad Pastor Hobbs was part of the group tonight. It seems like he held the conversation together. I can't imagine how sad he has to be. It was so unfair what happened to his wife, and she was incredible. He's had a lifetime of helping other people carry their sadness at the worst times of their lives, so I'm glad the others at the table helped him through his."

"It was a good night, for sure. Looks like it ain't night no more, though." Laticia pointed to Austen's one window in the dormer above her desk on the other side of the room. The sky was a milky white with an accompanying promise of sunrise.

"Looks I'll be sleeping my day away if I can even go to sleep with everything on my mind right now. I hope I haven't kept you from something important today."

"No work today for me, so I'll be sleeping, too. It's been real nice catching up with you, Austen. Thanks again for last night. None of us are ever gonna forget it."

"I am so glad you stayed close to hear their stories. I can't stand waiting until next Thanksgiving to reach out to them. I almost want to fast forward a year to introduce myself to them and then rewind to live out the year."

"How you gonna make yourself wait that long, girl?"

"I have an idea brewing, but I'll need your help to make it happen."

ALSO BY A. AINSWORTH

Christian Fiction

Lonesome Reunion: A Lonesome, Party of Six Novel

Find under author name Al Ainsworth.

Memoir

Lines in the Gravel

Stories from the Roller Coaster

Biography

Playing for Overtime: The David Lee Herbert Story

Sports Action

Coach Dave Season One

Coach Dave Season Two: All-Stars

Coach Dave Season Three: Middle School

Coach Dave Season Four: Travel Ball

Coach Dave Season Five: The Next Level

Made in the USA
Columbia, SC
16 March 2021